LONE HEARTS OF TOPAZ

TRUE HEARTS OF TEXAS

BOOK THREE

K.S. JONES

Lone Hearts of Topaz
Paperback Edition

Wolfpack Publishing
9850 S. Maryland Parkway, Suite A-5 #323
Las Vegas, Nevada 89183

wolfpackpublishing.com

Paperback ISBN 978-1-63977-986-4
eBook ISBN 978-1-63977-985-7
LCCN 2023934366

To Jennifer Brown

You are that thin, bright light that sews the dawn of day to sunrise, and the same breathtaking light between sunset and dusk. I see you every day, and I know that you are extraordinary.

ACKNOWLEDGMENTS

A special thank you to my husband, Richard, who takes over household duties and just about everything else that matters when a book deadline is looming. And to Michelle Ferrer, my talented writing friend who understands my silence, but is always there to listen when needed. Also, to Mary Gail Winston for her willingness to answer my florist questions; to Debra Gifford, who happily responds to my silly inquiries late at night with such seriousness; to Sheri Groom, who always comes through in a pinch; and to Barbara Rettig, who can see the light at the end of the tunnel even when I cannot. A special thank you to Lisa Montanaro of the Women's Fiction Writers Association, as well as Anna Fernandes and Alethea Busby for pulling me out of my Italian crisis. And to Rachel Santino for her expert editing work. Most of all, though, I want to thank Carla Teves Page for inspiring this story, and her daughter, Toni, for finding me. My last conversation with my childhood friend was filled with fun, laughter, and many memories. I am sorry, Carla, that I never came back. I didn't know you were waiting for me. Rest in peace, sweet lady. You were an inspiration in more ways than one.

Lone Hearts of Topaz

CHAPTER 1

They'd groomed the horses and cleaned their saddles after a muddy morning ride, returning to the horse barn when the cold rain turned to snow. Two inches had already fallen. They'd sat on hay bales, watching the flakes fall beyond the open doors, wrapped in each other's arms. A white Christmas in Central Texas was beyond rare, so it had been a fitting day for Shane to propose.

Memories of the people she'd loved and lost were strong today. Kelsey-Rose stood in her florist shop, staring out the window at the busy sidewalks of the town's colorful turn-of-the-century buildings. She glanced at her delicate wristwatch—a vintage gold Timex once worn by her grandmother. Ten 'til noon. *He should be here by now.*

Topaz had been in decline for decades, but the restoration of its historic town square had brought life to its shops again. Bargain hunters, tourists, and day-trippers flooded the downtown, many searching for festive feelings found only in the biggest cities, or smallest towns, as holiday season neared.

Like so many other timeworn communities, the Texas town might have moldered away in neglect and disrepair had it not been for her father, Harley Flowers, and her friend Robert Wood, publisher of *The Blue Topaz Times* weekly newspaper. Together, they had saved the downtown from ruination.

Dazzled by the annual fall foliage show, visitors walked the square, admiring the vibrant reds and yellows of the oaks, sycamores, maples, and flameleaf sumac. Ordinarily, Kelsey-Rose would spend hours gathering autumn leaves and multifaceted branches for fall floral decorations and arrangements, but her mind had been elsewhere this season.

In the diagonal crosswalk that led from one street corner to the other, she spotted Robert, dressed in a grape-colored pinstriped shirt and beige khakis, his hat shading most of his face. He angled across the street toward her shop—his gait slower than her recall wanted.

The bell above the door tinkled when he pushed it open.

"Is it done?" Kelsey-Rose asked him, knowing the answer but fearing it nonetheless.

"It is." Robert opened his arms when she went to him and pulled her close to his heavyset frame.

In a hug, she said, "What am I going to do without you? You're my best friend."

He gave an affectionate pat to her back, but then he took her shoulders and held her out at arm's length with steady eyes on her. "Kelsey-Rose, it's time you found a new friend—one your own age. You deserve someone better than a worn-out eighty-year-old like me."

But she'd lived her entire life—thirty years almost

—in the understanding embrace of this man. She didn't know how to get through a day without him.

He smiled and curled a strand of coppery-red hair behind her ear. "I'll always think of you as that pretty little redheaded girl who'd come knocking on our door for some of Martha's fig jam." He wiped a tear from her cheek. "And look at you now. You're still a pretty redheaded girl, but you're all grown up. Remind me again, how long have you owned this shop?"

"Five years next month," she said. "But you know I worked here all through high school."

Robert lowered his gaze, memories sliding his hands into the front pockets of his khakis. With a slow shake of his head, he muttered, "Five years." He raised his gaze. "I never thought we'd get you off that horse, yet here you are, a fine, upstanding young businesswoman, Kelsey-Rose. I'm proud of you."

Her floral shop, Say It With Flowers, and his newspaper stood on adjacent street corners, connected by the crosswalk and a line of sight.

Kelsey-Rose felt tears welling, but she refused to unleash them. "Who'll help you find your hat when you lose it now?"

He laughed and patted the rounded crown of his black wool cowboy hat. "I'll just have to keep it on my head, I guess."

She knew Robert well enough to know that the glisten in his eyes was about to turn him around and walk him out the door, and she wasn't ready for that yet. With a forced smile, she took his hand and tugged. "C'mon. You need one more cup of my coffee before heading off into retirement."

In the back of her shop, Kelsey-Rose poured two

cups, adding creamer to hers, then the two sat together at the bistro table in the tiny back room.

"The young man who bought the newspaper from me looks to be about your same age," Robert announced before taking a sip, his eyes angling a glance toward her. "Good-lookin' boy, too."

"Are you trying to marry me off?" It was no secret she'd turned down Dax Porter and his marriage proposals every year, and Robert had never told her she was wrong.

"No," he said with a single shake of his head. "I'm just saying maybe you should go over to the newspaper office and introduce yourself. Welcome him. Be a friendly face."

"I'm always friendly, aren't I?"

"Yes." He nodded. "And that's what I told him."

"You told him about me?"

"Sure, I did, Kelsey-Rose. Why wouldn't I?"

She sat back, arms crossed. "And I suppose Daddy helped out a bit, too, didn't he?"

Harley Flowers wasn't just a local rancher who provided the town with the iconic Texas Longhorn cattle when needed to promote Living History events; his Forty Flowers Ranch also raised the Longhorns for stock show events, rodeos, parades, parties, political gatherings, and movies. He sold many of the animals to Texas corporations as mascots and as marketing tools, and he also supplied the biggest restaurant in town with Longhorn beef for their menu. But when the cattle industry went into decline a decade ago, he cut his herd in half and opened the only real estate office in town, partnering with his oldest daughter, Mae. She managed the office and listed and sold residential properties while he specialized in selling land and ranches when the need arose. When Robert had asked, he'd listed the newspaper for sale for him.

Robert leaned forward, closer to her, with a grin. "Seems like your dad did mention that you were one of the prettiest Flowers in town."

Her arms fell to her side and her head dropped back. She stared at the pressed-tin ceiling. "Don't tell me Daddy's still telling people that!"

Robert chuckled. "I've always thought it was cute."

Kelsey-Rose propped herself up and glared at him. "It stopped being cute when I was in eighth grade."

"Well, it always made my Martha laugh, rest her soul. And I'm sure I'll get a few more grins out of it before my time is up, too."

Her muscles tensed. Having Robert move south to Galveston was hard enough, but the thought of him moving on to heaven someday was unimaginable. He was the only man who had never judged her for the mistakes she'd made.

She needed a change of subject. "So, what's his name?"

"The new owner? It's Colton *something*..." Robert reached into his shirt pocket, pulled out a business card, and then put on his glasses to read: "Colton Wilde." He handed it to her.

Kelsey-Rose fingered the glitzy bronze metallic lettering, *Wilde Publishing*, on the snow-white card. After glancing at the address, she said, "He's from Texas? I guess I never asked. I just thought the buyer would come from the West Coast or the East Coast."

"You're partly right. He says he is originally from California, but he's been in the Dallas area for the last thirty-plus years. His family owns about a dozen or more newspapers. Some of them big. Colton was the managing editor for one of them, but evidently, he and his father don't get along too well. He decided to try it on his own. This is his first solo venture. He says he plans to do it without any family help. If he can make a go of it, he plans to buy more."

"A silver spoon?" She wrinkled her nose. "Not my type. You know I'll have a hard time being civil if he's a spoiled rich boy who doesn't know what it's like to have callused hands."

"You never know what's buried deep inside someone until you dig a little. Give him a chance."

Kelsey-Rose laughed. "Spoken like a true newspaperman."

The front bell tinkled with the arrival of a customer, bringing Kelsey-Rose and Robert to their feet. They came together in a hug.

"Call me when you get there, okay?" she said. "I want to know you've arrived safely."

"I will," he promised, kissing her forehead.

In the front of the shop stood Tommy Lee King, his back to them as he pulled a premade vase of roses from the floral cooler. Kelsey-Rose greeted him but then focused on Robert's exit, giving him a wave when he looked back. She watched until he crossed the street, disappearing behind the newspaper office where he always parked his car.

"Can you deliver these today?" Tommy asked, handing Kelsey-Rose the vase.

She tensed. "Are these going to your wife, Tommy Lee?" This was the only part of her job she hated.

"Nah." He grinned like a schoolboy caught in the act. "Dory's seven months pregnant." Tommy reached for a playful pinch to her chin, but Kelsey-Rose swayed from his hand. "Aww, c'mon now. Don't be that way."

She took the vase from him and then went to the cash register. She handed him a blank enclosure card. "Write what you want." She took out an order sheet. "Who's it going to?" Her voice was gruff, and she knew it. She didn't care if her tone sounded mean.

Tommy held up the plain white card. "Don't you have a prettier one?"

She snatched the card from him and handed him an XOXO card with hollow hearts on it.

"That's a better one." Tommy smiled. "Thanks." He wrote: *Would love to see you, baby.* Then he handed the card back.

Florists had a code, a certain etiquette, an unspoken privacy pact with their customers. She bit her tongue to stop a brash comment from tumbling out. "What's the delivery address?"

"Send it to Dani's house." He waited until Kelsey-Rose glanced up from her order book. "You know where she lives."

Yes, she knew where Danielle London lived. The three of them—Kelsey-Rose, Dani, and Tommy Lee—had all been assigned to the same precalculus study group in their senior year of high school, and Dani was the reason why she'd passed the class with a B-minus grade instead of failing. They'd had many study nights together in the big Victorian house on Twilight Shadows Road, and the once-upon-a-time best friends had gotten into more than enough trouble there, too.

The pretty blonde had a head for math, earning herself a scholarship to Trinity University in San Antonio, but before the semester began, Dani's parents died in a boating accident, leaving her—a legally adult orphan—to inherit the big blue house. College for her was out after that, but the eighteen-year-old survived.

She turned the front parlor of her home into an office, acquired an accounting degree online, and opened London Business Services.

But Kelsey-Rose also knew that the twice-divorced Danielle tended to get bored quickly, and it was a slow time of year for accountants.

Tommy pulled cash from his wallet and handed it to her. "Don't need a receipt," he said, "but make sure you deliver those flowers by five o'clock today."

He left, climbing into the same twenty-year-old F-150 he'd driven all through high school, then backed out of the angled parking space on the street in front of her shop.

Kelsey-Rose fingered the handwritten card. She thought about writing a replacement, addressing the envelope to Tommy's pregnant wife, Dory, and then delivering the flowers to her instead, but a decision like that could jeopardize her business.

Kelsey-Rose was the middle child of three girls, but she was the only wholly independent daughter of Harley Flowers. She needed to keep a professional head and not embarrass the entire family. She'd done enough of that already.

With the click of a switch, she turned on her laser printer and input Danielle's name and address. In an instant, the delivery information printed out onto the enclosure card envelope. As much as she hated to do it, she slipped the handwritten card inside and secured it with a colorless cardholder pick.

With Rita, her longtime half-day employee, on vacation for the week, Kelsey-Rose reached for the phone, intending to call her part-time helper, Lexi, but then remembered it was Friday—a school day for the high schooler—and it was just one o'clock in the afternoon. She wouldn't be available for deliveries until a quarter to five. Instead, she dialed her younger sister.

"Hey, Rainey, can you deliver for me this afternoon?" She couldn't bring herself to take the flowers in person.

"Sure," Rainey said, "but my last class doesn't end until two thirty. We had a pep rally."

The high school dance instructor had once been a brilliant dancer herself. She'd had everything needed to make it to Broadway—her dream. Grace, poise, beauty, and talent. She would have made it, too, had she not met Harry Dunn, part-time actor, part-time husband, full-time cheater. Despite the chiding of her sisters, Rainey loved him like an addiction.

"I just need the flowers delivered by five."

"No problem," Rainey said. "I'll pick up Emma from daycare and head over after class."

Kelsey-Rose hung up the phone. Her hand drifted to her worktable. She fingered the roll of red satin ribbon with the scripted words *I Heart You!* printed in white. Experts said *Love* was cliché. Overused. Boring. She'd since learned dozens of ways to say *love* without using the word at all. In her business, clandestine wording turned stale platitudes into chic verses. She'd written plenty herself, proud of her creativity.

Five years ago, she'd thought herself clever by renaming The Secret Florist Shop to Say It With Flowers. It seemed ingenious, considering Flowers was her last name. Being relied upon by the townspeople for celebrations of love, weddings, births, milestones, and even deaths made her contributions to the small community feel significant. She was giving back. Making amends. Finding redemption.

Flowers gave everyone a chance to say the things that might never be said otherwise, true or not.

On the notepad she used to create new verses, she scribbled, *True Love is Rarely Real*, but then she scratched it out, crumpled the paper, and tossed the thought away.

CHAPTER 2

Colton Wilde stepped out of the car, his gaze assessing the downtown. Topaz had more character than most people, with its artsy shops, cafes, and historic two-story limestone-block courthouse set prominently in the center of the town square.

The Blue Topaz Times hadn't been his first choice. It wasn't even his second. His sights were set on any Pacific Coast Highway town, but prices in California were too far out of his reach. And the criteria had been harder to find than he'd expected: a thriving small town—population 25,000 or less—with a major highway, situated in a county that had, at minimum, ten neighboring communities with businesses capable of advertising. And he hadn't forgotten about the living conditions. It had to be tolerable. He needed to live in the town, build up his business and bank account, and hire a managing editor before moving on to the next bigger and better newspaper purchase. But he'd never dreamed it would drag him to this sleepy little Texas town more than an hour northwest of Austin. What it all came down to was that Topaz was the best attainable platform available for his entrepreneurial leap. And it was just a year, he kept telling himself. A person can live anywhere for one measly year.

Five hours of driving from North Texas had given him a stiff neck and a headache. He'd barely made his eleven o'clock closing on time. After signing the legal papers, Colton exchanged his cashier's check for the keys and title to *The Blue Topaz Times*—lock, stock, and barrel. He owned the two-story corner building, the business, and the three-thousand-square-foot apartment on the upper floor. Now all he had to do was win over the newspaper's four longtime employees and the townspeople and learn to make a living without any help from his father. He couldn't go home again. That had been made clear.

Colton opened the heavy wood door and stepped inside. It had been over a month since he'd toured the building with an inspector and his accountant. Everyone had been friendly and upbeat. Today, however, it felt oddly cold.

"Mr. Wilde." The middle-aged receptionist jutted up from behind a window-like opening centered on the wall facing the long, narrow lobby.

"Lillie, isn't it?" Colton asked, already knowing the answer. She had his mother's name.

"Yes."

He walked to the counter where she stood and peered into the room behind her. Two men and a woman stared back, silent. "It's nice to see everyone again." He pointed to the door that separated them from him. "Can someone buzz me through?"

"Oh!" Lillie hurried to the door and opened it for him. "I'm sorry. Robert always used the back entrance."

Colton walked into the news office, his inherited staff standing in wait. For what, he didn't know. "Well," he said. "My first day." He took off his waxy cognac-colored leather jacket and draped it over a chair back.

"You workin' today?" one of the men asked. "Robert only left twenty minutes ago. We thought we wouldn't see you 'til tomorrow."

With his finger pointed thoughtfully at the man, Colton said, "You're Mackenzie, right?"

"Mack." The man corrected. "Just Mack."

Marion Mackenzie had shed his first name in elementary school. It was the first step in toughening up his reputation. People thought twice before trying to intimidate a man named Mack. And it had worked well for him as a newspaper reporter.

"My moving van won't arrive for a few days, Mack," Colton shrugged, "so I don't have anything to do but spend time getting to know each of you. Who does what around here?"

Mack sat, his legs straddling the corner of a well-used wooden desk that probably hadn't moved an inch off its spot since the 1980s. He motioned to the man standing next to him and then to the fashionable silver-haired woman. "Scott is our sports editor, and Beth manages the office and takes care of the classifieds." Then pointing to Lillie, he said, "Lillie's the receptionist and part-time proofreader. What else do you want to know?"

"And you're the staff reporter, right?" Colton said.

"Right."

"Where does that leave me?"

"What do you mean?" Mack asked.

"What do I do around here except rake in the money?" Colton laughed, but no one else did.

Serious, Mack said, "You're the publisher—the editor in chief—you do all the rest."

"All the rest?"

"Yeah," Mack said, glancing person-to-person for support. "You handle the day-to-day operations, plus the advertising, proofreading, paginating, front page, opinion page, circulation, complaints...you know, *all the rest*." He looked around at the others and then turned back to Colton. "Robert said you'd done this before."

Colton lowered his head, concealing a grin. "I was born into it, Mack, and I'll turn thirty-five next month. Back when I started, most reporters still loved their typewriters. I've got my first Royal packed in a box somewhere." He glanced at Lillie, whose focus was glued to him while stationed at the reception desk. He'd called twice in the last month. "You're good on the phones," he said to her. "You have a nice, friendly rapport with callers. Are you willing to handle some circulation duties, too?"

Lillie nodded, giving a wary glance to the others.

"And you, Mack, how would you like to be the new managing editor? Your old boss told me that you always took over for him during his vacation and did a fine job."

"Sure, yeah." He shot Scott and Beth a look. "Okay."

"Good. The front page is yours." Colton then nodded to the fidgety sports editor, fortyish, skinny with glasses, wearing an oversized brown corduroy jacket. "Scott, I have a promotion for you, too." When the reporter straightened his stance as if he'd just been called to duty, Colton said, "Mack's going to need a good staff reporter and photographer, so I'd like you to do more than sports for us, okay?"

"Okay," Scott said. Smiling, he quickly tucked his hands into the pockets of his blue jeans.

Robert Wood had sent recommendations and twenty weekly issues home with Colton on his last visit. He'd scoured every word twice. For a small-town newspaper, these guys had decent writing talent.

"Beth," Colton said, "I need an advertising manager. Are you willing?"

"Depends." She crossed her arms. "Does it include a raise and a bonus based on sales?"

"It does." Colton glanced at his staff. "I have a bonus structure worked out for each of you."

With tensions easing, Beth pulled a cigarette from its pack and lit it. After an exhale of smoke, she said, "This might not be so bad after all."

Colton tossed a look at a badly stained ceramic cup with just a swirl of old coffee inside. He picked it up and held it out to Beth. "Sorry, no smoking inside the building."

Beth blew out the puff of smoke she'd just inhaled, hesitant. When Colton kept a steady hand on the cup, she dropped her lit cigarette into it. "I've been smoking longer than you've been alive."

"And you can keep right on smoking, but not in this building." Colton walked back to the office kitchen with the cup and then returned, wiping his hands on a paper towel. "Who cleans up around here anyway? The kitchen looks like it hasn't been touched in a month."

"Longer, probably," Lillie said. "I do what I can, but I still have kids in high school, and I can't stay past five o'clock."

"Isn't there a cleaning service in town that does that kind of thing?"

"Yes," Beth told him. "There's Minnie Maids and Scuff-Away. Both clean houses and offices. Want me to call and get prices?"

"That'd be great." But then, with second thoughts, Colton turned to Mack. "They've got to be trustworthy—no snooping around. We break the big stories around here, not the maid. Do you think that'll be a problem?"

"Well..." Mack rubbed his chin, his head tilted in thought. "Might need Minnie to do it herself."

"Okay, your judgment's good with me 'til it's not," Colton told him. He waved his finger back and forth between Mack and Beth. "I'll leave it up to the two of you. See if we can do a trade-out for her services. Free newspaper advertising in exchange for once-a-week cleaning."

The building, historically known as the State Bank Building, was built in 1899 utilizing limestone blocks from the area. When the bank closed in 1949, F.W. Woolworth purchased the two-story structure. It was the only department store in town for the next thirty years.

With the town on the brink of abandonment in the 1980s, *The Blue Topaz Times* bought the place for nearly nothing, turning it into its newspaper office. Publisher Robert Wood owned it for four decades. Now it belonged to Colton Wilde. The building had history and character, just like the town. All it needed was some fine-tuning and a deep cleaning.

Colton took the interior back stairs up to the second floor—his home for the next year.

The stagnant air inside the vintage flat drew a musty scent from the well-seasoned wood of its wide-plank floor, heavy oak doors, and varnish-worn window frames. Expansive, the place was occupied when he'd seen it last. Now vacant, it looked different. Smelled different. Colton hung his jacket on a bronze wall hook near the door and then walked across the hollow-sounding living room to the three double-hung sash windows overlooking the town square. He fingered the heavy, outdated floor-to-ceiling drapes, watching dust flee the folds only to hang in the sunlit air streaming through the panes. He unlatched the catch on the window and lifted to open it, but it didn't budge. Painted shut. Probably for decades.

Colton stood, staring out from the tall middle window, studying the shops below. Rough stone sidewalks from a rustic bygone era outlined the square in cobblestone style. It was the first Friday in November, and the picturesque town square was teeming with shoppers and sightseers carrying holiday gift bags.

The newspaper should have been crowded with advertisements this week, but it wasn't.

Wishbone's Western Wear and Gem Rockhound's Natural Stones on the east side of the big courthouse were separated by a long, narrow alley-shaped bootmaker's shop. To the south, a handcrafted furniture store whose Talavera tiled entry, shared with Pottery and More, stood next to a Mexican eatery. To the west was an artsy farmhouse-décor store, Jo's Homestyle Bakery and Coffee Shop, and a florist. Sharing the north side of the square with the building he now owned was an old theater renovated into a performing arts center and a shop named Candle Sense.

His gaze shifted from one business to another—advertising dollars on his mind.

He'd spent two-thirds of his savings on this building

and its newspaper. It needed to turn a profit within the first year, or he was risking unrecoverable failure. *He had to make this work.* After the falling-out he'd had with his father, there was nothing left for him. His inheritance had been pulled out from under him like a rug on fire.

Still, he stood by his decision, even though it had lost him his family.

Looking down from his second-story window, his gaze landed on the crimson pinstriped awning that shaded the single-story florist shop owned by the real estate agent's daughter. She might be his first ally on the square if he played his cards right, and he would need help integrating into the historic Texas town that boasted of fourth and fifth-generation families.

Colton grabbed his leather Armani and headed down the outside back stairs. The breeze urged him to don the jacket, but the seventy-degree day quashed the need.

He crossed the street, letting the angled crosswalk lead him to the florist shop. *Say It With Flowers,* lettered in white, was painted on the barely tinted glass door.

When the bell above Colton's head tinkled, the woman at the counter turned, bringing his first footfall inside to a standstill. Door half open, he breathed, "Hi." Her dark coppery-red hair, softened by shy undertones of gold, fell over her shoulders, landing in an artful bounce. "You wouldn't be the Flowers girl who owns this shop, would you?"

Her expression shifted, easing into a poised shopkeeper's smile. She walked from behind the counter and extended her hand. "I'm Kelsey-Rose...Flowers," she added. "And you're the new owner of *The Blue Topaz Times*."

Up close, he saw that her eyes were the most stunning blue he'd ever seen—unexpected given her red hair and fine French rosé complexion. He reached, accepting her hand. "You're right." *In so many ways.* "I'm Colton Wilde."

CHAPTER 3

To be fair, it wasn't that Kelsey-Rose had never seen a man as striking as Colton Wilde before, but for the life of her, if she had, she couldn't remember when or where. The mere sight of him captured her breath long before her brain registered the allure. His chocolate-brown hair, wind-stirred in such a way that one strand curled onto his forehead like a fishhook baiting her, drew her gaze to the glimmer in his blue-gray eyes. The man was drop-dead gorgeous. And he had wealth and privilege written all over him.

"Welcome to Topaz," she said.

Attentive, he smiled, still holding her hand. "I'm liking it better and better all the time."

"You've only been in town a day." She laughed, pulling back her hand as her eyes zeroed in on the small mole tucked ever so slightly into the folds of his smile. A beauty mark, it was indeed. "This is really a great little town." *Be professional. Friendly.* "Is there something I can help you with today?"

Colton tracked the sweep of her hand, which presented an array of flowers and gifts.

"It's all very nice," he said before turning to point at his newly purchased building. "Did you know I can see your shop from my new apartment on the second floor?"

Kelsey-Rose nodded. "Yes, I'm familiar with the building. I've been inside many times."

"You have?"

"Robert was my closest friend."

"The old man?"

A prickle tingled her. "If you mean the man you bought the newspaper from, yes." Robert was eighty years old, but to call him an old man sounded disrespectful. Her glare at Colton was a defensive move. Her heart was already breaking from the loss of her friend. "I'm going to miss Robert. A lot. He was like family to me."

"Sorry. That probably sounded rude, didn't it?"

The newcomer's leather jacket probably cost more than her monthly building rent, and his dark blue chino pants and chambray shirt screamed highbrow, not hardworking.

Kelsey-Rose shifted her attention from Colton to a display table without addressing his remark. She began straightening its Western floral décor items, cowboy boot vases, and colorful neckerchiefs tied into bows. "Would you like to order flowers or buy a gift for someone?"

"No." Colton glanced at the lasso-style phone holders on the table. "Actually, I just came in to meet you."

When the bell over the door tinkled again, both Colton and Kelsey-Rose turned.

"Hi, Rainey," Kelsey-Rose greeted her sister. "Thanks for helping me out today." She started for the refrigerated case that cooled the vase of roses Tommy had purchased.

"Man, I love the fragrance in this place." Then Rainey's focus froze on Colton. "Hi," she said to him. "You're new here."

Colton dropped his gaze to the floor with a grin. "Does everybody know everybody around here?"

"Yeah," Rainey told him, sweeping her long strawberry blonde hair over her shoulder. "It's the curse of a small town."

He lifted his focus. "I moved here from a small town where I was very involved with the community, and even I didn't know *everybody*."

"How small?" Rainey asked.

"Coppell's got a population of about forty-two thousand people."

"Well, Topaz has almost twenty thousand, and maybe half of the people live out in the county. So, in town, we all know each other, mostly anyway. We're also not part of the DFW metroplex like Coppell is, which makes your small town not so small. Here in Topaz, we either entertain ourselves, or we're not entertained at all." Then Rainey waved her finger at him. "And I'm not trying to be rude or anything, but you stand out like a sore thumb in those designer clothes, oxfords, and that gorgeous salon-styled hair."

Kelsey-Rose sputtered a laugh before she caught herself, plastering a stoic look on her face instead. She handed the vase to Rainey. "Where's my niece?" she asked. The two-year-old was also her godchild.

"In the car." Rainey tossed a glance outside to her

cherry-red Camaro. "She fell asleep on the way over. I better get going." She turned for the door but stopped to look back. "Who am I delivering these to anyway?"

"It's on the card." Kelsey-Rose pointed to the small white envelope.

On her way out, Rainey called over her shoulder, "Welcome to town, whoever you are."

As the door was closing, Kelsey-Rose gave a soft slap to her own forehead. "I'm sorry. I didn't even introduce you."

"Your sister, I gather?"

"Yes, I've got two." She gave a penitent sigh. "That was Rainey, my younger sister. She teaches dance twice a week at the high school. Mae is my older sister. She owns the real estate office in town with my dad. You've already met him, Harley Flowers. He was your Realtor."

"I know. When Mr. Wood suggested I come and introduce myself to you, your father seconded the notion."

"I heard. Sorry about that."

Colton smiled. "I'm glad they did." His gaze was plastered to her. "What time do you close?"

"Six o'clock. Why?"

"I was just wondering if you'd consider having dinner with me tonight?"

"Oh, I don't know about that…" Instinctively, Kelsey-Rose took a step back. She had no real reason to refuse. She didn't have plans, and she would swear that she wasn't in a committed relationship. Dax Porter was not her boyfriend, she'd made that perfectly clear to him too many times, but because they'd been together on and off for nearly a decade, he still assumed he had a claim. Having dinner with another man—*this man* who could turn heads without even trying—was sure to cause a stir.

And the auto shop where Dax was a mechanic happened to be across the street from The Purple Sage, the best restaurant in town. It was where her father regularly sent newcomers, so she had a feeling that was exactly where Colton Wilde wanted to go. Under the circumstances, dinner there probably wouldn't fare well for either of them. If Dax caught sight of her with another man, his protective ire would rise, and even worse, he'd have hurt feelings, and she just wasn't up to smoothing ruffled feathers or consoling him.

"My treat," Colton said. "Your father recommended—"

Kelsey-Rose held up her hand. "I know. The Purple Sage."

"From the sound of it, that must not be your favorite. Is there another place you'd rather go?"

"Do you like tamales?" The words had popped out before she could stop them.

"Never had one."

Her brows jutted up. "Really? You're from Texas, and you've never eaten a tamale?"

"Nope." Colton shook his head. "I have an Italian mother, so I grew up on a staple of pasta, tomatoes, and olives."

"Well, I can't get through the day without one." Kelsey-Rose took his arm in a friendly manner and walked him closer to the window. She pointed to a fiesta-colored shop front on the adjacent street. "That's Marta's Homemade Tamales. The best in the county. I could meet you there at six thirty?"

"Six thirty is perfect."

COLTON WALKED BACK ACROSS THE STREET TO THE newspaper building. He had a date with what must surely be the most beautiful woman in Topaz, but he'd sensed a bit of opposition. Was it because he'd bought the business that used to belong to her friend? Or because she had a boyfriend? He hadn't even asked. In jest, her father had called her a "single Flower," so he doubted she was married. Maybe she just didn't like him—lots of people didn't. He'd been called cocky and arrogant, though he'd never seen it in himself.

Colton opened the front door to *The Blue Topaz Times* and walked up to the counter. "Lillie," he said. "What can you tell me about the lady who owns the florist shop?"

"Kelsey-Rose?" When Colton nodded, Lillie leaned back in her chair with her fingers steepled. "A lot. She's a close friend of Robert's, and she's the middle daughter of Harley Flowers—he has three. She loves her dog, and she's single, but she has a protective boyfriend. A leftover from high school days." She slanted a wary eye at her new boss.

"Well, okay then," he said, tapping his palms on the reception counter. "Buzz me through again, please?"

Colton walked across the cluttered newsroom, oblivious to the eyes of his staff, making his way to his new office at the rear of the building. He shut the door behind him.

Floor-to-ceiling bookshelves, built permanently into the walls of the vintage office, held dozens of reference books, a plethora of editorial style guides, and shelves of outdated printing press manuals, which *The Blue Topaz Times* no longer used.

The antique mahogany desk, with its black hide writing surface, had exquisite scrollwork. Roaring lion heads shaped the desk corners, and each short pedestal leg resembled the foot of a beast. Colton walked along the desk edge, his hand brushing the surface, appraising its carvings. His best guess was that the desk was at least as old as the building itself. It seemed to be the one thing respected well.

On an interior wall was a brown brick fireplace, its mahogany mantle vacant of all but a ten-year-old trophy awarded for General Excellence in journalism. On the adjoining wall were two double-hung sash windows, side-by-side, with blinds half closed, and pushed up against the wall nearest the door was a library table. Beside it stood a newspaper rack displaying the last eight weekly issues of *The Blue Topaz Times*.

Dust, fine as ash, covered all but the elegant desk, which had been polished to a shine.

SUNDOWN NUDGED THE WARM AUTUMN DAY INTO cooler Texas sweater weather. A light breeze blew against Kelsey-Rose as she crossed Main Street, cutting through the grassy square where the courthouse stood to Marta's Homemade Tamales. She opened the door to the vestibule, her focus falling on the periodical racks lining the wall. Atop one of the display stands marked *FREE,* set a bundled stack of the monthly real estate *FOR SALE* magazine—its high-gloss cover featuring

HF Realty's newest listing. She threw her purse strap over her shoulder and then used both hands to carefully pull the top issue out from under its fastening strap. With it in her hand, she opened the interior door to the restaurant.

"Hey, Kelsey-Rose." The woman came from behind the hostess station with a menu. "Where's your jacket, sweetie? There's a cold front moving in, so it's too chilly to eat out on the back patio this evening. You want a table inside near the window instead?"

Kelsey-Rose glanced around the dining room. Regular patrons, all of them. "A window table is fine, Sofia." When the dark-haired woman turned with a nod, Kelsey-Rose reached for her forearm, stilling her. In a hushed tone, she said, "I'm actually meeting someone."

"Your papa or sisters?"

"No, his name is Colton Wilde."

Sofia pulled back, her brows jutting upward. "A man?" She leaned in, whispering, "A date?"

"No," Kelsey-Rose said. "Nothing like that. He's new in town." With Robert's voice echoing in her head, she said, "I'm just a friendly face."

At the table for two near the window, Kelsey-Rose opened the real estate magazine to its *Featured Listing of the Month* page. A photo of her father, Harley Flowers, wearing his favorite straw Resistol cowboy hat and a smile, hung in the top left corner, crediting him as the listing agent of the spotlighted property—a sprawling 598-acre cattle ranch with its main residence nearly as big as the Topaz courthouse in the town square. The aerial shot, probably taken by her father's new photography drone, showed a pool, tennis court, and a nine-hole golf course. Texas ranches had become trendy—

hobby farms for the world's billionaires, and she hated the change.

"Here's sweet tea for you," Sofia said, setting down the glass and straw. "Fresh chips and salsa are on the way."

"Thank you."

But the waitress lingered. "I heard Robert left today." Sofia slipped her order book into a pocket on her tricolor folkloric skirt. "You'll miss him, huh?"

Kelsey-Rose nodded, her focus on the straw's paper wrapper. "Yeah." She looked up at the waitress. Sofia was the same age as Mae, her oldest sister, but the two women were entirely different. Sofia had an innocence —a sweetness—that Mae had never possessed. "It won't be the same around here without him."

The waitress laid her hand on Kelsey-Rose's shoulder. "I know, sweetie." She patted, then turned when another patron called out to her, hurrying away.

With her gaze focused out the window, Kelsey-Rose spotted the Corvette Stingray, arctic white with silver and black stinger stripes, pulling into a parking space. Even before seeing the driver's face, she knew it was Colton Wilde.

She sipped her tea and watched him step out of the sports car, wearing his leather jacket. Rainey was right —he stood out like a sore thumb, but he was a stunning sore thumb. He wasn't at all like anyone else in Topaz. He was movie-star quality but different from her brother-in-law, Harry Dunn, who earned his living as an actor playing bit parts in movies, commercials, and stage plays. There was no comparison between the two men. One had class. The other did not.

Why had this man chosen Topaz when the town was obviously not his style?

His gait was graceful up the cobblestone walk to the restaurant door, and once inside, his charismatic persona, evocative of a man of noble mien, drew all eyes. Sofia gave a side glance to the table for two at the window and then pointed.

Colton approached the table with a smile for Kelsey-Rose.

"Am I late?" He gave a nod to her glass of iced tea, then pulled off his jacket and hung it over the chair back before seating himself. "Have you already ordered?"

"No." Kelsey-Rose tipped her raised glass. "It's my usual drink. I come here all the time. Sofia brings it out without me asking for it."

She handed him the menu. "They serve tacos and enchiladas, but you wanted to try the tamales, right?"

Not answering, Colton glanced behind him, then around the small dining room. "Is the waitress coming back?"

Kelsey-Rose swiveled for a look. "She's at Shannon's table. Her grandkids are in town." She turned back to Colton. "It might be a while, but I can probably answer any questions about the menu."

"Actually, I wanted to order a margarita. I feel like celebrating."

His new ownership. He owned her best friend's home and business now. She needed to remember that her sadness wasn't his fault. "House 'rita, strawberry 'rita, or pickle 'rita?"

"*Pickle* 'rita? Are you serious?"

She flipped the menu over in front of him, and even though the print was upside down to her, she pointed to the drink offering on the menu. "It's the only margarita my brother-in-law will order. He loves pickle juice."

Brows raised, Colton said, "Pass."

"So, a house margarita, then?"

"Top shelf."

Kelsey-Rose laughed. She got up from the table. "There's only one shelf." She walked to the bar lit with twenty-year-old neon scrolls.

Within minutes, she returned to the table with an icy saguaro-stemmed margarita glass. "I forgot to ask whether you wanted frozen or on the rocks, but I'm guessing you're a traditional kind of guy." She set it down.

Colton fingered the salted rim. "You didn't want one?"

"I'm good with tea."

He held up his margarita for a toast, clinking her glass when she lifted it. "To Topaz and a new future."

After a sip, Colton said, "So, tell me about yourself. Something you wouldn't normally tell someone on a first date."

Her eyes flared briefly at the unexpected question. "Sorry." She gave a smile reserved for misunderstandings. "But this isn't a date."

Colton sat back in his chair. "It was just an expression. An icebreaker. I'm interested in...*people.* In general." He leaned forward. "I'd like to know more about you."

Sofia approached, interrupting their talk before ever reaching them. "The other table took longer than I thought." She pointed at the margarita. "But tequila makes waiting easier. What can I get for you two?"

Colton grabbed up his single-sided menu. "I haven't even looked yet."

"Two tamale plates," Kelsey-Rose ordered. "One with extra jalapeños and one without."

"Is the one without for me?" He peered over the top of the menu at her.

"Yep. I doubt you're ready yet."

They both laughed. After Sofia left, he said, "So, back to my question..."

Kelsey-Rose scanned the restaurant, her thoughts searching for something safe to admit. *Something she wouldn't usually tell someone.* It was much too late for that. Everyone knew her secrets. Except for this man.

"My mother died when I was four."

Colton sat back. "Wow. I'm sorry."

"I don't really remember her. My father did great with us, and I had my two sisters, so we sort of helped raise each other. Dad remarried when I was ten."

"Did you get the proverbial evil stepmother?"

"No, Nina's been great. They've been married for twenty years, so she's been 'Mom' to us for a long time." She directed a single nod to Colton. "Your turn."

"My turn, huh?" He glanced at the dingy, cork-paneled ceiling, focusing on a brown water stain. "I love history. I like the outdoors. And one of these days, I plan to write a novel."

"Really?" Kelsey-Rose sat up straighter. "I love to read. What's it going to be about?"

"Probably a saga about a rich and powerful family and their one and only son who nearly brought down the empire by revealing a dark truth."

"Hmmm... A child who shamed the family, or a family who shamed the son?"

He looked hard at Kelsey-Rose. "Maybe both."

When Sofia set their plates down, Colton waited until she left before picking up his fork and poking the cornhusk on his tamales.

Kelsey-Rose sent a stealthy glimpse across the table,

waiting until Colton shot back a sly glance of his own before she unwrapped her tamale husk, pulled it off, and set it aside. With her fork, she cut through the tamale, allowing the corn masa-scented steam to escape. When the seemingly self-reliant man mimicked her technique, she felt the tug of a smile.

"You're right," Colton said after a taste. "These are fantastic. I don't know why I've never tried them."

"I love authentic Mexican food. Tex-Mex, too."

By the time Sofia picked up their empty dishes, Kelsey-Rose had talked about her flower shop, her family and her sisters, her friendship with Robert, her Jack Russell terrier, and her little green house on Mustang Drive.

"You're a really good newspaperman."

"What do you mean?" he asked, then smiled as if he already knew.

"You managed to get all sorts of information out of me, yet I still don't know much about you."

Colton smiled. "I enjoyed tonight." He reached across to her hand, his eyes never leaving hers. "If you agree to see me again, I'll promise to tell you all about myself."

The slow burn—one barely hot enough to keep her sensuality alive for the past decade—blazed at his touch. Her gaze sharpened. His eyes were honest, and his interest was genuine. He had a wholly embraceable spirit. He'd slipped under her radar and fallen right through the door to the soft spot in her heart. She'd never intended to leave herself open ever again.

Kelsey-Rose pulled her hand from his and stood. A sense of panic had hit. She needed to get out. She needed to get away—home to her backyard where she could be alone, wrapped in a blanket under the stars, surrounded by the memories that would forever be her cross to bear. She needed Free, her Jack Russell terrier, who knew her burdens but forgave her anyway. If solace were to be found tonight, it would come from him. Not this stranger. Not this man. No matter how much she wanted the night with him.

CHAPTER 4

It was a chilly fifty-six degrees when Kelsey-Rose stepped into her backyard, wrapped in a plaid flannel blanket, and slid into her backyard Adirondack chair under the stars. She patted her knee, encouraging Free onto her lap. The terrier nuzzled his little white body, spotted with black and tan markings, beneath the blanket and then rotated himself, settling in.

Mustang Drive was in the older part of town and only had a few homes. It was on the outskirts, barely inside the city limits, with easy access to the road leading to the Forty Flowers Ranch. There were no streetlights and no edged sidewalks or curbing. The scraggly front lawns had simply surrendered when the decades-old blacktop refused to give up more ground.

Her half-acre yard was treeless and unfenced, but at the back of her house were two metal posts, strung with a supporting wire, where a star jasmine vine grew. Over the years, the woody evergreen had spread ten feet wide and grown three feet tall. It bloomed pinwheel-like blossoms every spring and summer, sending out a rich, sweet floral scent.

At the sound of heavy work boots crunching dry leaves, blown over into her yard from the neighbor's Spanish oak, Free bolted from under the blanket, barking before his paws hit the ground.

"Hey, Free. It's me, boy, Dax." He emerged from the night shadows—his steps lit up by the bright beam of a flashlight. "You star watching again?" he asked Kelsey-Rose, readjusting her second Adirondack chair until it was closer to her, and then he sat.

"Yeah." With her head tilted upward, she pointed. "Orion is right overhead tonight."

He looked up without acknowledging the constellation. "What took you so long to get home?"

His voice was kind. Caring when it needed to be. It was one of the things she loved most about him if she loved anything at all.

Dax Porter lived across the road in a rental house that his parents had owned for decades. He might have been best man at her wedding if Shane had lived. Unlike so many others, he'd never outwardly blamed her for the accident. But her own self-imposed punishment gave him rights to ask questions she didn't want to answer, and over the years, she'd given him privileges no other man had.

"Robert left for Galveston today," she said, her stargazing more intense. Clutching her cell phone, she swung her hand up, resting her elbow on the arm of the chair. "He promised to call when he arrived, but I haven't heard from him yet." She looked at Dax. "I don't know if I should be worried or mad."

"Just call him," Dax said, popping open the can of beer he'd carried over, then taking a swallow.

"You know him. He's not going to answer if he's driving, and if he doesn't answer, I'll worry more."

"It's a five-hour drive. He probably stopped off for food." Dax reached for a curled wave of her coppery-red hair, then slipped his hand to the back of her neck, gently massaging. "Did you eat?"

Kelsey-Rose nodded. She didn't want to have this conversation. "I think I'll turn in early tonight." She stood, pulling the blanket tighter around her. "C'mon, Free. Time for bed."

When the Jack Russell terrier came running, Dax stood, too. He pulled Kelsey-Rose to him and kissed her, first on the cheek, then on her lips, moving to a spot just below her ear. He pressed himself to her.

"Any room for me under the blankets tonight?" he whispered.

Lightly, she pushed back, stepping away. "Not tonight, Dax. I've got a lot on my mind."

With Free on her heels, she crossed the yard to her back door and opened it. When she glanced back, Dax was still standing midyard, one hand on his hip, staring at the ground.

"I'm sorry," she called to him, then she stepped inside with Free and closed the door.

The house lights were off, but the short hallway to her bedroom had a lit nightlight. Once inside her room, she closed the window blinds, then turned on her bedside lamp. There was no need to peek through the slats to see if Dax was okay. She already knew the answer. He would stand there, in that same spot, for another few minutes, hoping she would come back out, and then when she didn't, he would walk back across the street to his house, sulking the whole way.

Kelsey-Rose slipped into her knee-length, holly-berry cotton gown and brushed her hair and teeth. She'd just grabbed the remote control off the night-stand when her phone rang. She glanced at the caller ID and then answered.

"Robert, where are you? I've been worried."

"It's a long drive to Galveston, Kelsey-Rose. I stopped off at that little pork schnitzel place we ate at a few months back."

The sound of his voice pulled the stress out of her tense shoulders. "Was it as good this time?"

"Better, maybe. But I'm here now. The management company did what it promised. The condo was cleaned and sanitized, and it's all set with my belongings. Everything is unpacked and put away, except for what I brought with me."

"Is the heat turned on, too?"

"It's plenty warm." The phone reception skipped in and out. "I can see the lights of a freighter in the Gulf tonight. I think I'm going to like it here, Kelsey-Rose."

Her throat tightened. She took a breath. "It's the perfect place for a Navy man to retire."

"I've missed the water. Living inland all these years almost made me forget what salt air smelled like."

It was the retirement he'd always wanted. Galveston was an old coastal town, and it was ideal for a man who read as many books in one month as she read in a year—and for someone who loved fishing and boating, too, it was perfect. The Gulf Coast had been calling to him, and he'd finally answered.

"Get some sleep," she said to him. "Your first

morning walk on the beach as a retiree is just a few hours away."

After saying good night, she set down her phone and reached for Free, scratching behind his ear. "He's happy, and that's all that matters, right?" she said to the dog.

The Jack Russell cocked his head, listening, his bright, round brown eyes staring at her from atop her teal-colored bed quilt.

COLTON STOOD AT THE DEATHLY QUIET RECEPTION desk of the only hotel in town. The tan-painted walls, basket décor, and brown laminate check-in counter smelled of stale cigarettes and ammonia. The lobby chairs behind him—some in autumn plaid fabrics, some in solid shades of beige—all sat empty. The wall-mounted television was dark.

"Hello?" he called out.

He glanced around, listening for approaching footsteps, but heard none. Between him and the elevator stood a hallway table with a glass beverage dispenser filled with water and lemons and an espresso machine, so new it still had its price tag. A stained, handwritten sign hung tacked to the wall above it: *Compliments of Beck's Hardware*.

"Hello?" he called again, louder.

"I'm comin'," an unseen woman answered back.

Irritated, he tapped his credit card on the counter. The next closest hotel was nearly forty miles east. For all he knew, it could be worse.

A heavyset woman lumbered up behind the check-in counter, holding a broom, dustpan, and a red plastic caddy filled with various spray bottles.

"I have a reservation," Colton said to her.

Without looking up, she set her cleaning supplies down. "Okay," then, after a few taps on the keyboard, she said, "What's your name?"

"Colton Wilde."

Her head jerked up, her focus landing directly on him. "The newspaperman?"

"Yes."

The woman wiped her hands down the front of her white canvas apron and reached across the check-in desk for a handshake. "I'm Tammy Hye. Lillie's Aunt." When Colton didn't respond, she said, "She works for you at the newspaper."

"Oh," Colton said with a nod. "Sure. Lillie." He reached for the handshake. "A pleasure to meet you."

Staring a moment too long, she said, "I forgot you were comin' in tonight." She swiped his credit card through the terminal, then slid a key card inside an envelope where she'd written his room number. She handed it over. "Take the elevator to the third floor, turn right, and go to the end of the hall. I upgraded you to a corner suite. You've got views of the town square and the river."

He nodded, grabbed the handle of his hard-side spinner, and picked up his duffel. "Thank you."

Once inside his room, Colton went straight to the desk, where he saw a pad and pen. He sat his bag down and then wrote: *Check advertiser list for The Gem Hotel and Beck's Hardware.*

The suite was in orange, yellow, and cream colors and had a corner of windows. Colton slid the sheer curtains back. The courthouse subtly lit the downtown to the west, but the north-facing window overlooked the countryside darkened by night. A blanket of black beneath the near-moonless night lay still over the raw natural land and its river.

He turned his gaze back to the square, studying the buildings. Had he done the right thing moving here? This rural Texas town was different in almost every way from the bustling Dallas metroplex. The lifestyle. The land. The weather. The people. He was a fish out of water in this place, but the reality of it was that he had no choice about it now. The decision had been made, and his money invested.

Colton unpacked, hanging his clothes inside the accordion-door closet. After showering, he turned on the television. The *Austin Nightly News* boasted of coverage in fourteen counties, followed by a Blanco War veteran's story. He retook the pad and pen and wrote: *Need list of Austin advertisers.*

He turned down the bed and then sat on the edge, his phone in his hand. It felt odd not to call anyone to say he'd arrived safely. Usually, it was his mother, who always saw him as a child even though he hadn't lived at home for over fifteen years, but neither parent had bothered to see him off, say goodbye, or wish him well. Their cold shoulder wasn't just icy; it was as hard as granite.

And the minute Carly, his former fiancée, found out his father had cut him out of the will, she'd broken off their engagement. Kept the ring. Then virtually disappeared. It'd been over two months since she'd taken a call from him. It was clear their relationship had ended. Maybe it'd never been real at all. He wouldn't fall for love ever again.

Was it all worth it? Were his damned ethics—a

code of honor he never knew he had—worth losing everything and everyone he'd ever loved? It sure didn't feel worth it tonight.

Except for that girl. Kelsey-Rose. There was something hauntingly wonderful about her.

CHAPTER 5

It had been seventeen years since Marjorie Boyle died. Yet every November, on the sixth day of the month, her husband, Andrew, came into the flower shop like clockwork to order calla lilies for her grave.

At the tinkle of the bell, Kelsey-Rose looked up. The sight of the eighty-six-year-old man wearing a herringbone Irish flat cap melted her heart. Without more than a few words, he gave her hope that maybe, *maybe,* a true promise to love lasted. For some. A few. Perhaps just one, but it was all the kinship she needed.

"Mr. Boyle, hello," she greeted. She came from behind the counter. "I put in a special order of calla lilies last week. They've arrived, and they're beautiful." She motioned him into the back room. "Come take a look."

In the back, she opened the refrigerated case where five-gallon buckets held an array of newly delivered flowers.

"I know you like the white ones for Mrs. Boyle, but

look at these—they're called Picasso calla lilies." Kelsey-Rose pulled one from the container. "Their white and purple contrast is so lovely." When he nodded without a response, she slid it back into the plastic floral bucket and lifted a bloom from the next container. "These are Mahogany calla lilies. They have such an elegant look, don't they?"

She wanted to make an impactful contribution to the ritual she so admired.

Mr. Boyle stepped closer, peering inside the cooler. "What kind did you say those were?"

"Picasso calla lily," she told him.

"They are beautiful, but Margie never liked Picasso. Too abstract, she said." He turned to Kelsey-Rose. "It was kind of you to order these other colors, but if you don't mind, white lilies were always her favorite. She would tell you they were pure and honest. I'd hate to disappoint her. Do you think I can have a dozen, just wrapped in tissue paper?"

She put her hand on his shoulder. "Of course. I'll get them ready for you."

While she was ringing up the purchase, the bereaved man pulled an enclosure card from the countertop selection rack. He took a pen from his shirt pocket. As he wrote, she shifted a glance to his words:

I haven't forgotten. I still miss you every day. Andrew.

After she handed him the bouquet, he tucked the card between the stems. "Thank you," he said to her, leaving the shop with the flowers.

Behind the cash register, her appointment calendar for the upcoming year hung on the wall. Kelsey-Rose flipped the pages to next November and wrote herself a reminder to order white calla lilies for Mrs. Boyle.

When the bell over the door tinkled again, she looked up.

"Jack," she said. Kelsey-Rose went to her grief counseling companion with a hug. "Is it time to restock my flower seed packets already?"

"Maybe not." He smiled after releasing her from their friendly embrace. "But I had to restock a few other places in town, and I thought I'd stop by and see if you needed more." He held up a bluebonnet seed packet. "These are really popular this year. You'll want to tell your customers to plant these now. They'll reward them in March or April."

Kelsey-Rose walked with him to the table holding the corrugated display box labeled *TXUS Seeds*.

"Any chance you could find me a wood display box?" Kelsey-Rose asked. "Something that might fit my Western décor? I'm really into old barn wood these days."

Jack looked at her. "Hey, that's a really great marketing idea. I'll ask Paige to come up with something, and I'll let you know."

"Thanks. So…" Kelsey-Rose dragged out the word. "Are you still seeing Addy?"

Jack glanced at her. "Yeah." Then his hands went to his hips, and he smiled. "I haven't messed it up yet. Suddenly, everything seems easy because of her. Juli loves her. I guess I do, too."

"I'm really happy for you, Jack," she said. "It's been…what…four years since Kaitlin died?"

"Yes, and about ten years for you since Shane died, right?"

"Yeah," Kelsey-Rose lowered her head. "Ten years in December."

Jack set down his seed carrier and focused his attention on Kelsey-Rose. "You know, I never thought I'd ever find someone else after Kaitlin. Never in a million years. But when I met Addy, something clicked right away. I mean," he laughed, "how could two people, so different, find each other? But I knew right away that she could change my life. There was just no way that I would admit to it because if I did, I'd have to admit that I was willing to let Kaitlin go, and you, of all people, know how that feels." Jack gave a slight, understanding smile at her unease. "There was no way I was willing to do that." Kelsey-Rose listened without interruption. "I had a hard time confessing my feelings for Addy. About loving her." He moved his hand to her shoulder, giving her a comforting squeeze. "Kelsey-Rose, I almost lost her because I wouldn't admit to anyone, most especially me, how I felt about her. I was afraid that if I did, I'd be cheating on Kaitlin. You need to know I was wrong."

"Well," she said to Jack. "It sounds like our grief counseling paid off for you."

Jack pulled her into a hug. "Your Addy is right around the corner. I just know it. And I am always here if you need to talk. You are never alone."

"You either," she said.

Jack refilled the TXUS Seeds display rack, and as he was packing up to leave, he said, "If Paige can find a wooden display box for your table, I'll bring it next month."

Jack Brown was one of the truest trauma friends that she had, and her connection to him was real.

"Thanks, Jack," she said as he left the store. He had

found an amazing woman who knew how to bridge the gap between his past and his future. But that was a once in a blue moon kind of thing. It was silly to think it could be the same for her.

When the bell over the door tinkled yet again, she greeted, "Hello, Daddy." She went to him for a hug, pushing up the long sleeves of her oversized gold sweater.

Harley Flowers was a tall, slender man with short salt-and-pepper hair—salt outweighing the pepper. He wore his burnished bourbon calfskin boots and a straw Resistol with a cattlemen's crown year-round, no matter the weather or the work.

"My beautiful daughter," he said, returning her embrace.

Kelsey-Rose took him by the hand and pulled him into the back room. She dropped his favorite coffee pod into the maker, then pressed the brew button. "Take a look at these, Daddy." She showed him her delivery of flowers. "I think you should take Nina some mahogany lilies."

"She'd like that," he said, removing his hat and taking a seat at the bistro table. "I saw Mr. Boyle leaving with his annual bouquet of calla lilies when I came in. I'd sure love for him to list that beautiful old Victorian with Mae. It's too much house for him to take care of at his age. You know it sits on ten prime acres and has river access. That one listing alone could draw dozens of qualified buyers here from Dallas and Houston."

"Oh, Daddy. He's never going to leave Mrs. Boyle. He would be lost without her."

"You're probably right." He got up for his coffee, then sat back down while Kelsey-Rose trimmed the stems of the calla lilies for Nina's bouquet. "Speaking of men and women…"

She tossed a knowing glance over her shoulder. "I don't think we were speaking of men and women. We were talking about Mr. and Mrs. Boyle, and they're much more than that to each other. They're a couple whose love has transcended life itself."

"That's a romanticist's description if I ever heard one." He laughed. "My point was—"

"I already know your point, Daddy." Kelsey-Rose stopped fiddling with the flowers and turned to her father. "Yes, I've met Colton Wilde. Yes, he's gorgeous. And single. And smart. And, and, and…" Her hands went to her hips. "Why is it still so hard for everyone to accept that my promise to Shane was real? I'll never love another. I gave my solemn oath, and I intend to keep it."

Her father grinned and then lowered a smug look to the floor. "What makes you think I was talking about Colton Wilde?" He raised his focus, settling on his daughter's deep blue eyes. "My point was—we need to talk about Dax."

"Oh," she said, taken aback by her own insolent presumption. "What about Dax?"

"He drove out to the ranch to see me this morning." Her father sipped his coffee. "You know I only want what's best for you, don't you?"

"Sure. Yes, of course."

"Kelsey-Rose, you've got to send that boy on his way or marry him. It's been a long time since Shane died, and Dax has been there waiting every day, just wanting you to love him. Maybe not the same way you loved Shane, but enough to share a life together. I'm not saying he doesn't have faults, but overall, he's been loyal to you these last ten years, and he promised me that he will stay committed to you." He stood and went to his daughter, pulling her into his arms and hugging her. "You're not the only one who made a deathbed promise to Shane that day. Dax made one, too. He promised to take care of you, and he's made a good mechanic of himself with a steady job." Softer, he said, "But all any of us wants is for you to be happy. To be in love. To have a family. To let that day go."

After a moment, Kelsey-Rose stepped back—her vision blurred by welling tears. "Daddy, I am happy. And I already have all the family I'll ever need. I have you and Nina, and my sisters. Their husbands, and sweet little Emma, too. And I do love Dax, just in a different way. But Shane will always be the only man I'll ever truly love, just like I promised."

"Kelsey-Rose." He shook his head. "Shane's been dead *ten years*, honey. You can keep right on loving him, just like I still love your mother, God rest her beautiful Irish soul. But you deserve to fall in love again. Just like I did with Nina after your mother died."

She turned back to the flowers. Quiet, Kelsey-Rose inserted each stem into a water tube and then wrapped the calla lilies in waxed tissue paper before handing them to her father.

"I'll think about it." Her pat answer usually satisfied him enough to put an end to these conversations. When he took the bouquet from her, she raised up on tiptoes and kissed him on the cheek, hoping to send him off happy, knowing he'd given her the advice he thought she needed.

But instead of leaving, he said, "You're not getting rid of me that easily today." He laid the tissue-wrapped lilies on the table. "We're not done talking yet."

Her father was a man of well-chosen words, never more said than was needed, so she had expected her kiss to put an end to their conversation.

"I'm not trying to get rid of you." Kelsey-Rose had her focus on the floor instead of him. "I'm always glad to listen to whatever you have to say."

"That's good to hear, but you're probably not going to like this next thing any more than you did the last one."

Curious, she looked up at him. "What is it?"

Her father shifted, taking a deep breath before slowly exhaling. He firmed himself into a sturdier stance. "It's time for you to come home, Kelsey-Rose. I'll be sixty in January, and I still have a lot to teach you. You've got to learn more about our ranch operations and the managerial process of it all. The production, recordkeeping, finances, and marketing will all fall to you one day, and it takes time to learn it all. The ranch needs you. I need you."

Kelsey-Rose shook her head. "Daddy, I've already said no dozens of times. I'm not that girl anymore. You've got Ty and Cullen. They'll do whatever you ask. And Nina is good with bookkeeping and customers."

Her father lowered his head and hesitated, which is what he always did when he needed time to form the right words.

"Nina still has seven more years until she can retire from the health tech company, and even though she mostly works from home, hers is a full-time job. She can't do both." He glanced up, refocusing on his daughter. "Besides, she's not the rancher in the family."

"I know, but—"

"Honey, you can't just give up on who you are when life throws you a curve ball. You got knocked down good and hard—nobody is saying you didn't—but you've drifted away from everything that was ever important to you. Ty and Cullen are good cowboys, but they're ranch hands. Their last name isn't Flowers, and they're not my heirs. You know where you belong."

"I have the flower shop now."

Stern, her father stood glaring at her. "You can do whatever you want with this shop, but the ranch is your inheritance, Kelsey-Rose. Mae never had any interest in it, and Rainey, God bless that girl, has had her head in the clouds since the day she was born." His focus dropped to the floor with a shake of his head. "Maybe if we'd had sons..." Then he looked up at her again. "But we didn't." His smile was forced when he gave a soft pinch to her chin. "God gave us you instead, Kelsey-Rose. You've loved the ranch since the minute we put boots on you—the cattle, the horses, the land, the life. All of it. It's in your blood." He gave her a look that only fathers who are disappointed in their daughters can give. "You've had enough time. You need to come home now."

Kelsey-Rose picked up the bouquet of calla lilies off the table and handed it back to her father. "I stopped loving all of those things the day Shane died. He was the son and the heir you deserved—not me."

Sometimes her memories were too strong to hold.

With lowered head, Kelsey-Rose walked out of the back room and across the shop to the front door and opened it. "I need to get back to work." She forced a businesswoman's smile from a daughter's heart. "I appreciate the talk, Daddy, but I'm fine. You don't need me out messing up the ranch. I'm fine right where I am. Really. Tell Nina I'll make a salad for Sunday's supper, will you?"

From the doorway, Kelsey-Rose watched her father get into his F-350 pickup truck and drive away, turning onto the road that would take him past her little green house on Mustang Drive, leading to the turnoff that would take him back home to the ranch—the place where all her dreams died.

The shop was silent except for the clicks from the refrigerated floral coolers.

She went to the music system and pressed play on guitar instrumentals, hoping to quiet her thoughts.

There were moments this past year when the loneliness of her promise had almost been too much, but she'd never spoken to anyone about it.

Alone in the shop, she closed her eyes, raised her face, and then lifted her arms as if she were young again, waiting to feel the embrace of the loving arms she knew awaited her someday. If she spoke, would Shane hear her? If she cried, would he comfort her? After a breath of reason, she lowered her arms and opened her eyes, for she knew the answer. She'd known it all along.

CHAPTER 6

It'd taken a week, but Colton had managed to search nearly half the files in the newsroom's row of five-drawer metal cabinets.

"Find what you wanted yet?" Mack asked him.

Amid a stack of thirty or more manila folders Colton had set aside, he stood, holding four files. "I've got a good start on the December issues. These stories are interesting and probably memorable for those who have lived here for at least ten years."

The Blue Topaz Times had never run a "This Week in Local History" column, and in the past, Colton's twist on updating an archived event—making it a human-interest story rather than a regular news day story—had become one of the most popular features at his former newspaper. It was a look back in time. A walk through the reader's memories. Starting the same column here would help familiarize him with this new town and its storied history, plus he had already been able to sell a sponsorship to Watkins Funeral Home.

"Beth?" Colton looked around the room, and when

he didn't see her, he called out to Lillie instead. "Do you know where she is?"

"Smoke break," the receptionist called back.

There were no modern cubicles or partitions in the newsroom. It was just one wide-open space with maps framed in picket fence wood, walls of file cabinets and bookcases, long library tables with a chair or two at each, six maple-varnished wood desks set six feet apart, of which only three were used as intended. The other desks sat piled high with stacks of books, magazines, and papers of one kind or another. It was cluttered. Dingy and outdated. And no maid service had shown up in a week. Colton was used to a certain level of cleanliness and comfort, and this wasn't measuring up.

He walked out the back door into the parking lot.

The exterior stairs, leading down from his second-story living quarters, landed next to a park-like bench, double-bolted to the back wall of the limestone-block building. Beth was seated, intently reading on her phone, oblivious to his arrival. Smoke from her cigarette curled above her and vanished into the morning air.

"Hey, Beth," Colton called. After an acknowledging glance from her, he said, "Any news on finding someone to clean the office?"

"Yeah." Beth stood, dropped her cigarette to the ground, and then stepped on it, giving it a twist under her shoe. "Minnie starts tomorrow after the office closes. She's coming by today for a key."

"What kind of a deal did we get?"

"She'll clean once a week for a quarter-page ad." Beth shrugged. "But she doesn't think newspaper advertising works, so if she hasn't picked up any new clients by the end of the month, the deal is off. She says she's not working for free."

Colton gave a half laugh. "Okay." He did a midstep pivot and headed back to the door.

"Oh!" Beth raised her voice, jutting her hand into the air to stop his retreat. "I forgot to tell you. The flat-screen is coming tomorrow for the newsroom like you wanted. They said they'd mount it, too, but someone has to show them where you want it. You never specified."

"Perfect. Will you call and tell them I'll need my personal televisions mounted upstairs, too? My moving van arrives today, so this is good timing."

"What if they charge extra?"

"Just do a trade-out for it."

Beth snickered. She walked past him on her way back inside the newsroom. "You'll never make a profit using the barter system, and those bonuses you promised us will be a long time coming if you're not taking in any actual cash." She turned with a last glance. "Anything else you need, boss?" Her tone was snide. She nodded to his Corvette parked at an angle across parking lot lines. "A free carwash? An interior decorator for your new apartment? I'm sure we could do a trade-out for those services, too."

The slim, well-dressed older woman, almost elegant in her poise, pulled open the door but stopped and looked back.

"By the way, today is Lillie's birthday. Robert used to bring her flowers and buy a cake for the office." Then she stepped inside, pulling the door shut behind her.

Colton stood alone in the parking lot, statue still, and pushed out a sigh. Somehow, he'd done it again. He had a knack for offending people, and he had no idea how or why. But if he took a broader focus, he could usually find a positive hidden within the negative. This was no different.

He needed to buy flowers, and that meant he had a legitimate reason to see Kelsey-Rose.

CHAPTER 7

It was almost eleven o'clock when the moving company's semitruck arrived. The big yellow diesel downshifted to a halt at the crosswalk that linked Say It With Flowers to *The Blue Topaz Times*. The rig made a wide left turn, pulling up alongside the newspaper building and taking up the entire northbound lane.

Kelsey-Rose stood at her shop window, watching. It wasn't that she wanted a glimpse of the wealthy man's personal belongings. It was that she wanted a glimpse of the man himself.

Colton hadn't stopped by the shop all week, which was good, she'd decided, except that she hadn't been able to get him off her mind. One casual tamale dinner together had set her soul on fire, but admitting it, even if just to herself, would make it harder to disengage her desire for him. Her daydreams, but most especially her night dreams, had secret yearnings for a night alone with this man. She imagined herself with him in ways that made her feel like a woman in love, or maybe just a woman in lust. Thoughts of a covert affair—a crazy rendezvous under cover of darkness and discretion—had crept inside her, and she hadn't been able to shake it.

Shane had been the first man to whom she'd been intimate. After his death, she'd given herself exclusively to Dax—the only one who had loved Shane as much as she had. They'd been together the entire last decade, but there had never been a spark between them. No passion had touched her soul. No urges beyond need.

But Colton Wilde affected her differently. She couldn't explain it, but she was drawn to him in every way. He was a smart, sophisticated man who probably knew what to do with a woman. At almost thirty years of age, she longed for more. She *needed* more. In small towns, though, everyone judged morals. And few knew about her what they should. As far as the people in Topaz were concerned, she belonged to Dax. When she was ready to give her true heart away, he merited the reward, if that's what it was. Everyone said so.

When Kelsey-Rose spotted Colton on the sidewalk across the street, her heart doubled its beat. His physique had perfect balance and composure. He didn't wear a cowboy hat or ball cap, and his leather oxfords were certainly not cut from the same leather as a pair of burnished boots. Even from this distance, she could see that his style and class were not all Texan. It was obvious. He had a worldly finesse to the way he handled everything.

She nipped at her fingernails. The magnetism was real—for her, anyway—but Colton's absence this week had been bothersome.

She blamed herself. Her comfortable wardrobe wouldn't flatter any figure. She was plain. Unimpressive. Just a small-town girl without any magic. She was boring in every kind of way.

OUTSIDE, COLTON GREETED THE DRIVER OF THE moving truck. "You're here earlier than I expected," he said with a handshake.

The man gave a thumb to the highway behind him. "Stayed at the rest area west of town last night." He handed Colton a clipboard with several pages. "If you'll just sign showing we're at the right place to unload, we can get started."

Colton took the pen and signed, and then he handed it back. "Everything is going up to the second floor, but you've got three ways up. This building used to be a department store, so it has a freight elevator inside. It also has a set of Scarlett O'Hara stairs."

"A set of what?" the driver asked.

With a half smile, Colton said, "Sorry. I'm an old movie buff. There's a wide, elegant-looking staircase inside, completely out of character in this building." Then he pointed to the rear parking lot. "But there's also an outside entrance in the back."

A tangle of younger men piled out of the truck's extended cab, gathering on the sidewalk.

"Can you and I take a look before we get started?" the driver asked.

"Sure. Follow me." Colton and the man entered the building together. After a tour of the empty apartment and its entrances, he said, "Do you need me for anything right now?"

"Just furniture placement. Once it's in, we'll unload the boxes according to how they're marked by room."

"How long before you're finished?"

The man looked at his wristwatch. "We should be done by three, I think."

Colton glanced across to the florist shop. "Great. I've got to take care of something real quick, but I'll be right back."

In a jog, Colton crossed the street to the shop owned by Kelsey-Rose.

"Hello." She greeted him even before the glass door closed behind him. "I see your moving company arrived."

He turned for a look, only then realizing the big truck was blocking half the traffic lanes. "Should I ask them to move before they start unloading?"

Her hand swished the air. "They're fine. It's not like we have a lot of traffic on weekdays. Besides, if Eddie has an issue, he'll let you know."

"Who's Eddie?"

"Our police chief. He's married to my sister, Mae."

He'd forgotten how beautiful this woman was, and he was having a hard time pulling his gaze away. Her eyes were bluer than they had any right to be on a redhead, and her casual country-girl style bore an earthy wildness. She was a free spirit, not a silk-stocking socialite.

"I've thought about you all week," he said.

"Really?" She stood straighter. "I couldn't tell."

"Yes, really." The sweet smell of roses was in the air. "I should have come sooner."

"You're here now."

He gave an embarrassed shrug. "Actually, to be honest, I came in to buy flowers for Lillie," he said. "Today is her birthday."

When the light in her eyes dimmed, he reached for

her hand and took hold. "That's the excuse I'm using anyway."

"Colton, you don't need an excuse." Kelsey-Rose went to the floral cooler where she kept her special premade arrangements. "Lillie loves Gerbera daisies." She pulled a tin French flower pail out and held it up. It was filled with a dozen colorful flowers accented with fresh bear grass. "How about these?"

"Perfect." On the word, his lilt softened. He walked to the cash register and pulled out a credit card.

Kelsey-Rose cleared her throat, then with lowered head, she cast a sly upward glance, hoping to catch his eye. "You wouldn't want to join me for dinner again tonight, would you?"

"I was planning to ask you the same thing."

"You were?"

"Yes, but I was going to use the pretense of needing your decorating opinion."

She smiled. "I love decorating."

AT SIX O'CLOCK, KELSEY-ROSE LOCKED THE FRONT door to her shop and turned out all but the interior security lights, but before leaving through the back door, she dialed her neighbor.

"Hi, Leah, I'll be in town a little longer than usual tonight. Do you mind feeding Free and letting him out for me?"

She didn't feel the need to give a reason for her delay, and thankfully, Leah hadn't asked.

With keys in hand, Kelsey-Rose left through the back door, locking it, and then walked to her sea blue Santa Fe, glancing across the street to *The Blue Topaz*

Times building. She dropped the keys back inside her purse, deciding to walk instead. The last thing she needed was rumors, and having her car spotted after dark at the home of the new man in town would light the match.

At the top landing of his outside stairs, she took an extra deep breath, slowly exhaled, and then knocked.

Colton opened the door wearing brown penny loafers, dark rinse jeans, and a plain white T-shirt instead of his earlier work attire.

"Hi there." His gaze swept the figure of her, lingering much too long. "Please, come in." He stepped aside for her. "I meant to change out of these old clothes before you got here, but I lost track of time. You'll never believe the mess I've made in just a few hours."

She pointed to his jeans first, then to her own. "Your clothes don't look old. Actually, we look alike now."

He smiled. "Yeah, but you look great. Me, not so much."

The apartment in the historic building had over three thousand square feet, being the entire upper level to the newspaper offices below. It had high, fourteen-foot ceilings with tall windows on three sides, and although the unpacked boxes were neatly stacked, there was barely enough walk space between them to maneuver through the big open room.

Colton led her through the cardboard maze, finally ending in the kitchen. He opened both sides of the stainless-steel French door refrigerator and felt inside. "It's starting to get cold, but as you can see, it's quite empty." He closed it, then said, "So, I have nothing but tap water to offer, which I can't do because I haven't found the drinking glasses yet."

"Well, then, we'd better get you unpacked. I might get thirsty." When he laughed, she did, too. She gave a wave with her phone. "Why not order pizza tonight? They'll deliver plastic cups with a liter of whatever to drink."

"Great." He took his phone from his pocket. "Who am I calling?"

"Salvatore's Pizza." She showed him the number displayed on her phone. As he called, she said, "Their bacon cheeseburger pizza is the deal of the week. It's a town favorite."

"Does that mean it's the high school football team's standing order?"

She laughed. "Why, yes, it does."

Colton placed the order, gave them his address, and paid over the phone.

"Where should I start?" Kelsey-Rose scanned the room.

"I didn't really expect you to help unpack boxes, but without you, I might be living out of cardboard for months. I guess I should have hired white-glove service for the delivery and setup, too." He did a three-sixty turn, stopping where he started. "The moving guys hooked up all the appliances and assembled the bed, and I managed to hang the clothes from the wardrobe cartons earlier, so," he hesitated while scanning the boxes again, "maybe we should focus on finding the drinking glasses, coffee cups, plates, and silverware." Then he laughed. "But finding the sheets, pillows, and blankets is pretty important, too. I don't want to have to sleep at the hotel again tonight."

"Right," Kelsey-Rose agreed. "Let's just start with these boxes in the kitchen first, and then we can look for the bedding."

COLTON HAD NEVER PACKED OR UNPACKED A BOX IN his life until today—he'd always had other people to do that for him, but after Beth's comments earlier, he wasn't keen on admitting that to the only friend he had in town. Besides, his life had changed drastically in the last two months. He needed to start doing things for himself. Following Kelsey-Rose's lead, he inspected the boxes, finally finding labels on the side of each carton with a partially itemized list of the contents. "Hey, this one says the coffeemaker is inside."

"Well, great! You open that one, and I'll look for the box with dishes." She pushed and then swiveled a few boxes, reading more labels.

But Colton stood, scoping the kitchen.

"Problem?" she asked.

His hands landed on his hips. "I used scissors to open the wardrobe cartons earlier, but I left them somewhere." Jokingly, he said, "You wouldn't happen to have a knife or anything to cut the tape off these boxes, would you?"

"Oh, yep!" She maneuvered back through to the living room, where she'd left her purse earlier. She carried it back to the kitchen, pulled out two utility knives, and handed him one.

Brows raised, he said, "Do you always carry box cutters in your purse?"

She shrugged. "I thought you might need them. I brought them over from the shop. I open shipping boxes just about every day."

"You're a handy girl."

But she was more than that.

Kelsey-Rose had four and a half boxes unpacked by

the time their pizza arrived. She was putting plates into the cabinet when the door buzzer sounded. A glance out the kitchen window showed Toby, Dax's youngest brother, standing on the stairway landing with their delivery. She moved to an inconspicuous spot away from the window.

Colton opened the door and greeted the teen, then took the pizza and the liter of Pepsi from him, setting them on a stack of nearby boxes. He pulled a five-dollar bill from his wallet.

"Oh, hey," the teen said. "You already gave me a tip when you ordered. It went on your charge."

"It's okay. That's extra for climbing all those stairs."

"Thanks," the boy said, accepting the bill. "Next time you call for delivery, be sure to ask for Toby, okay?"

After closing the door, Colton glanced over a row of boxes into the kitchen. "Kelsey-Rose, where are you?"

"Here," she answered, weaving through stacks of boxes, finding her way into the living room where Colton had taken their dinner delivery.

He set the flat box and the liter bottle down on the coffee table, then pulled napkins and plastic cups out of a bag marked *Salvatore's – The Real Deal.*

"This is the only table in the whole place that isn't stacked with boxes."

Kelsey-Rose sat on the leather sectional. "Did they remember to put packets of red pepper flakes in the bag?"

Colton reached in, pulling out two fiery chili packets and two clear packets of parmesan. He handed her one of each and then sat beside her on the couch. He lifted the box lid but then stopped. He stared at the pizza before shifting a look to Kelsey-Rose. "It has pickle slices on it. And fried bacon."

"It's a bacon cheeseburger pizza. Don't you eat pickles on a cheeseburger?"

"On a burger, yes, but not on a pizza."

"I love pickles." She reached for the pizza, put a slice on a paper napkin, and handed it to him, reserving a good-humored smile. Then she took a slice for herself and bit into it.

Colton waited for her reaction to the sourness he expected, but when she had none, he gave his slice another look. After a moment, he picked off a dill round and offered it to Kelsey-Rose. "Want mine?"

"Where's your sense of adventure?" She laughed. "Be brave. Just try it."

"Adventure, huh?" Her wheedling coaxed a smile from him. "Be brave, the lady says." Colton popped the pickle into his mouth and then bit into the slice and chewed. Nodding, he said, "Hey, not bad." Then, "This is actually *really* good."

"Told you." Kelsey-Rose laughed again, nudging him teasingly. "But it's the bacon that really sends it over the top." Her gaze caught his, roaming his face as if seeing it for the first time.

"You're amazing," he said. This playful woman had turned up the heat, and he doubted she even knew it.

"Why? Because I eat pizza with bacon and pickles?"

"No, because you're incredibly beautiful and because you're *yourself*. It's almost as if you don't know how extraordinary you are."

The mystery of this flame-haired beauty spurred wayward thoughts and more. Beneath the lighted ceiling fans, dimly lit, Colton leaned in, pressing his lips to hers. She hadn't pulled away. She hadn't stopped him.

~

AT HIS KISS, A FLUTTER OF BUTTERFLIES TOOK FLIGHT inside of her. The magnetism that drew a man and a woman together had eluded her for almost a lifetime, but here, so close to Colton Wilde, her body implicitly understood. The "spark" was real. A live wire was loose.

Kelsey-Rose set down her half-eaten slice. "There's nothing special about me." She faked a smile, regretting that she'd freed herself to feel things she had no right to feel. "A lot of single women live in this town, and they are all more exciting than me. Half already know about you. The other half will find out soon enough. People like you are hard to hide in a small town. Talk is flying about a gorgeous new bachelor in town."

"Is there now?" Colton laughed, then his knee brushed against hers.

Though an innocent touch, it ignited a fire low inside her, sending her glance downward. If only she had it in her to be forward. To daringly lean over and kiss Colton like he'd kissed her. To touch him intimately. No matter how many times she'd begged the heavens for just one chance to be the girl she wanted to be, she was afraid to risk it now.

She lifted her gaze. "Honestly, I'm the most boring person you'll ever meet. You'll find out soon enough, and I'd hate for you to be disappointed by surprise."

Her desire to be a woman no one in this town would recognize—someone this stranger might want in his bed for the night—might have been in her dreams, but it wasn't in her DNA.

Kelsey-Rose stood. She glanced at her grandmother's Timex on her wrist. "Look at the time. It's a quarter 'til nine already." She reached across a stack of boxes for her purse. "I should be going."

But when she turned for goodbyes, Colton was there, beside her.

"Don't go." His blue-gray eyes melted the thin layer of ice she'd kept frozen between them.

With a whisper, Colton's lips brushed hers. "I want you to stay."

Kelsey-Rose dropped her purse. Wrapping her arms around him, she pressed her body to his, her lips to his. The kiss awakened every one of her senses, unleashing a lust she'd repressed for too many years. The heat within her was rising fast. A dazed kaleidoscope of colors twirled and flashed through closed eyelids—white, red, blue.

Then a knock—metal to wood—rapped three times. "Police. Open up, please."

Startled, Kelsey-Rose jerked back away from Colton. "Oh, God, it's Eddie!"

"It's fine." Unfazed, Colton brushed a stray strand of her red hair back into place, then he started for the door, slowly weaving through the maze of boxes. "It's probably a welcome to the neighborhood visit."

"Doubtful," Kelsey-Rose answered, slinging her purse strap over her shoulder.

To the second knock, Colton called, "Coming." He pulled open the door to find a tall, muscled police officer with a backdrop of flashing lights from the parking lot below. "Good evening, Officer. What can I do for you?"

The policeman, dressed in a black uniform with blue and gold arm patches, held a long-handled flashlight as his doorknocker. He slipped it back into its holder on his belt.

"Are you the new owner of this building?"

"Yes, I am. Colton Wilde." He reached for a handshake but lowered his hand when it was ignored.

"I'm looking for Kelsey-Rose Flowers. She owns the florist shop on the corner. Her car is there, but she isn't. No one seems to know where she is, and you're the only stranger in town."

Kelsey-Rose skirted the boxes, then pulled the door open wider. "Eddie, I'm right here."

He swung a look between Kelsey-Rose and Colton. "Is everything all right? Dax said you didn't come home after work, and when he went to the flower shop to check on you, just your car was there."

"Everything is fine, Eddie." She glanced at Colton, then back to her brother-in-law. "I was just leaving." She pushed past Eddie and took the stairs down.

Kelsey-Rose crossed the street without looking back.

CHAPTER 8

Colton spent most of the night unpacking boxes and glancing out his window at the florist shop, which was closed up dark except for the dim interior security lights.

He couldn't get Kelsey-Rose off his mind. Her eyes, the color of fine cobalt-blue crystal, had eased his earlier doubts about settling down in this small town for a year. There was definite chemistry between them—unlike anything he'd experienced before. It felt natural, not showy.

Women had always found him attractive, but he wasn't blind to the power of his financial status. Because of his wealth, he'd had his pick of beautiful women all willing to cater to him, but having a real relationship, one that was authentic and honest was another story. Now, thanks to the change in his father's will, his endless cash flow and the charm it bought him were gone. All he had left now were yields and dividends from stock investments, a savings account he'd never seen so low, and a bank balance that would barely tide him over half a year until he could start making a profit off *The Blue Topaz Times*.

No matter how drawn he was to Kelsey-Rose, his focus needed to stay on business, not on that red-haired beauty, but she was stuck in his head like a debt he owed. He couldn't shake the feeling he had about her.

A year in this small Central Texas town was all he needed to become financially solvent again and rebuild his creditworthiness. After that, he could return home to Coppell or anywhere else in the metroplex where the lifestyle wasn't so "lights out at nine" rural. He could shake the quiet of this little town off his conscience and get his life back. He could prove to his father that he had worth after all.

In the morning, Colton went to the kitchen in his vintage apartment and made coffee for himself. He was at the living room window, sipping from his cup when Kelsey-Rose pulled into the parking lot of her florist shop. She got out, never looking his way, and disappeared into the store. He watched as the lights came on inside.

She had a boyfriend, he knew. But if it were a serious relationship, would she have kissed him last night? Would she have kissed him the *way* she had last night? His attraction to her was intense. He sensed a lonely lioness beneath her modest demeanor. She had been close to losing self-control—he'd felt it. And he was fairly sure he would have obliged the woman had the police chief not come knocking. Last night had to say something about the commitment she had to her boyfriend, didn't it?

Colton shook the woman from his thoughts, gulped

the last of his coffee before setting the empty cup in the sink, and then he showered and dressed for work.

He took the inside Scarlett O'Hara stairs down to the office where Mack, Scott, Lillie, and Beth waited, having their morning coffee klatch together.

"Morning, all," he greeted them.

"Heard you had a late night," Beth said to him.

Colton stopped, giving her a questioning look. "What do you mean?"

"You and Kelsey-Rose? You know she's got a devoted boyfriend, don't you?" she said.

He tensed. Straightening his posture. "How could you know about that?" He glanced at the oversized clock on the wall. "It's not even nine o'clock in the morning yet. That's less than twelve hours." Ire prickled him. He turned and headed for the kitchen. He needed more coffee. Over his shoulder, he shouted, "Why this town needs a newspaper, I'll never know. All you need to do is wake up around here, and news just flies through your window."

Inaudible chatter made its way into the kitchen but stopped once he returned with coffee.

"Is that cleaning woman you hired coming today? There's barely a clean cup."

"Tonight," Beth said, getting out of her chair and grabbing her tan wool coat. "I have a few appointments this morning," she said to Lillie. "Call if you need me."

After Beth left, Colton turned to Mack, who was still sitting on the corner of his desk. "Do you ever use a chair?"

Mack stood, hands raised. "Hey, don't take it out on me."

"Sorry, Mack." Colton sighed. "Didn't mean to take

it out on you." He turned to Scott and Lillie. "You two either. I was just caught off guard at how fast social news travels." Then he sputtered a laugh. "Sure is a lot faster than the newspaper."

"Don't worry about it," Mack said, going to his desk chair and sitting.

Colton turned to Mack as if he were the only person left in the room. "What did I do to make Beth dislike me so much?"

"It's not you," Mack told him. "She's just dealing with a bad hand of cards life dealt her."

Colton understood that. He'd gone from a winning streak to a losing one in the blink of an eye. "Good to know." He turned and headed toward his private office, talking as he walked. "I'll be working on 'This Week in Local History' this morning, but I've got a flat-screen TV scheduled for delivery sometime today that needs to be wall-mounted. Be sure to let me know when it arrives."

The four files he'd chosen were on his desk, arranged by date, starting with the first week in November. He planned to debut the new column in the last November issue, which meant he needed to get started on the update of the old story quickly.

He opened the first file, dated a decade ago: *Two Prisoners Escape, Kill Topaz Police Officer.* Colton read the whole story, making notes on a yellow legal pad.

At the time, Topaz employed four full-time police officers and two volunteer reserves for events and gatherings. The officer killed, Joe Pixley, was a veteran on the force, serving almost twenty years, when the two escapees robbed the gas station owned by Pixley's parents.

It doesn't get more local than that, Colton thought. He dropped the legal pad and pen into his satchel and then went to find his new managing editor.

At his desk, Mack sat hunched over his keyboard, typing.

"Say, Mack, do you remember the Pixley killing?"

Mack sat back. "Sure. Joe was a great guy."

"Is his family around?"

"Yeah, they still own the gas station out on Highway 29. Why?"

Colton grabbed his jacket. "I'm going out to talk to them. Call if you need me."

The northern tip of the Texas Hill Country offered an unusual allure with its rolling, hilly elevations sloping into fertile farmland and cattle ranches. Although woody pecan trees, various oaks, mesquite, and cedar shaped most of the landscape on Colton's drive north, breaks between the hills leveled into open prairie mixed with prickly pear cacti, bluestem, switch-grass, sumac and sage, and other native vegetation. For centuries, the Lipan Apache and Comanche had prized this land for its plentiful hunting.

All that was missing from this history-laden land for Colton was a quick way to get to the Dallas metroplex, where its eight million or so people, skyscrapers, music venues, museums, and arts, could give a spur to his existence. Although he had a keen interest in history, he missed the vibrant flair unique to his normally upscale life.

On the plus side, the Gulf of Mexico and its fresh sea breezes were just a few hours south of where he stood.

The GPS cautioned that his destination was one-quarter of a mile ahead. Colton slowed his Corvette, pulling off the road onto a dirt shoulder that led to a sixties-style gas station. It had a tall, separate double-bay garage behind it. The painted red and white wooden sign read *Pixley's Gas and Garage*.

Colton parked in front near the main window where the exterior ice machine took up too much space, and then grabbed his brown leather satchel with a legal pad inside and got out of the car.

He pulled open the glass front door to the interested eyes of several men, one who stood behind the cashiering counter, all ogling his white Corvette. He looked back at it before saying, "It's the new convertible Stingray."

"How new?" one man asked. "Does it have the Z51 performance package?"

A smile and nod came from Colton. "It does. You know your Corvettes."

"Man, I've wanted one of those cars my whole life."

Colton extended his hand. "Colton Wilde. I'm the new owner of *The Blue Topaz Times*."

"Should have guessed." The man shook hands, then said, "I'm Mel Smith. I own the only auto parts store in town." He turned to the other men and pointed. "Larry has the motorcycle shop you passed coming out here, and Ross is Pixley's shop mechanic." He nodded to the man behind the counter. "You probably already know Kyle."

Colton turned to the thirtyish man at the counter who wore a short-sleeve, blue and white plaid Western-style shirt with snap-flap pockets. He was thin and had curly blond hair that stuck out from beneath a ball cap. "You the owner here, Kyle?"

"Nah," he said with a smile. "One day, maybe. My granddad owns the place. I just work here."

Remembering the newspaper article, Colton asked, "Are you Joe's son?"

Kyle pulled back, brows raised. "Yeah. Did you know my dad?"

"No." Colton shook his head. He glanced back at the other men, then turned his attention back to Kyle. "I was hoping to talk to you and your grandparents about how things have been since you lost your dad. Maybe after you finish up with your customers?"

"They're not customers. Not really, anyway. They just stop in to talk." Kyle turned the conversation back to his grandparents. "Grandma passed away last July, but Gramps is around." He nodded to one of the men. "Probably out working on the car Ross overpromised to a customer today."

Ross pitched his empty water bottle into the trash can. "Yeah. I need to get back to work." Tossing a look at the other men, he said, "See y'all later."

Before long, a man wearing gray pinstriped coveralls came through the back entrance, scattering the remaining men out the door. He walked to the front counter, wiping his hands on an oil rag. When he noticed Colton, he said, "I'm John Pixley. Ross said you was lookin' for me?"

Colton reached for a handshake. "I'm Colton Wilde. The new owner of *The Blue Topaz Times*." He gave a nod to Kyle behind the counter. "I'd like to talk to you two about an article I'm writing."

"What about?"

"About Joe's death and how you've coped as a family without him."

"That was ten years ago." He stuffed the oil rag

deep into his coveralls pocket. "What's the point of bringin' it all up again?"

"I'd like to update the story."

Kyle said, "Is it okay, Gramps?"

John Pixley took a seat on a tall swivel stool at the cashiering counter, and said, "Yeah. Go ahead."

With a bursting grin, Kyle said, "I've never been interviewed by a newspaper before."

"There's nothing to it," Colton said. He put his satchel on the counter and pulled out his yellow legal pad and a pen. He focused on the grandfather. "Just to get started, why don't you fill me in on the details of the robbery? Did the convicts just walk in through the front door that day, or did they sneak in the back, or what?"

John nodded at his grandson. "You'll have to ask Kyle about that. He was here, not me."

Colton shot a look at Kyle. "You're the one who was robbed at gunpoint?"

He shook his head. "No, I was working on a truck out back in the garage. It was Shane who got held up."

With a cock of his head, Colton asked, "Who is Shane again?" He didn't want to admit that he didn't remember anyone named Shane in the story he'd read.

"He helped out as a mechanic sometimes when we were shorthanded," Kyle explained. "He was good with a wrench, but he was great in a saddle. Best saddle bronc rider I'd ever seen, but anyway, I'd asked him to work for an hour or so after Dax called in sick. I was replacing an oil filter when the bell on the door rang, so we knew someone had come in. Shane went up front to wait on the customer for me."

John interjected. "All of the boys were friends from high school. After graduation, they came to me and asked if I would teach them how to be mechanics. I agreed and hired Kyle and Dax full-time, but Shane wasn't really lookin' for a job. He was already working on a ranch. He just wanted to learn how to take care of his truck when he was out on the road going from rodeo to rodeo, so I just paid him by the hour whenever he could help us out. I'd planned for my son Joe to work alongside me and then take over someday, but he had other ideas." He gave a nod to Kyle. "I was glad to have my grandson show interest in the family business, and I needed the extra help."

Colton nodded, then asked, "So, Shane was up front—right here where we are now—when the escapees robbed the place?"

"Yeah," Kyle said. "It was almost closing time, and it was just the two of us."

John Pixley gave a hefty sigh. "I never should have left those boys alone that night."

"We were almost twenty, Gramps. It's not like we were kids." Then Kyle looked at Colton again. "Soon as Shane gave 'em the money from the cash register, they ran for their car."

"And then Shane called the police?"

"Nobody called the police. My dad drove up in the squad car, planning to help us lock up for the night after he found out we were here alone. Soon as the escapees saw him, they thought he was coming to arrest them, so they shot him."

For the next twenty minutes, Colton interviewed the two men, being interrupted only once by a customer needing gas.

"Well, that should do it," Colton said, flipping through his notes. "Except the original article mentions a man named Audley. I'd like to talk to him, and to Shane, too. Do you know where I can find them?"

"The cemetery, if you're lookin'," John said. "Audley was Shane's God-given name. Audley Shane Delany. A couple of weeks after the robbery, he had a bad accident."

"Did that happen here, too?"

"No," Kyle said. "He was working out at the ranch with his girlfriend when he decided to try ridin' a bronc that nobody ever rode. Shane was the real deal. He was a rodeo champ. He'd won just about every buckle he could get, even the all-around at the National High School Finals Rodeo the summer before. He had a good rodeo scholarship for college, too, but he'd delayed his first semester when his girlfriend threatened to break up with him if he left without her. She was a senior in high school, so she couldn't go with him yet."

"Shane was smart," John Pixley said. "He was gonna be a rodeo rider for as long as he could, but he knew that wasn't gonna last forever, so he planned to study animal science at Sam Houston, and then when his rodeo days were over, he and Kelsey-Rose would run her father's ranch together."

Colton's head jerked up from the notepad. "Kelsey-Rose?"

"Yeah," Kyle said. "She owns the flower shop on the square now. Next to the newspaper building. They was gonna get married and take over that ranch together someday."

"And Shane was killed in that accident?" Colton wanted clarification.

Kyle nodded. "Yeah. It was real bad."

John Pixley stood. "We were still mourning the loss of Joe when it happened, but Kyle and Shane had been good friends since first grade, so losing Shane was hard, especially so soon after Joe was killed." He offered his hand to Colton. "I need to get back out to the garage, but glad you stopped by." They shook, and then he handed Colton his business card. "Welcome to town."

CHAPTER 9

The Sunday family dinner was a weekly tradition, so rarely did anyone neglect the commitment.

It was a quarter until five in the evening when Kelsey-Rose arrived, later than usual. She stood in the kitchen of the ranch-style home, glancing out the bay window above the sink at her family, mingling and laughing just as they did every Sunday night in the tranquil, heavily treed but well-manicured backyard. The expansive flagstone patio was nearly the same square footage as the home, with trails that led through the trees on dimly lit paths to a footbridge that arched over a shallow creek near a secluded, lighted gazebo.

Kelsey-Rose slid the roasted, diced sweet potatoes out of the oven, setting the pan on a rack to cool, then finished tossing the mixed greens with pepitas and feta cheese for her favorite fall salad. She added the cooled sweet potato bites to the bowl and had just reached for the maple bacon balsamic dressing when the doorbell chimed.

"Coming," she called out. She left the salad bowl on the countertop and went to the door, pulling it open.

"Colton," she said. "What are you doing here?"

He was dressed in dark gray chinos, a gray cashmere pullover sweater with leather-ribbed shoulders, and underneath it, he had on a blood-red shirt with only its collar showing. Her heart skipped a beat at the mere sight of him.

Colton smiled as his gaze settled on her. "Your father invited me. I thought you knew." He held out the wine gift bag he carried.

"No, I didn't know." She took the bag and then stepped aside, inviting him in. "He didn't say anything at all to me about it."

"Are you disappointed?"

Did she sound disappointed? She didn't mean to—surprised maybe—because the truth was, had she known Colton was coming, she would have showered, worn something nicer, and prepared herself emotionally. She hadn't seen him since the night of their kiss.

"No," Kelsey-Rose said. "Not disappointed at all." She glanced down at herself, wearing jeans wore-thin and an old gray sweatshirt. Her hand went to her hair. The dark blue stocking cap was still on her head. "We're casual here at the ranch," she said, hoping to justify her lazy look rather than explaining that attractive, well-fitting clothes drew unwanted male attention, which she had expertly learned to shun. "And Sunday suppers are always outside unless Mother Nature says no, so everyone is in the backyard." She tipped her head into a side nod and said, "Come with me."

On their way, Kelsey-Rose grabbed the big wooden salad bowl off the counter. With the handles of the wine bag over her wrist like a bracelet, she opened the back door leading onto the porch, crossing the flagstone patio to an extensive outdoor kitchen where the family gathered.

"Hey, look who I found at the door." She set the bowl on the polished stone counter near the built-in grill and then handed the wine gift bag to her father. With a side-eye glare aimed at him, she said, "I guess you forgot to tell me Colton was coming tonight."

"Did I forget to mention it?" Harley Flowers reached past his daughter, shaking Colton's hand. With a turn to his family, he announced, "Everyone, this is Colton Wilde. The new owner of *The Blue Topaz Times*. I've asked him to join us for supper tonight." Then he turned back to Kelsey-Rose. "How was your ride?"

"Good. Cool temps." With a glance at Colton, she said, "That's why I am grungier than usual. I spent the afternoon on Backbone Ridge. I go riding up there whenever I get the chance."

When her stepmother approached on her way into the house, Kelsey-Rose gave another introduction, presenting Nina to Colton.

"We're so glad you came," Nina said to their guest, shaking his hand. Then she looked at Kelsey-Rose. "I forgot to bring out the pies. I'll be back in a few minutes."

When Nina left, Kelsey-Rose motioned to her younger sister who stood waiting. "Colton, you remember Rainey from the flower shop, don't you?"

"Yes, I do." Colton greeted her with a smile. "It's nice to see you again." Then he looked down at the little girl whose arms were clamped around Rainey's left leg. "This pretty lady must be the sleeper I didn't get to meet that day."

"Yep, that's her," Rainey said, running her fingers

through the girl's wavy blonde hair. "This is Emma. She's two years old, and she's very shy."

Colton laughed when Emma peeked at him from between her mother's legs. "She's a cute one." The wink he gave the girl caused Emma to bolt for Nina, who was crossing the patio with a pie. Rainey turned and ran after her, snatching Emma before she could tackle Nina from behind.

"Oh, good catch." Kelsey-Rose laughed with Colton when Rainey lifted the girl into a twirl.

When the two of them were alone, Colton did a 360-degree turn, taking in the expansive backyard. "This place is a surprise. When your dad said, 'Come out to the ranch,' I didn't expect this."

"What did you expect?" she asked him.

"A real working ranch, I guess."

"This *is* a real working ranch. It's dedicated to raising Texas Longhorn cattle, but before 2010, the Forty Flowers Ranch was a thirty-six-hundred-acre cow-calf operation with about eight hundred acres in managed pastureland and the rest in native pasture or woodlands, but the drought hit us hard. By 2013, Daddy decided he had to take the ranch in a different direction to stay profitable, so he sold off the Angus and built up our herd of Longhorn cattle. They're kind of a no-hassle breed because they have a natural resistance to a lot of the diseases and parasites that cause most cattle to get sick. Longhorns also take advantage of whatever type of forage the land offers them, so they put less stress on the pastures. It was a smart decision."

Colton had steady eyes on Kelsey-Rose, listening to every word. When she finished, he said, "For a beautiful flower shop owner, I'm surprised you know so much about cattle and ranching. You impress me at every turn."

"It's easy when you grow up here. I worked this ranch until I was twenty." She took a moment to contemplate the question, but then she asked him, "Have you ever seen a Longhorn up close?"

"No," he said. "I usually just see them as decorations in corporate pastures or on a parade route. I'd sure like to one of these days, though."

Kelsey-Rose glanced at her family who was all busy together at the grilling station in the outdoor kitchen. "Come on." She took his hand and pulled. "Daddy keeps his two best show guys in the pasture behind the barn."

At the stock corral, two longhorn steers, one burnt orange with white pinto-like spots and the other white with sienna speckles, stood at pitchfork-sized mounds of fresh hay, peacefully chewing. In the background was a natural pasture, separate from the show cattle, where other longhorns grazed.

Kelsey-Rose pointed, directing Colton's attention to the iconic cattle in the distance. "Longhorns have an incredible history to tell. The DNA of our herd can be traced back to the 1860s, but some herds can be traced back to the fifteenth century here in Texas."

Colton looked at her. "You know, this would make a great story for the paper."

"It would," she said with a pleased smile. "These are impressive animals who prosper on native grass that regular cattle cannot survive on alone, and they can go without water for days. They protect each other from harm, tend to fellow herd members who are sick or wounded, and they calve effortlessly. They will amaze you with their intelligence, and vet bills for a herd like ours are almost nonexistent." Kelsey-Rose glanced at Colton. "They're incredible animals." Her level of knowledge had given this moment a seriousness she hadn't intended, so she softened the mood with a smile, and then she pointed again. "These two are so docile you could saddle 'em and ride 'em. The mostly white steer is named Speckled Pete, and the burnt orange guy with the burnished horns is Sequoia Sam. Those curved beauties might measure ninety or more inches tip to tip."

When Speckled Pete turned his head, the last bright light from the setting sun glinted off his ivory-colored horns. Colton reached through the pipe fencing, feeling the bowed horn of the mellow steer. Gently, he rubbed. "I don't think any other breed of cattle captures the imagination quite like a Texas Longhorn."

"True," Kelsey-Rose agreed. "Longhorns are the real heart and identity of Texas."

It was almost dark when they returned to the family gathering where twinkle lights dotted the trees surrounding the expansive backyard patio.

"This must have been quite a place to grow up," Colton said. "You could get lost in the peace and quiet. It's a different world out here, isn't it?"

Kelsey-Rose glanced around at the house and the backyard, trying to see it through his eyes. "It didn't always look this way. My grandfather bought the ranch in 1940, hence the name Forty Flowers, and then he built this home using stone quarried right here on this land. When Dad and Nina decided to remodel the house about twenty years ago, there was nothing back here but an overgrown tangle of trees, dead grass, dying shrubs, and a big lopsided hole dug into the ground for a fire pit. Nina redesigned the backyard and hired a landscaping crew to make her vision of it come true. After the work was finished, this amazing refuge was here. That's when Dad started a new family tradition of having Sunday suppers out here, rain or shine. We've only had to move our gathering inside twice because of the weather. Once, we had an incredible ice storm that dropped temps down into the negative digits, which just doesn't happen this far south. And then one other time, a cat-four hurricane hit Corpus Christi, then swung upstate, bringing with it fifty-mile-per-hour winds. Otherwise, we deal with the elements we're handed. It's the only honest way to love Mother Nature."

When she looked at Colton, he was quiet but smiling. "I've been talking too much, haven't I?" she asked.

"Not at all," he said, his grin staying. "But I am curious…do you have any idea how much I want to take you in my arms right now and finish that kiss we started?"

"You do?" She smiled, glancing down. How could he possibly be attracted to her looking like she looked tonight? "I thought maybe I'd ruined the whole vibe between us when I ran out and left you standing there alone to explain things to Eddie that night, which by the way, he's never mentioned to me."

Colton's focus shifted into the distance over her shoulder. "Speaking of your brother-in-law, here he comes with a pretty redhead who might be glaring at me. I can't tell." He extended his hand as Kelsey-Rose turned. "Hello again," he said to Eddie.

"We were wondering where you two wandered off to," Eddie said.

The woman gave Colton an inquisitive look, one

that came naturally to older sisters. "So, you're the mystery man everyone is talking about?"

"Am I?" Colton laughed.

"And I can see why," she told him. "You're gorgeous. Are you married? Or have you ever been?"

"Mae!" Kelsey-Rose felt the rising heat of a flushed face.

"What?" Mae said to her sister. "It's a perfectly polite question." Then she gave Kelsey-Rose a head-to-toe scan. "I've seen you look better."

Suppressing a smile, Colton said, "No. Never married." In riposte, he asked, "You?"

Without missing a verbal beat, Mae looked at her husband. "Oh, I married Eddie right out of high school. He's the only man who ever showed any real interest, and I refused to go through my adult life as Mae Flowers. It was hard enough as a kid. My parents thought it was cute since I'd been born on May first, but the 'April showers bring May Flowers' teasing never ended." She reached out to Colton for a handshake. "I'm Mae Edwards now."

Eddie glanced at Colton with a sarcastic smirk. "Obviously, true love."

They both laughed, then Mae asked, "Can I get you a beer, or a glass of wine, or tea?"

After a glance at Eddie's amber bottle, Colton said, "I'll have the same. Thank you."

When Mae left to get drinks, Eddie said, "Hey, I know it was all perfectly innocent, but half the town is talking about you two being alone together in your apartment the other night." He reached out and gave an affectionate squeeze to Kelsey-Rose's shoulder. "The townsfolk are pretty protective of Kelsey-Rose and Dax, so you might get a few icy stares for a while."

"Already have," Colton said.

Kelsey-Rose shrugged Eddie's hand off her shoulder.

"Excuse me," she said to Colton. She walked away from the two men, past her family, taking the path behind the outdoor kitchen that led into the forested darkness lit only by the twinkling of strung lights.

Alone on the bridge that arched over a creek, Kelsey-Rose stood under the night's rising moon with a handful of old pecan nuts she'd scooped off the ground beneath the trees along the way. Life always found a way to humiliate her. One by one, she tossed the hulls into the steady flow of the water below, watching them float back toward her, only to disappear beneath the footbridge.

"Hey," came a tender voice.

Her glance caught sight of Colton.

He stopped beside her on the bridge.

She tried to smile, but it came out barely a grin. "Sorry to leave you holding the bag again on a conversation with Eddie," she said. "I'm usually better at fading away. No one misses me if I'm quick and quiet."

"I missed you," he told her. After a moment, he said, "I take it Dax is your boyfriend?"

She shrugged. "I guess so."

Colton nodded. His focus followed hers to the creek below. "Then I should apologize. I don't usually kiss another man's girl."

Kelsey-Rose hurled the remaining pecans into the creek.

"Hey." His voice was low and soothing. He took her hand, holding it until her clenched fist relaxed. "I'll apologize for the kiss if you want me to."

"And if I don't want you to?"

Their eyes met, unguarded.

"Then I'd like to kiss you again."

Softly, Kelsey-Rose said, "I don't want you to apologize."

Colton had her in his arms, his lips on hers, his tongue exploring her mouth. His embrace was strong, so tight she felt his manhood. An urgent ache—a desperate need—drove itself deep inside. *What was wrong with her! Why couldn't she control herself with this man?* She started to push away, but instead, her hands, in a will of their own, slid up under his gray sweater—his tucked shirt a cruel barrier from her touch. Her mouth opened wider, wanting more, imagining this man in ways she never dreamed possible.

She had to stop! Kelsey-Rose pulled back and drew a breath. Summoning her strength of will, she forced herself to take a step away, but her gaze stayed glued to the blue-gray eyes that studied her.

"Colton, I can't help myself when I'm with you. I don't know why, but I can't." Welling tears blurred her vision. "We can't see each other like this again. I can't let everyone down."

Softly, he asked, "How would being with me let anyone down?"

"You wouldn't understand."

"Try me." When she didn't answer, he said, "Does this have anything to do with Shane?"

Eyes wide, she stepped back again. "How do you know about Shane?"

He gave a one-shoulder shrug. "I'm a newspaperman. I met with the Pixleys a few days ago. I wanted to update the story of Joe's death and the robbery. Shane came up."

"Oh..." she whispered.

"I haven't been able to fit Dax into the story though. Are you in love with him?"

"No," she said softly.

"Then why are you with him?"

"I promised Shane."

"That you'd be with Dax?"

She shook her head. "Before he died, I made a promise to Shane that I would never love another man. Dax promised him—he promised everyone—that he would take care of me."

"So, you're both keeping a deathbed promise?"

Kelsey-Rose nodded.

"Well, that's just crazy."

His remark jarred her. "Don't call me crazy."

"No…" Colton said. "I didn't call *you* crazy. The *situation* is crazy. You can't live your life on a promise like that just because you made a vow that no one in their right mind can expect you to keep." He gave her a long look. "Is this Dax guy in love with you?"

"He says he is." A runaway tear escaped, tracing down her cheek. "We've been together for ten years, more or less. The whole town is expecting us to get married. And I know I owe it to them."

"I don't understand."

Her focus landed on Colton. "Shane was the hometown hero. He was an only child, and he came from a very influential family. His father is a county judge, and his mom is the principal of an elementary school, but they used to be the town's famous rodeo couple. His dad competed and won national titles in team roping and tie-down roping, and his mom junior rodeoed and was crowned Miss Rodeo Texas when Shane was just ten years old. Everyone expected Shane to put us on the map after he earned rodeo scholarships from the

Texas Rodeo Cowboy Hall of Fame and the National High School Rodeo Association. He was accepted into Sam Houston State in Huntsville to study animal science. He was really smart. He was bound to win the College National Finals Rodeo. Shane was so good. He had already graduated from high school, but I was still a senior, and I didn't want him to leave without me. I wanted him to take me, too. I just didn't want to be left behind." Her gaze dropped. "Half the town still blames me for his death, and the other half feels pathetically sorry for me. Dax is the thing that everyone has in common. When Shane died, Dax stepped in for his best friend and promised he would take care of me. Everyone loved him for that. They still do. I can't disappoint all these people again. They're still waiting for me to make amends for Shane's death."

Colton lifted her chin until their eyes met. "Are you in love with Dax?"

She wanted to answer, but all she could do was search Colton's eyes for a reason why the words wouldn't come.

"I have to be honest, Kelsey-Rose. This love story, tragic as it may be, doesn't sway me at all, if for no other reason than to give you a friend who doesn't think of you as the girl who belongs to Shane or his stand-in."

CHAPTER 10

Thanksgiving was fast approaching, and the Say It With Flowers floral shop was booming with orders. Holiday centerpieces, fall wreaths, door swag, baskets, trays, and vases of cut flowers flew out the door, whether by delivery or walk-in customers.

Kelsey-Rose was putting the final touches on a special-order request when her part-time helper, Samantha, came to the back room.

"There's a cute guy out front asking for you," the girl told her, all the while knotting her long brown hair into a bun. "Do you want me to finish that order, so you can go wait on him?"

"Actually," Kelsey-Rose said, "I'm done. Can you take Free out for me real quick?" She grabbed a leash for the Jack Russell terrier and handed it to the high schooler. "He's been scratching and whining at the back door for his afternoon walk."

"Sure." Samantha took the leash and snapped it onto Free's collar, and then said, "Come on, boy."

Three customers were in the shop when Kelsey-Rose walked through on her way to the cash register.

"Honey?" A well-kept, gray-haired woman in an autumn-colored dress called out.

Kelsey-Rose stopped. "Hello, Mrs. Cummins. Did you need something else today?"

"I need my fall wreath for the door. My grandkids will be here any minute from Tulsa to stay with me through Thanksgiving, and I always have my wreath hung."

Kelsey-Rose gave a quiet gasp. Aiden's first day was today, but it wasn't until now that she realized she hadn't seen him in hours. She'd given him seven orders to deliver, but Mrs. Cummins should have been his first stop.

"Aiden has your wreath out for delivery."

Mrs. Cummins shook her head. "No, he hasn't brought it yet, and you said I'd have it by noon today. That was three hours ago. My grandkids are driving together without their parents this year, and they're supposed to be here by four." She glared at Kelsey-Rose. "It's after three o'clock now, and you know I always have my wreath up before company arrives!"

Kelsey-Rose took out her cell phone. "Let me call him..." With the phone to her ear, she turned for privacy only to spot Colton standing back, out of the way, watching. As her gaze landed on him, he smiled. When Aiden answered with *yeah?* she quietly spoke into the phone. "Mrs. Cummins is here for her wreath."

"Who is this?" Aiden asked.

"It's Kelsey-Rose." When she was met with silence, she said, "From the flower shop."

"Oh," Aiden said. "Well, I'm at that lady's house, but nobody's home."

"Okay." Kelsey-Rose cupped her hand around her voice so that her whisper wouldn't be overheard. "She leaves her wreath hanger up year-round on her front door. Can you just hang it and finish the other deliveries, please?"

Kelsey-Rose glanced at Colton, her thoughts jumping to their last kiss and the seductive scent of him.

When the call ended, Kelsey-Rose held up a *patience, please?* finger to Colton then went back to Mrs. Cummins. "Aiden is at your house now. He's hanging the wreath for you."

The woman shook her head again. "I should get a discount for having to come all the way down here on a Friday afternoon. You didn't keep your promise."

Promise. She had learned to hate the word. Its meaning could not be trusted.

"I apologize, Mrs. Cummins." Kelsey-Rose took a clear vase holding ivory and orange Peruvian lilies from the floral cooler and handed it to the woman. "Please accept these with my compliments. They'll look lovely on your breakfast table."

She walked the elderly woman to the door and opened it for her and then turned back to find Samantha assisting the remaining customer, leaving Colton waiting in the corner.

"Hey there," she said on approach.

"You're busy today," he noted.

"Yeah. Holidays are crazy around here. Sorry you had to wait."

"I needed a break anyway." Colton stood awkwardly quiet for a moment, then cleared his throat. "News is, I need holiday décor on my building since the newspaper is part of the Revival Coalition on the Square. I didn't even know I was a member. Is my office just messing with me so that I'll put up holiday decorations, or is that real?"

"Oh, it's real." Kelsey-Rose laughed. She rattled off the holiday events: "Thanksgiving, Christmas, Easter, Memorial Day, Fourth of July, Labor Day, and the Fall Festival in October. Every business on the square agreed to decorate their windows, or at least their entrances, for those seven annual events to liven up the tourist trade." She motioned him into the back room then pointed to her table of autumn-like supplies. "If the town has a parade, or a Friday Social on the Square like we have tonight, decorations are expected, too."

"Tonight is the Social on the Square?"

"One of them, yes." Kelsey-Rose gave a half shrug and nodded. "Starts at five o'clock." She lifted a large fall harvest wreath off the worktable, holding it for Colton to see. "How about this one?"

"Yeah," he said. "It looks great. Did someone forget to pick up their order?"

She set the pumpkin and cornucopia wreath down. "I just finished it for the real estate office, but they're not on the square. If you want this one, I can make them another." She motioned to her remaining autumn-colored supplies. "I need to free up space anyway. My Christmas supplies will start arriving on Monday."

"That'd be great." He pulled out his wallet. "I'll need a hanger for it, too."

"Robert keeps an adjustable wreath hanger in the downstairs storeroom. Just ask Lillie. She knows where it is."

Kelsey-Rose slid the wreath into an oversized plastic bag and started toward the cash register with it, talking as she walked. "The annual holiday parade is tomorrow. Don't forget your Whitetail Christmas Bucks."

"My what?" Colton asked, hurrying to keep pace with her through the shop.

At the counter, she set down the wreath. Brows raised, she said, "Uh-oh. I forgot to mention it, didn't I?"

"Yeah, I guess so."

"*Whitetail Christmas Bucks* is a play on words. We don't actually have a white Christmas around here, but we have plenty of whitetail deer, and by now, the bucks have showy antlers like reindeer, which they'll be shedding soon. Since the parade kicks off special holiday events on the square, all the merchants in the Revival Coalition start giving away *bucks,* which are used just like real money, but only redeemable at the businesses on the square until Christmas. Then after the New Year, the spent bucks are turned in to the mayor's office for a tally. The business owner with the most bucks wins a prize from every merchant on the square. Robert gave a one-year subscription to the newspaper and one month of free advertising, but you can do whatever you want. Once the total bucks are tallied, the number gets equally divided between the participating merchants. Then they contribute that amount—in real dollars—to the following year's downtown restoration costs."

Brows raised, Colton said, "That's a pretty big deal to forget to tell the new guy about."

"Sorry," she said. "Your 'Welcome to Topaz' chamber of commerce packet mentions it, but it was up to me to dole out the bucks."

"So, you handle these bucks?"

"Yes and no," she told him. "Robert always handled the printing, but when you bought the newspaper, he left his personal bucks with me for safekeeping." She shrugged. "I completely forgot about them until now. They're at my house, but I can bring them to you before the parade tomorrow if that's okay?"

Colton smiled. "That's okay by me, but how do I distribute them?"

"You can hand them out however you want. All at once, or you can stretch it out until Christmas." She reached across the counter, lightly touching his hand. "I'm really sorry that I forgot. I promise I'll get them to you early."

He glanced at her hand atop his, then nodded. "I trust you," he said, smiling.

"Good." Kelsey-Rose withdrew her tingling fingers. "I should also probably tell you, you'll need door swag for Christmas." She gave a pursed smile. "Sorry. It needs to be up by December first."

Colton raised a brow. "And where do I get that?"

"You can order from me or from anywhere, even online, but if you want me to make it for you, you'll need to order soon. Everyone on the square who buys from me has already placed an order."

"Can I do that now?"

"Of course." Kelsey-Rose pulled an order pad from her apron pocket. "What would you like?"

"Your choice. Just let me know when I can pick it up."

"Sure, what's your price range?"

With a grip on his wallet, Colton shifted from one foot to the other. "Would you be interested in advertising? We could work a trade for today's wreath and the Christmas wreath."

Kelsey-Rose smiled but then readied herself at the cash register. "The only trades I take are cash in exchange for merchandise. Swapping services doesn't pay the bills."

"Yes, it *does* pay the bills. A trade-out is just free advertising dollars, which you'll use to bring in more paying customers, resulting in higher revenues."

She rang up the wreath sale, but before pressing total, she glanced at Colton. "It isn't *free* advertising dollars. The materials used to make this beautiful wreath have already come out of today's profits. If I give it to you without collecting any money, I can't recoup my costs or make a profit."

"Not today," he said. "But the extra customers that a newspaper advertisement brings in will more than make up for it."

"Colton." Kelsey-Rose kept a business face even though his blue-gray eyes had a way of hijacking her thoughts, sending them far from work. "My best friend used to own the newspaper that you own now, and I never even advertised with him. And I don't like newspapers. They ruin people's lives." When the bell above the shop's door tinkled, she displayed her hand. "See? I'm swamped. I'm the only florist in town, and everyone already knows where I am. Why do I need to advertise?"

Colton leaned across the counter, and in a low voice, he said, "Because I need you to."

Kelsey-Rose sputtered a laugh and entered his order into the cash register, but when his expression didn't change, she stopped. "No, you don't," she skeptically joked. "You're wealthy, remember?"

"I never said I was wealthy."

"Yes, you did." Her smile faded at his stone-faced expression.

"No." Colton straightened. "I didn't. My father, Peter Wilde, is wealthy. That doesn't mean I am."

She focused a blank stare on him. "But I thought..."

He held up his wallet. "Can we do a trade, or do you still want cash?"

"A trade is fine." Her words tumbled out.

"Okay." He slipped his wallet back into his pocket. "I can send Beth by on Monday to work out the details."

"No," Kelsey-Rose said. She shook her head. "Heavens no. I'd rather work out the deal directly with you."

"Is there a problem with Beth?"

"It's not that. Not really, anyway. It's more like... she hates me."

Colton eased into a smile. "I can't imagine anyone hating you."

"Well, imagine it or not, Beth does. She holds me responsible for Shane's death." Kelsey-Rose wrote out the order, showing zero paid with *Trade* written across it. She initialed it, then handed him a copy. "And I can't say she's wrong."

BY FIVE O'CLOCK, A BAND BLASTING COUNTRY MUSIC with a rock and roll beat had their sound speakers cranked up full volume, making it hard for Colton to hear Lillie say good night on her way out.

He followed her into the narrow lobby, locking the door after her, but then stood at the row of front windows, looking out at the town square. The courthouse lawn was crowded with people. Drink vendors under party tents or in concession trailers bordered the sidewalks, and a food truck emblazoned with *Dizzy Dog BBQ* had angled itself on the concrete near the dumpsters in the courthouse parking lot.

It was an excellent opportunity for Colton to meet more of the business community, but why hadn't his newspaper advertised the event?

He bounded up the stairs to his apartment, took a shower, shaved, and then dressed in blue jeans and a quarter-zip Sherpa sweater. On his way out, he grabbed a dozen new business cards and slipped them into his wallet.

At the park, Colton wandered through the crowd, not knowing anyone. People were friendly, sharing smiles and laughter, but they seemed most sociable with those whose first names they already knew. He had that fish-out-of-water feeling, searching the crowd for a recognizable face.

From behind him, Kelsey-Rose called, "Colton, you came."

He turned. The sight of her brought a smile. "Glad you found me. I haven't seen a single person that I know."

"You will. Everyone comes to the Friday Social on the Square events. Even farmers and ranchers who live miles outside of town. It's a big deal around here."

"So…" he said, her blue eyes striking a stammer in him. After a moment, he unleashed another smile and tried again. "Can I hang out with you until you get tired of having a tagalong?"

"Of course," she said. "Let's grab a drink."

On the way to a white tent marked *Topaz Tea and Coffee*, Kelsey-Rose introduced a half dozen businessmen to Colton, but it wasn't until they were in the waiting line for drinks that he realized the two of them had drawn looks and whispers.

Nonchalantly, Colton leaned close. "Are the stares because you're so amazingly beautiful, or for some other reason?"

Kelsey-Rose glanced about, then turned her eyes to Colton. "I'm being judged. Don't let it bother you."

His brows jutted upward. "Because of me?"

She nodded. "I'm out with the new guy in town."

"Wow." Colton shifted. A kiss crossed his mind. "We could give them a real reason to gawk."

"Oh, please don't." She laughed.

They inched their way forward in line until it was their turn.

"Kelsey-Rose!" The order taker bellowed, half-heartedly drying her hands on the yellow bib apron she wore. Without glancing at Colton, the woman pulled Kelsey-Rose halfway across the serving table for a hug.

When the bear grip ended, Kelsey-Rose introduced the two. "Colton Wilde, meet Diana March. Mrs. March was my tenth grade homeroom teacher."

"And her head rodeo coach. She's the reason we took second in our region. Never have gotten that close since." The husky woman leaned toward Colton in a whisper. "That girl could barrel race with the best of 'em. She was always my favorite, but don't go tellin' anyone." Then she said to him, "You want Texas sweet tea, sugar?"

The entendre swirled a moment. "Do you have tea without sugar?"

"Unsweet?" The woman's voice carried a blasphemous lilt. When Colton nodded, she turned with a shout, "Bobby, you make any plain tea today?" When no one answered, she swung a look back to Colton. "He must be off somewhere again. Hang on. I'll go look myself."

"No, that's okay," Colton snapped before Mrs. March could walk away, giving a glance to the growing line behind him. "Do you have bottled water?"

"Sure, but I'd be glad to go look for plain tea."

"Thank you, but a bottle of water will be fine."

Diana March pulled a clear plastic bottle from an ice chest, handed it to Colton, and then shifted her attention to Kelsey-Rose. "Sweet tea, darlin'?"

"Yes, please."

When the two emerged from the tent with their drinks, Colton spotted a vaguely familiar face. When their eyes locked, the man raised his arm in greeting, then he and the two men with him started toward Colton, all bunched together like baby birds trying to find their wings.

"Hey, Mr. Newspaperman. Remember me? Kyle Pixley."

Kelsey-Rose turned.

"Oh, sure, yes," Colton answered. The smell of whiskey and beer lingered on them.

"When's that story coming out in the newspaper? I've looked through the last two issues."

"It'll be out the last week of November. After Thanksgiving." Colton intended to further the conversation but cut it short when the man wearing dark sunglasses gave Kelsey-Rose a long, drunken kiss on the lips.

"I'll tell Gramps," Kyle said. "He wants to buy extra copies."

A camera flash turned Colton. "Hey, boss," Scott said, lowering his Nikon. "Mack said to get pictures today."

Colton's mind whirled with questions, but the sight of Kelsey-Rose entangled in the arms of another man made maintaining a businessman's stature almost impossible. The urge to pull the two apart thundered inside him. He forced himself to focus on Scott and business. "Do you know why we didn't advertise this event?"

"Sure," Scott told him. "Because everybody already knew about it. It didn't need to be advertised."

"That's not the point." Aggravation raised the tenor of Colton's voice, spurred on by the sounds behind him.

"It isn't?" Scott asked.

"No. The purpose of advertising is not always to bring in more people. It also creates a healthy, positive image for the town and the businesses in it, making the desire to be here—to shop here—long-term." Colton turned for a glance. The kisser's arm hung draped over Kelsey-Rose's shoulder, his fingertips playfully grazing her sweater at breast level. He turned back to Scott. "We can discuss it at our Monday meeting." He pulled his iPhone out and tapped in a reminder note for himself. "Ten o'clock sharp, okay?"

With a mumbled "Okay," Scott wandered off, leaving Colton to work his way into the group again.

He reached in for a handshake, intentionally summoning the right hand of the man too friendly with Kelsey-Rose, even though she hadn't dissuaded the affection. "Colton Wilde," he said. "I don't think we've met. I'm the new owner of *The Blue Topaz Times*."

The man unhooked his arm from around Kelsey-Rose and shook hands. "Dax Porter."

Dax. He should have guessed. Without a flinch, Colton offered his hand to the other man.

"I'm Clay Barrow," the other said. "Our grandma works for you."

"Your grandma?"

"Yeah. Beth Barrow."

"Beth is your grandmother?" Colton, caught unaware, forced a friendly smile. "Good to meet you."

Kelsey-Rose stood flush-faced beside Dax as he downed a last gulp of beer, tossing the empty can into a trash container. "Clay and Dax are cousins," she told Colton.

Chin lifted, Colton gave an understanding nod. It made sense as to why Beth and Kelsey-Rose weren't on friendly terms. Dax was her grandson—the man at the other end of the deathbed promise. The one who Kelsey-Rose had not yet married.

"I've heard of you," Colton said to Dax, civility intended, but the dark brown eyes staring back at him doused his attempt at diplomacy.

"I'll bet you have," Dax said, pulling Kelsey-Rose closer. "When you mess with another man's woman, talk seems to happen."

CHAPTER II

Dax Porter wasn't the type of man Colton expected. His blue sweatshirt and jeans bore oil stains, but then again, so did the clothes his friends were wearing. He stood about the same height as Kelsey-Rose with ebony-black hair buzzed short and a well-trimmed mustache and box beard, but nothing about him was particularly good-looking or charming.

"Hey," Colton said to Kelsey-Rose, intending to defuse tension. "I think I'll take a walk around and see if I can meet some people."

Kelsey-Rose broke away from Dax. "I'll go, too. I promised to introduce you."

But Dax pulled her back with a glare at Colton. "You're with me, Kelsey-Rose," he said. "Not him."

A protective mood overtook Colton. With clenched jaws, he stepped forward but stopped. He needed to walk away while his temper was intact. "It's all right, Kelsey-Rose. I can find my way around." *Did she want to stay?* Colton shifted to a better, firmer stance. "Will you be okay?"

"You don't need to worry whether my girlfriend is okay or not."

Kyle Pixley gave a playful shove to his friend, then to Colton, he said, "Don't mind Dax. Kelsey-Rose is fine."

Dax locked eyes with Colton and lowered his tone to a serious one. "Kelsey-Rose belongs to me. Everyone around here knows it. Maybe you didn't, but you do now."

Colton glanced at Kelsey-Rose, who turned her face away. He lowered his head to gain control of any rash temperament. He was probably no more than a few years older than Dax, but he felt like a lifetime existed between himself and this man right now.

If he'd learned anything at all, it was that it wasn't his place to save anyone. He'd learned that lesson the hard way. *But this woman…* Colton raised his head, taking in the man. Easy, he said, "What I know is that she deserves better." The red-haired beauty he found so intriguing—so alluring—gave him a glance he couldn't read. He shifted. "Is this what you want, Kelsey-Rose?"

"It's fine," she told him. "You go on and enjoy yourself. I'll catch up later."

Colton hadn't been trying to make her choose, although he'd hoped she would. Now that she had and her choice hadn't been him, there was nothing left to do but walk away with some semblance of dignity.

~

WHEN COLTON WAS OUT OF SIGHT AND OUT OF earshot, Kelsey-Rose shoved herself away from Dax.

"You were so rude!" If the heat in her cheeks were any indication, her eyes were blazing. "I've never been so embarrassed!"

Dax stepped back but then took hold of her arm. He pulled her with him to a spot behind the dumpsters, away from his friends and the crowd. Inches from her, brazenly, he said, "How do you think you made *me* feel? Everybody in town is talking about how you're drooling over this guy, and here he is telling me that I'm not good enough for you!" Dax shrugged off Kyle's hand when it landed on his shoulder and stayed focused on Kelsey-Rose. "Every time he goes into the flower shop looking for you, I have to hear about it from somebody! And do you want to talk about the night Eddie found you inside that guy's apartment while I was out running around looking for you, thinking you were hurt or in trouble?" The tightness of his grip eased off her arm, but his glare persisted. "I haven't given you grief for any of it, but here you are tonight, out in public with *him* instead of me!"

"Dax." She glanced at the two friends who had come to stand beside them. She hadn't meant to shame him. "I didn't think..."

"Damn right, you didn't think."

To Kyle and Clay, Kelsey-Rose softly said, "Can you guys give us a minute, please?"

Clay nodded and gave a friendly squeeze to Dax's shoulder. "We'll be at the beer barn."

The dumpsters weren't the ideal place to have a serious talk, but time came when it came.

"I'm sorry if I embarrassed you," she told Dax. "I never meant to, but my feelings about us haven't changed."

"You said you'd wait 'til the first of the year to decide, Kelsey-Rose."

"I know I did." Quietly, she said, "But December fifth will be ten years since Shane died. I thought the anniversary might bring me some answers."

"Maybe it will." His voice softened. "It's only a few more weeks."

Kelsey-Rose touched his cheek, her fingers brushing the dark stubble. "You know that I love you for all the years you've given to me, don't you?"

"I love you, too." Dax gently grasped her shoulders. At arm's length, he looked into her eyes. "I promise, Kelsey-Rose, we'll have the biggest wedding this town has ever seen. Everyone will come. All you have to do is say *yes*." He released his touch. "One of these days, I might get tired of asking, and everything from the past is going to come up again if I do."

Her throat tightened. Fighting tears, she said, "Dax, I can't say yes. Not today anyway. Maybe not ever." Kelsey-Rose firmed her voice. "I've always been truthful with you. You know that I love you, but I've never been *in love* with you. You deserve a woman who loves you like I can't."

Dax stepped back. "I don't want to hear this again. I don't want anyone else, and besides, you promised you'd wait until December." He pointed at her. "And you're the girl who doesn't break promises." With no more words than that, he turned and walked off toward the beer barn.

~

AS THE AUTUMN HAZE OF A GOLDEN-GRAY SKY blurred the setting sun, Colton wandered through the crowds of people gathered on the courthouse lawn, some dancing the two-step to the live music. Why did losing this woman bother him so much? Kelsey-Rose was the opposite of everything he'd ever wanted. She wasn't an elegant, refined, or a high fashion female. Instead, she was a natural beauty—a raw jewel in his otherwise cultured and polished world. And the thought of her drove him wild.

"Hi there."

The voice pulled Colton from his thoughts. He turned to find a woman flashing him a smile.

"Hello," he said.

The buxom blonde wore a Venice blue V-neck blouse. Her long, relaxed ringlets hung to her thin waist, cinched tight by a rhinestone belt and indigo blue jeans. With long, manicured nails painted barely blue, she held out a limp hand to him.

"I'm Danielle, and I already know who you are."

"Well, that makes introductions easy." Colton clasped her hand.

"A handsome man like you shouldn't be standing here all alone." With a tug, she said, "Come buy me a drink."

Every square folding table inside the event tent at The Best Margarita Bar in Texas was full, so Danielle led Colton outside with their plastic drink cups. They sat on a concrete bench beneath a tree near the bronze statue of the town founder.

To wrangle his male impulses, Colton looked up through the limbs of the stately pecan, sparse with leaves and probably as old as the courthouse itself. He steadied his thoughts and then focused on the woman again. "There are lots of people here today. I was hoping to meet a few business owners. What about you?"

Danielle took a sip of her margarita, holding the cup prominently in her ringless left hand. "I came to meet you."

Colton's gaze dropped to her cleavage. He hadn't meant for his glance to turn into a long, lusty stare, but it had. When he regained his composure, Danielle met his eyes with a smile.

"It's all right, darlin'," she said. "I'd be hurt if you hadn't looked."

He cleared his throat, trying to keep his eyes above her shoulders. "So, how is it that you know about me, but I know nothing about you?"

"Everybody knows about you. Your name is Colton Wilde. You're from Dallas. You bought *The Blue Topaz Times* a few weeks ago. You come from a long line of newspapermen. You've made every man in town envious of your sports car…" Then she pointed across the square to the two-story limestone building on the corner. "And you live in that big upstairs apartment all alone."

With a half smile, Colton said, "And let me guess, someone told you I was wealthy." His former fiancée, Carly, had found that to be his most endearing feature, but he had learned that too late.

Danielle took another sip of her margarita. "I didn't need anybody to tell me that. You're too classy to be just a regular Joe, which brings me to the burning question I have for you—why would you settle for this little nothing town?"

Colton had started to wonder about that himself. He hated to be wrong about anything, but second thoughts had entered his mind. Advertising was the moneymaker for any newspaper, yet even his staff here didn't believe in it. But he'd done his research. He'd jumped in with both bank accounts. Even if he had made a mistake, he couldn't walk away now. He'd bet it all on his own calculated hunch.

"Topaz is a unique town. It has character." He looked at the blonde who sat cross-legged, twirling a ringlet of hair around her finger. "There must be something you like about living here, isn't there?"

Kittenish, she smiled. "Well, I like it a lot more now that you've moved in."

Colton straightened on the bench. "No, really," he said, wanting to know. "Why do you stay?"

Danielle tipped her clear plastic cup back and drank the last of her margarita, then stood. After a shake of the ice, she set her cup down on the concrete bench. "I have too much invested in this town to walk away without a really good reason."

"Invested how?" Colton stood, too.

She reached into the back pocket of her tight blue jeans and pulled out a business card. She handed it to Colton.

He read its glossy black print. "You own an accounting firm?"

She laughed. "I *am* the accounting firm."

Colton took out his wallet, slid her card inside, pulled out one of his own cards, and then handed it to her. "I came here tonight to meet business owners, and I've been talking to one for fifteen minutes and didn't even realize it."

"Business talk is boring. I'm glad you didn't know right off." She slid Colton's card into her back pocket, then closed the gap between them with a step. "My services are available…if you need an accountant." She used her forefinger to trace the line of his jaw. "By the way, the phone number and address printed on the card are my personal number and home address. Feel free to call or stop by anytime."

It had been too many long weeks, months maybe, without a woman in his bed, and the urge to take this one made itself embarrassingly known. Colton readjusted his stance. He'd toyed with many femme fatales in his lifetime, but this one set the red flag warning ablaze. Tempting as the woman was, playing with fire in a small town almost always left someone burned.

KELSEY-ROSE SEARCHED THE EVENT FOR COLTON SO that she could apologize. She checked the tents, concession trailers, the dance area, and even the line to the portable restrooms, all with no luck. He was nowhere to be found.

At Dizzy Dog BBQ, she came across her father and Nina.

"Hey, you two," she said.

"Hello." Her father stood from his picnic table seat, offering it to her.

"No, it's okay," Kelsey-Rose told him. She leaned and kissed her stepmother, Nina, on the cheek. "I'm headed home to fix myself popcorn and see if I can find an old movie on TV."

Harley Flowers looked at the time on his phone, then gave her a glance. "It's still early. The main event band hasn't even started yet. Is everything okay?"

Nina reached for her hand. "What's wrong, Kelsey-Rose?"

She wasn't ready to admit how she felt about Colton or how she'd messed up any chance she might have had with him. She looked at her father. "Dax and I had an argument. I just need some alone time."

Nina got up from the table and pulled Kelsey-Rose into a hug. "I'm sorry, honey."

Kelsey-Rose forced a smile and nodded.

Her father stood and planted a kiss atop her head. "Why don't you stay? Let me buy you a plate of barbecue."

"I think I just need to be alone." She hugged him. "And Free is still at the shop. I need to get him home anyway."

"Okay," he said. "But will you promise to call us if you need anything?"

"Promise," she said.

Kelsey-Rose made her way through the crowd, crossing the street to her shop. Her cell phone rang as she unlocked the back door. She looked at the caller ID, then answered.

"Robert, is everything okay?"

"Hi, Kelsey-Rose. Things are just dandy. Are you at the Social on the Square?"

She smiled at the sound of his voice and the way he remembered every event in Topaz. "Just leaving," she said.

"So early?"

"Yeah." Other than Free, Robert knew more of her secrets than almost anyone else, but she hated to burden him with her problems. "I tried to break it off with Dax again tonight."

There was silence, then, "How did it go?"

"It didn't." She stepped into the back room of her flower shop, greeted by Free and his overactive docked tail. "Maybe I should stop stalling," she told Robert.

"Just get married. It's not like it would change much in my life. And everyone would be happy."

"Would *you* be happy?" he asked.

She couldn't say she would. "Relieved, maybe?" A lump formed in her throat. "Sad, too, maybe. But in all honesty, I'm not sure I would know how to be me without him."

"Say, Kelsey-Rose, why don't you pack a few things and you and Free come down and stay with me for the weekend? If it's not too cold, we can walk on the beach, and I can introduce you to a few of my new friends here in Galveston. A change of scenery might do you good."

"Really?" she asked.

"Really."

"Does your condo allow pets?"

"Yes, and if you leave first thing in the morning, you'll be here by noon. I'll take you out for an early Thanksgiving dinner before you head back on Sunday."

She'd have to talk Rainey into running the store for her, or close it on one of the busiest Saturdays of the year, but a weekend away with the friend who knew her heart better than anyone else sounded exactly like what she needed. This sad loneliness that she couldn't shake was smothering her. "Can I bring anything?"

"Just you and Free," Robert said.

"Okay."

After so many years of being cried out, the tears came unexpectedly. Kelsey-Rose took a tissue and dried her eyes, knowing these droplets were no longer falling on a memory. These fell for a future that was dead and buried.

CHAPTER 12

Kelsey-Rose called Rainey first, glad that she was willing to keep the store open on Saturday for her, and then she called her father with the news that she was leaving to spend the weekend in Galveston. "Be home Sunday evening," she told him.

She hung the *Closed* sign on the front door and called her three part-time employees to tell them that Rainey was running the shop until she returned. With each phone call, the stress knotting her shoulders faded.

She locked up, then got into the Santa Fe with Free, and they started for home.

Nothing was stopping her from leaving tonight. An extra evening away, sleeping beneath the stars in her backpacking tent with Free like she loved to do, might help gather her thoughts. Maybe she'd make a new plan for her future—one *without* Dax. But the sinking truth was, she wasn't sure she knew how to be *her* without *him*.

If she could just reconcile herself to marriage,

everyone would be happy. And she knew she owed it to them. Maybe if she stopped overthinking it and gave in to Dax's proposal, she could be happy. But if that were true, shouldn't she feel a tinge of happiness at the thought of being his wife?

Perhaps time away would bring the clarity she desperately needed.

At her small green house on Mustang Drive, she packed her travel bag, then Free's small duffle with his food and two bowls, his favorite blanket, and a toy, and then she grabbed her tent and sleeping bag. Even though she would only be gone until Sunday, she watered her plants and then called Leah, her neighbor, to say she was leaving town, and taking Free. She grabbed the extra stack of Whitetail Christmas Bucks from her desk drawer and dropped them into a plastic grocery bag for Colton. She'd promised to deliver them, and she intended to do just that. She would leave them at his apartment on her way out of town.

When she pulled open the car door, the tricolor terrier jumped into the front passenger seat, perching like a navigator on duty.

Backing out of the driveway, she glanced at the house across the street where Dax lived. Usually, she would leave a note, but she needed to stop drawing him into her world until she was sure about their future. Still, he might worry.

She pulled into his driveway and parked, then tore a page from her flower delivery book and wrote: *Dax, I'm sorry about our argument tonight. I hope you understand. I'm taking Free. We'll be gone for the weekend.* She signed it, not *Love, Kelsey-Rose* as usual, but just plain Kelsey-Rose. She slid the note between the doorjamb and his screen door, returned to her idling Santa Fe, and drove away.

To avoid traffic on the square, she took the back route to *The Blue Topaz Times* building. After dropping off the bucks, she would hit the freeway and not stop until she was forty-five minutes south of Houston. Going further meant driving the Galveston Causeway Bridge at night, and that wasn't something she was comfortable doing until daylight.

With the Social on the Square still in full swing, Kelsey-Rose parked behind the building, on the far side of a dumpster where just the sea blue rooftop of her vehicle was visible from the side street. She hated rumors and innuendos and saw no reason to instigate any. It was easier to go sight unseen.

Free took the back steps up two at a time with just his dragging leash slowing him. At the top, Kelsey-Rose scooped him up. "Calm down," she scolded the terrier. "We're not staying. Robert doesn't live here anymore."

But as she reached for the knob to hang the plastic bag, the door pulled open, bringing a low growl from the dog.

Colton smiled when he saw her, giving a glance to the dog before looking side-to-side and then returning his gaze to her. "I thought I heard voices. Were you talking to the dog?"

"Yes, sorry." She glanced at Free, who growled again—his dark, round eyes steady on Colton. "I didn't expect you to be home. I thought you'd still be at the social." She held up the plastic bag with a banded bundle inside. "I was dropping off the Whitetail Christmas Bucks."

He opened the door wider. "Whatever the reason, I'm glad you're here. Come in."

She'd only intended a brief stop, a furtive moment to keep a promise, but she stepped inside anyway.

Colton closed the door behind her, and then asked, "Is he friendly?"

"Free?" she asked.

"The dog…yes. His name is Free?"

Kelsey-Rose put the Jack Russell down on the floor but kept his leash taut. "Weird name, I know, but it's not my fault."

"You didn't name him?" Colton reached down, limp-handed, so Free could sniff him.

"I never knew his name. He just showed up at my house about three years ago. I'll bet I knocked on a hundred doors trying to find his owner, but no one knew where he belonged. I even printed flyers and put them up all over town, and Robert ran an ad in the lost and found section of the newspaper." When the little Jack Russell tugged on his leash, Kelsey-Rose unhooked it from him. He wandered from one furniture piece to another, sniffing. "I never planned on having a dog, so I would put him outside and tell him he was free." She made a shooing motion with her hands. "'Go,' I kept saying. 'You're free! You're free!' But he just stayed. He hung around for days. Every time I would tell him he was free, he would jump up, ears perked, tail wagging. I guess he thought his new name was 'Free,' so I gave it to him."

"He got a name he liked, and you got a dog."

Kelsey-Rose laughed. "I suppose." She took off her navy blue sweatshirt jacket and laid it on the wood floor near the unlit fireplace. It had been a favorite sleeping spot for the dog when Robert had lived there. "Free," she called. "Stop sniffing everything. Come lay down, boy."

After the dog curled up on the sweatshirt, Colton gave a side nod to the kitchen. "I was making a salad to go with the frozen lasagna that I have in the oven. Can you stay for dinner?"

"Sorry, no. I'm on my way out of town. I need to get away for a day or two."

"By yourself?" Colton asked. When she nodded, he turned for the kitchen, saying, "Where to?"

"Galveston." She walked behind, following him. "It was either that, or a weekend at Dad and Nina's house, or popcorn on the couch with the shades down, watching old movies." She laughed, making light of the choices.

"I love old movies."

"You do?" She smiled, watching as he pulled a salad bowl from the cabinet.

He no longer wore the luxe Sherpa sweater he'd had on for the social, donning a simple white T-shirt instead.

"If you'd stayed home, would popcorn have been your dinner?"

"Yes," she admitted.

Colton set the bowl next to a cutting board with a few long leaves of romaine, a container of cherry tomatoes, and a cucumber. "I've got a family-size lasagna in the oven. Any chance you just can't resist a frozen dinner?"

Kelsey-Rose glanced back at the living room where Free lay sleeping, then sent a look to the front door, trying to buy time before committing one way or the other.

Softly, he asked, "Would one of my favorite old movies sway you?"

In the lingering silence, her gaze pulled to him.

When their eyes met, Colton said, "The truth is, I feel bad about the way I left things tonight at the social. I'd like to make it up to you."

"It wasn't your fault." Kelsey-Rose glanced away, pulling out a tall stool opposite Colton at the granite-topped kitchen island, and sat.

A moment passed before he said, "I had no right to tell your boyfriend he wasn't good enough for you. I just lost my head."

"Well, if it helps, you're forgiven." She forced a smile, not knowing whether it was true or not. It had been Dax he'd offended, not her.

Though nothing much had changed in the big kitchen since Robert moved out and Colton moved in, everything seemed different, even the air in the place. The soft, cozy aroma of leather and lavender warmed the apartment, imparting a sense of subtle masculinity.

A few cardboard boxes, neatly stacked, still lined the back living room wall, but mostly the apartment was tidy with well-placed furnishings. The wall art hung tastefully on freshly painted walls. It *felt* good.

Colton went to the twelve-bottle wine rack, pulled out a Tuscan red, and presented it, propped against his forearm. "Good?" he asked her.

"None for me. Thank you," Kelsey-Rose said. "Water is fine unless you have tea."

He lowered the bottle. "Would you prefer a Merlot or Pinot? I'm relying on a nice glass of wine to improve the taste of the frozen lasagna."

Kelsey-Rose shook her head. "I don't drink." A subject she didn't want to discuss.

With a furrowed brow, Colton said, "Just wine? Or any spirits?"

She gave a well-practiced, make-believe smile. "I'm a coffee and tea kind of girl."

Colton slid the bottle back into its rack. "In a celebration, you'd join me in a champagne toast, though, wouldn't you?"

"Nope." She forced another smile, making light of the subject in hopes of dissuading the newspaperman from what felt like an investigation. "But I've been known to bring balloons for special occasions."

Uneasy, he shifted, then tossed a side nod to the sparsely decorated counter. "I'm sorry. I don't even own a tea maker."

She drew a deep breath, feeling as though she'd just taken a step into a walk-in freezer.

"It's not a big deal." Kelsey-Rose got up and went to the cabinet that held the drinking glasses she had unpacked for him weeks ago. She reached for the tap to fill the glass, but before she turned on the water, Colton gently laid a hand on her wrist, his fingers curling around it.

"I'll buy one if you promise to come back again." He hesitated. "Any chance you'll come back?"

She tried, but she couldn't pull her gaze off Colton. His thick chocolate-brown hair, styled in waves the way Mother Nature surely intended, accentuated the warmth of his blue-gray eyes. For the first time in almost a decade, her body unequivocally knew what it wanted.

Her pulse skipped under his fingertips, then quickened. A vulnerable response, she knew, but his touch was deeply sensual.

Colton Wilde didn't need to do anything but look at her to set her womanhood afire, stirring urges she'd expected long ago from a man but never felt. The desire was unfamiliar. Uncomfortable, *but not*.

Kelsey-Rose took a breath, waiting for her scattered nerves to settle, then set down the empty glass. Quietly, she retook a seat on the high stool.

She shouldn't be there. Shouldn't stay. But at this moment, the sense to walk away had deserted her.

She crossed her legs tighter, willing the heat between them down to a simmer. The past ten years had jaded her cynical view on love and sex—love was off the table, and sex had barely been worth the trouble—but this man was intoxicating.

Shifting on the barstool, she said, "Colton, there's a lot you don't know about me." Those who knew her had almost forgiven her wild-child past, but Colton hadn't known her then.

He handed her a glass filled with water. With his palms flat on the granite countertop, he leaned across, staring into her eyes. "So, tell me."

Kelsey-Rose swallowed hard. "Things that I don't talk about."

The last thing she wanted to be was the girl she'd been—or the woman she was now. She didn't want to be the girl everyone expected her to be either. She wanted to be someone new. Someone sexy and exciting. A woman so beguiling that a man like Colton Wilde couldn't resist.

Colton reached for her hand, grazing her fingers as they curled around the glass she held. "What do you say we forget about our pasts tonight? The people. The places. The problems." He straightened into a stand, his eyes still speaking to her.

He stood well over six feet, so her gaze rose with

the length of him. In a sultry whisper she'd tried in vain to harden, she said, "Deal."

A harmony balanced between them as if it belonged there.

Flustered by her thoughts, she stood, saying, "Let me make the salad. It's the one thing I do well."

Colton laughed, stepping back. "I seriously doubt that."

THE 1934 MOVIE *IT HAPPENED ONE NIGHT* PLAYED ON Colton's big-screen television while he and Kelsey-Rose sat together on his leather sectional the color of a fine Cuban cigar. They ate their lasagna and salad from the coffee table, both sipping from their glasses of plain water.

The low hum of white noise in the classic black-and-white movie had little effect on the heartrending words of Clark Gable, telling an inconsolable Claudette Colbert to go back to bed.

Rapt in the scene, Kelsey-Rose scooted to the edge of the sofa, intently focused. But Colton wasn't watching the movie. He was watching her.

Teary-eyed, she turned to him. "I can't believe this movie is making me cry."

Her coppery-red hair fell in a cascade of layers, flipping up at the ends. Colton reached for a long tendril and curled it behind her ear, exposing more of her flawless complexion. His gaze swept her face. Softly, he said, "I can't believe you've never seen it. It's a favorite for old movie buffs."

She was delicate in a rugged sort of way. Unlike any woman he'd known. The desire to touch her—to feel her passion so deeply it might change him forever—was nearly unbearable. But hers wasn't a heart he wanted to break. He no longer wanted to be the man he had been.

"Your old movies are different from mine," she said. "I meant old like *You've Got Mail* old, not Frank Capra old, although I do have a few great ones from the '40s and the '50s."

She ate the last bite of her lasagna, then stood with her plate, reaching for his. "Can you pause the movie so I can clean the dishes? I don't want to miss a word."

"Oh, no, you don't." Colton stood and took the plate from her hands. "That's what dishwashers are for, and you're my guest."

With the movie on pause, she walked with Colton to the kitchen, carrying her water glass. Free was on her heels, having a bounce every other step. "Hey, boy," she said to the dog. "You need a treat?"

Beside Colton, Kelsey-Rose set her glass inside the sink, then turned in a stretch, lifting the edge of her soft sky-blue T-shirt to push her hand into the front pocket of her loose-fitting denim jeans.

Colton's focus caught the slender figure she usually hid beneath exceedingly relaxed or bulky clothing. He stopped rinsing plates. When she pulled a tiny treat out of her pocket and fed it to Free, Colton set their dinner plates down.

The apartment was quiet except for the low whine from Free, begging for an extra treat.

But when Kelsey-Rose started for her pocket again, Colton reached for her. Not willfully. He had not intended to seduce this fragile woman, yet his fingers were involuntarily spreading over her hips, drawing her a fraction closer.

When she didn't resist, he pulled her to him and

kissed her, his heart racing when she slipped her arms around his neck, accepting his advance as if it were warranted.

Colton wrapped one arm around her thin body, and then with his other, he swept her up off her feet. Effortlessly, silently, he carried her to his bedroom and set her down on the white goose feather comforter atop his bed —her beautiful blue eyes soothing his doubts about the decision.

Sounds from the Social on the Square drifted up. Music. People. Traffic, leaving for the night.

His newly installed blinds, raised high, gave the tall trio of windows in his bedroom an unobstructed view of the full moon, its light uncontested except for the barely noticeable flame on a lavender-scented candle lit atop his bureau.

Colton stood looking down at her, imagining how her long red waves might tumble down her bare back. He sat beside her on the bed, noticing a quiver.

He reached for her hand. "You're trembling," he said warily. "I want to be with you tonight, Kelsey-Rose, but I need you to tell me it's okay."

Intimately, she raised her hand and touched his face.

"It's okay," she whispered.

CHAPTER 13

At the sound of a barking dog, Kelsey-Rose sat upright, withdrawing from Colton's embrace. *Free.* Scooting to the edge, she said, "I'm sorry." Guilt was a bigger burden than she imagined. "I only stopped by to drop off the bucks." She stood, pulling down her T-shirt as moonlight cast long shadows across the room. "We were headed to Galveston," she said lightly, a reminder to herself more than Colton. Her gaze washed over him as he rose from the bed.

Free scratched outside the closed door, barking again.

"I should go." She stepped away.

Tenderly, Colton said, "I want you to stay." He took her hand, stilling her with a kiss, then led her across the room to the tall trio of windows. He pointed up. "It's just me and you and that beautiful moon tonight." He caught her gaze, which took her breath.

"I should be halfway to Houston by now. If people knew..."

"No one needs to know you're here."

Kelsey-Rose nodded, her eyes avoiding him.

Gently, Colton tilted her chin upward. "Forget the past tonight and anyone or anything from it." He swept stray strands of hair behind her ear. "Stay with me, Kelsey-Rose. You can leave for Galveston tomorrow morning."

He drew her closer, his lips meeting hers. She moaned, deepening the kiss.

"Sweet God in heaven." Her knees weakened at his touch.

Free barked again. He was at the door, sounding a warning alarm. The line she was about to cross would surely be a one-way ticket. Her whole life could change. *Her whole life could change!* Wasn't this exactly what she'd wanted? Just one night to know whether a man could free a passion so dead within her that she would feel alive again?

Her fingers curled into Colton's white T-shirt, trying to find a grip on a world spinning out of control.

Free barked again.

Kelsey-Rose pressed her forehead against Colton's chest. Flustered, she said, "I need to take care of Free." She looked up at him. "His bag is in my car."

"I'll go with you."

"No." She stood back with her hand up. "It'll just take a minute." Before leaving, she raised up on tiptoes and placed a kiss on his lips.

When Kelsey-Rose came back with Free tethered on his leash, she had the duffle. Colton held open the front door for her, taking the bag as she entered. After closing and bolting the lock, he set the bag on the couch, watching as she unzipped it, pulling out a water bowl, a faux fur mat for sleeping, one plush toy, and a rubber Kong stuffed with treats. In exchange for her sweatshirt, Kelsey-Rose laid out the dog's mat. Colton filled the water bowl.

She knelt, releasing the clip on Free's leash, then placed the terrier on the mat with his toys. "Listen, Free," she said as the dog cocked his head to one side, staring at her. "Everything is okay, okay? Be a good boy, and don't pee on anything." She stood.

"He doesn't really do that, does he?"

"Pee?" Kelsey-Rose laughed. "Yes. But we try to confine it to the outdoors."

Colton laughed. "Touché."

With his smile holding, Colton reached for her hand, beckoning Kelsey-Rose back to the bedroom.

But a moment to think had settled. Softly, she asked him, "Colton, what are we doing?" She brushed a hand down his arm, lingering at the feel of his olive skin beneath her fingertips. "I don't want us to have any regrets tomorrow."

He held her gaze, a promise of honesty in his blue-gray eyes.

"I'll only regret tomorrow if I let you walk out of here."

She'd never expected this now—she had never expected *him*.

Kelsey-Rose hadn't intended to, but she tensed, blurting out, "I don't want to be in love."

There it was, out in the open. It should have felt liberating. Instead, her throat tightened, and tears welled.

"My heart is still broken from the first time I fell in love. I can't do it again."

Colton nodded, dropping his focus to the floor.

After a moment, his gaze lifted, meeting her eyes again. "What do you want me to say, Kelsey-Rose?"

With a falter, she lightly answered, "I just thought you should know."

When a tear spilled, Colton pulled her to him, her head chest high against his thin white T-shirt. His hand caressed the back of her neck, brushing through her hair. "If I agree not to let you fall in love with me, will you stay the night?"

She laughed at the ridiculous sound of it. Looking up at him, she wiped a late tear. Then sincerely, she said, "I'll try, but I can't promise anything before the sun comes up."

"I'll take whatever time you'll give me." Colton took her hand, leading her back to the bedroom and closing the door. On his bureau near the lit candle, he took a remote and clicked. When Louis Armstrong's rendition of "What a Wonderful World" began, he pulled her to him.

KELSEY-ROSE DIDN'T REMEMBER FALLING ASLEEP, but when she awoke, she was beneath crisp white sheets. Sleeping soundly beside her was Colton. *It hadn't been a dream.*

Faintly, she heard a scratch on the door. Kelsey-Rose scooted out from under the sheets, her bare feet landing on the cold wood floor. She quietly slipped into yesterday's blue T-shirt and jeans, grabbed her canvas shoes, and then tiptoed to the bedroom door, opening it just a crack to squeeze through without letting Free into the room.

Overnight, the waning scent of leather and lavender had given way to the stubborn odor of fresh paint, but the solitude inside the apartment was as quiet as the world outside. Not a thing stirred except her and Free. There was no early morning Saturday traffic, and it was too soon for the shops to open, so as sunrise dawned in colors of persimmon, amber, and barely blue, Kelsey-Rose pocketed her keys and took Free for a walk.

On her way back through the parking lot, she stopped and retrieved the weekend bag from her Santa Fe and carried it up the stairs.

Inside, she took the leash off Free and went to the kitchen to make coffee, only to find Colton waiting, barefoot, his brown hair mussed, wearing only his jeans.

"I was afraid you'd left until I realized the dog's bed was still here." He went to her and, cradling her face in his hands, kissed her lightly on the lips.

"You thought I'd sneak out in the middle of the night?"

Colton gave half a shrug. "I thought maybe."

Kelsey-Rose smirked. "I can't imagine any woman in her right mind ever leaving you in the middle of the night."

Colton poured two cups of coffee from the pot he'd made and handed her one. "Well, let's see." He glanced at the ceiling, then down again to Kelsey-Rose. "Carly left in the evening. Does that count?"

She hadn't expected him to answer. He'd meant it as a joke, hadn't he? When his serious face held, she awkwardly said, "Oh…" then she went to the refrigerator, pouring milk into her cup for coffee creamer. When she turned back to him, she said, "Do you want to talk about it?"

Colton grabbed a bag of bagels and two plates, and then he set them on the center island along with a serrated knife. With a container of strawberry cream cheese from the fridge, he sat, pulling out the stool beside him for her. After a sip of coffee, he said, "You should know. Carly and I were engaged to be married. I guess she decided it wasn't a good idea."

Kelsey-Rose sat, a bewildered scrunch creasing her forehead. "What reason did she give?"

"She didn't." When her mouth dropped open, Colton said, "The reason was obvious, I guess."

"What do you mean?"

"An hour after my father cut me out of his will, Carly left."

"Did you go after her? To be sure, I mean?"

"For six weeks." He flashed a contrite grin. "I can be persistent when I need to be. But she was more in love with my inheritance than she was with me. It took me a while to come to grips with that. When my money was gone, so was Carly."

"Wow." Kelsey-Rose spread cream cheese on half a bagel and then took a bite, thoughts wrinkling her brow. "So, you really don't have any money?"

Stone-faced, Colton lowered his gaze. Hesitant, he said, "No. Is that a problem?" He didn't look at her.

Kelsey-Rose slid off the stool and went to him. "Hey," she said, resting her hand on his shoulder. "I'm glad you don't have any money. It changes people into someone they're not. They become people who don't understand what's important in the world." When he looked at her, she kissed him. "Money is so overrated. And I think Carly needs her head examined."

Colton grinned, swiveling to pull her closer to him. "How badly do you want to go to Galveston?"

"I promised I would." She kissed him again, running her fingers through his dark brown hair—soft and baby-fine but full of disheveled curls.

"Maybe you don't keep this promise."

"I always keep my promises. Why wouldn't I keep this one?"

"Everyone thinks you're gone for the weekend, right?" When she nodded, he said, "So stay. Call your friend and tell him you're not coming." He pulled her closer for another kiss. "Then let's make love all weekend."

She laughed. "I can't do that."

"Yeah," he said with a nod. "You can."

"But today's the parade. Everyone will be downtown. Someone will see my car."

"So what? You're a grown woman." Using his fingers, Colton combed through her hair, his hands trailing down, smoothing her wrinkled T-shirt. "You don't need permission, Kelsey-Rose." He kissed her neck, then a trail of kisses moved upward to her ear, where he whispered, "Say it for me."

Kelsey-Rose pressed against him, desire wanting to feel the weight of him again. Softly, she asked, "Say what?"

Colton gently pulled back, gazing into her eyes, his look searching her face. "Say you don't need permission."

Feeling a swoon, Kelsey-Rose mumbled, "I don't need permission."

"Say it again."

Her head tilted back, a moan escaping. Coppery-red waves, not yet brushed, tumbled over her shoulders. Louder, she said, "I don't need permission."

Colton brushed his lips over her arched neck. "That's right. You don't need anyone's permission to be here." Then he stood, sweeping her up off her feet, and carried her back to the bedroom.

CHAPTER 14

By midmorning, autumn's bright sunlight brought the sounds of traffic and parade floats to the square downtown. Tractors and trucks with heavy diesel engines whined and rumbled, almost drowning out the sound of the Topaz High School band tuning up. Twirling majorettes in blue, gold, and white uniforms were awhirl on the courthouse lawn.

With Colton in the shower, Kelsey-Rose slipped her T-shirt on again and then dialed Robert.

"Hi," she said when he answered. "Sorry to call with a last-minute change of plans, but I've decided to stay in town this weekend."

"Why?" His tone was worried. "Is everything all right?"

"Yes." Kelsey-Rose glanced back at the unmade bed and the crumpled pillows—her focus falling to the pile of his and her clothes on the floor. "Actually, everything is perfect." The sultry tone of her own voice jarred her. She tensed. "The parade is today."

"Yes, but you knew that yesterday," Robert said. "Kelsey-Rose, what changed your mind?"

At age eighty, Robert was still her best friend, but she couldn't confide in him about the wild, wonderful time she was having with possibly the most amazing man she'd ever met, yet she wasn't going to lie to him either.

"I just think I need to stay here…to figure out my future. It's been ten years, and—"

"It's been ten years in an emotional prison for you, Kelsey-Rose. It's about time to pardon yourself, don't you think?"

He'd always been able to tell what she was thinking. "Maybe so," she said.

~

AS MUCH AS COLTON WANTED TO PULL KELSEY-ROSE into the shower with him, he was in a hurry for a reason. He needed to get dressed and find his staff before the festivities began. They needed to dole out his dividend of Whitetail Christmas Bucks. If it worked, he'd be able to slip away and return to Kelsey-Rose for the day.

Dressed in black jeans and a smoky-brown long-sleeve shirt, Colton walked to the living room, finding Kelsey-Rose staring out the window, deep in thought. He went to her, caging her in his arms from behind, then softly, he leaned over her shoulder and pressed a kiss to her cheek. "I promise to be back as soon as I can. I hate leaving you here."

She turned, her arms encircling his neck. "No, it's fine," she said. "If you think about it, it's my fault. I should have remembered to give you the bucks sooner. If I had, you wouldn't have to leave this morning."

Colton swept a tendril behind her ear and then kissed where it had been. "This won't take long." Then he released her and started down the hallway leading to the Scarlett O'Hara stairs, which would take him to the newspaper office below. Before he descended, he glanced back.

At the foyer, Kelsey-Rose stood leaning against the interior brick wall. Dressed only in her thigh-length sky-blue T-shirt, she watched him. Her red hair was mussed but beautiful. He had an almost uncontrollable craving for this woman.

"Promise me you'll be here when I get back?" he said to her.

Cool and collected, she replied, "Well, let's see..." With a smile in her eyes, Kelsey-Rose looked up at the high ceiling. "I need to shower, put on some clean clothes, tidy the kitchen, and watch the end of *It Happened One Night*." Teasingly, she looked at him. "If you're back before I can do all of that, I promise to be here."

Colton loved her sassy attitude. All he wanted was to rush back then and there and give her a reason to cry out his name again.

He pointed to her. "Don't leave."

When he got downstairs, he pulled the bundle of bucks out of the plastic grocery sack and then looked around the quiet office. None of his staff had arrived.

Colton dialed Mack. "Hey, where are you?"

"Home," Mack replied. "Why?"

"Isn't the parade about to start?"

"Starts at ten o'clock." Mack hesitated. "It's not even nine yet."

"I need you to hand out our Whitetail Christmas Bucks today."

Mack gave a hard sigh. "I wasn't plannin' on coming to the parade, Colton. Are you sayin' I have to drive in and work today? It's Saturday. You should have told me. I hate those damn parades."

Colton's business demeanor kicked in. "Well, if you'd told me about this promotion in the first place, I wouldn't have been caught off guard, Mack. So, yes, I need all of you down here to start doling out these Christmas bucks. You know how to do this annual event. I don't."

"Yeah, okay," Mack said, blowing out another sigh. "You need me to call everyone and tell them to meet you at the office?"

"No, I need you to call everyone and tell them to meet *you* at the office." Colton knew he sounded unreasonable. "Sorry, Mack," he said, "but you're the managing editor now."

After the call ended, Colton divided the bucks into four envelopes, each with a name, and set them on Mack's desk. When he did, he spotted a notepad. Written on it was the name Trent Nolver along with a phone number. He hadn't seen that name in many months. One he never expected to see again.

Troubled, he tore off the page and carried it with him to his computer, and logged on.

Two emails had arrived late yesterday—one from Trent, a reporter at the *Lone Star Herald*, a rival North Texas newspaper, and the other from his mother's personal assistant, Richard Kane. Colton opened the reporter's email first:

Hey Colton,

Didn't realize you'd left the metroplex. Took me a while to hunt down your new contact info. I'd like to get a statement for the Herald *from you about your father ASAP. Call me: 214-211-8586.*

Best,

Trent Nolver

Colton stood, staring at the email for a long minute. Why would he want a statement now after so many months? The trial wasn't scheduled to begin for another twelve weeks.

He closed the email and opened the next:

Dear Colton:

It is imperative that I reach you.

Sincerely,

Richard Kane

Obvious *modus operandi* language. Never put into writing something private that could be intercepted or anything that could be used against you. He wondered which it was.

Colton logged out, shutting down the computer. Too many possibilities ran through his head. After the story broke, he and Trent Nolver had agreed not to communicate again, so why was the reporter emailing him? And why did Mack have his name and phone number written on that notepad?

He folded the paper and slid it into his pocket for safekeeping.

It was Richard Kane's message that held a bigger meaning.

~

Concerned about how quiet Colton had been since he'd returned from downstairs, Kelsey-Rose took a guess, offering, "It's okay if you need to go to the parade, you know?"

Colton stood at the living room windows, looking down at the event. Without turning around, he said, "No, I'd rather be here with you."

But he had barely looked at her in the last thirty minutes.

Business was likely on his mind—unless he was already regretting her. Kelsey-Rose put a hand on his shoulder. "Hey," she said softly. When he turned, she asked, "Is there something you want to talk about?"

"Like what?"

"Whatever it is that's on your mind." She took hold of his hand. "Unless…" she had to force out the words. "Unless you want me to go. It's okay if you do."

Colton's eyes widened. "Oh, no." He took hold of her shoulders. "No, Kelsey-Rose." He shook his head, "I don't want you to leave." He raised his hands, cupping her face. Her attentive eyes relaxed the tenseness in his shoulders. "You're the best thing about this day."

Relieved, she smiled.

The last time she'd had an honest smile and felt true happiness seemed a lifetime ago. A distant memory, as though it belonged to someone else now.

Colton pulled her into his arms and held her. "It's just that I've been trying hard to leave my past behind. Trying to start over. Hoping to be a different man. But a voice from my darkest days found me again, and I'm just trying to decide whether I should reopen the door."

Kelsey-Rose stepped back. She couldn't imagine

him ever having dark days or what that might mean to a man like him. "You're not in trouble, are you?"

"No," he said. "No..."

"Thank goodness." Her hand flattened against the beat of his heart. She studied the worry lines on his face and his distant, troubled blue-gray eyes. Clearly, he was still unsettled. "Colton, is this something you need to take care of today?"

Again, he said, "No," but he'd said it hesitantly.

Kelsey-Rose raised up on her tiptoes and pressed a kiss to his lips. "Okay then," she said, trusting his words. "Aren't you the one who said we need to forget about the past this weekend?"

The small mole on his cheek disappeared into the folds of a tender smile.

While Colton had been downstairs, Kelsey-Rose had showered and then put on her indigo jeans and a brushed knit blouse—its bright colors and designs reminiscent of a chapel's stained-glass windows. Her top had a mid-length zippered front, which she'd purposely left half zipped.

"I'm feeling better already," he said to her.

Colton Wilde was every dream she'd ever dreamt. He was a fit, gorgeous, virile man who had class and manners, even in the bedroom. She'd felt his restraint last night and knew he was holding back. She'd barely been handled as a woman, and it was probably painfully obvious to a man like him. She guessed even experienced women had their hands full when he unleashed—*she wanted him unleashed*. If there was anything she wanted him to take off, it was the kid gloves.

In a gentle caress, she stroked his shoulders, her fingers trailing down his biceps, wanting to remember every inch of him long into Sunday night when she would have to leave this fantasy behind and return to the prison of her ordinary world.

RESPECTFUL OF HER BROKEN HEART, COLTON stepped back. The last thing he wanted to do was to take Kelsey-Rose down a path that might frighten her away. Right now, he needed her. Right now, he wanted her. But he wasn't fooled by the feelings that had gotten him into trouble before. He'd be gone in twelve months or less, and this woman's life already had enough turmoil. He was tired of ruining the lives of the people closest to him and his own, too, in the process. She'd been clear. She said she didn't want to fall in love, and neither did he.

At her behest, Colton brought out an old photo book and stood at the granite-topped kitchen island, holding it in front of Kelsey-Rose.

"Are you sure you want to see this?" He laughed. "It might change your impression of me."

Kelsey-Rose reached for the handcrafted album. "Hand it over and come sit by me." She patted the seat next to her.

With a sigh, Colton gave her the album and then sat. "Don't say I didn't warn you. You'll never look at me the same way again."

The opening page was an eight-by-ten glossy of a Tuscan-inspired stone-clad estate with an Italian barrel tile roof—a rich Mediterranean red. The property was well lighted and stood on manicured grounds with mature landscaping. In the twilit distance, a series of smaller buildings connected by arched walkways could be seen. All around were Shumard oaks, eastern redbud trees in bloom, boxwood, and nandina shrubs.

"What was this beautiful building? Your school or something?" She focused on the magazine-like photo.

Colton sat straighter on the kitchen barstool. "No, that's my childhood home." He waited.

Drop-jawed, Kelsey-Rose said, "This is your *house*?"

He nodded, then gave her a long glance. "I warned you that you'd never look at me the same way again."

She looked back at the photo book. "How many bedrooms are in this place?"

"Six. It has twelve thousand square feet. Maybe a little less, I think."

Kelsey-Rose sat back, wide-eyed. "Wow."

Colton nodded again. "I know."

"How many kids are in your family?"

"Me. Just me." He turned the page, pointing to a half-page photo of a young boy riding a Welsh pony. "This was me at five years old with my first horse, Bruno. Actually," he laughed, "Bruno was the only horse that was ever truly mine. All of the others are polo ponies and they belong to the estate."

She glanced at him. "You never mentioned to me that you ride."

"That's because I ride differently than you, but I love horses." Colton leaned in, looking closer at the photo. "I mean, come on, how could you not love horses when you start out with a guy like Bruno," he teased. "I almost won the trophy at the USPA General Patton Cup two years ago." He laughed with a glance at Kelsey-Rose. "You'll notice I said *almost.*"

"I'm impressed. I see you more as a sports car kind of guy, not a horse and rider kind of guy."

"Well, ranch riding and polo riding are two completely different things."

"A horse is a horse."

"And a rider is a rider, but I'll bet you are way out of my league."

Kelsey-Rose laughed, focusing again on the photo. She brushed her fingertip across the image of the brown-haired boy and his pony. "You were both adorable." She glanced at him, and then with splayed fingers, she reached, combing through his soft chocolate-brown curls, her hand wending around the line of his jaw. "You and Bruno had the same color of hair." Her caress lingered on his natural olive-colored skin.

Colton swiveled on the high kitchen stool, his gaze deepening on the woman who had touched a part of him no one had ever reached before. One that he wasn't even sure he knew existed.

After a deep inhale, Kelsey-Rose pulled back her touch, forcing her focus back onto the pages of the family album. "So, on to the next photo," she willed herself to turn the page. "Those are cypress trees, aren't they?" She pointed to a picture of the estate grounds where a row of tall, pencil-slender conifers grew. "I didn't know cypress grew in Dallas."

He nodded. "Italian cypress. Our gardener affectionately called them *special needs trees*. They require special attention and care. In Italy, the trees live hundreds of years, but in North Texas they only live a fraction of that time. Still, my mother insisted on the variety." Fixated on the photo, he said, "She's from the Chianti region in Northern Italy. She's spent almost a lifetime missing her home. She used to sit quietly, staring at those trees almost as if they could talk to her. I think she was lost in memories she couldn't let go of."

He brushed his finger across the row of trees. "Our groundskeeper would plant one every year at her request. If you count them, you'll know how many years she has been gone from Italy, her home, and her family. Those trees mean a lot to her. It's kind of sad, actually."

Kelsey-Rose listened so intently that it seemed she was watching the words flow from his mouth as he said them.

"It's heartbreaking," she said when he finished.

"Yes." Colton nodded, his heart warming to her compassion. He turned to the next page in the album.

With a softened voice, Kelsey-Rose asked, "Were you born in Italy?"

"No, not me. But it's where my father met my mother in the early eighties. She's Italian, and he was a correspondent from the San Francisco Bay Area. When they decided to marry, she chose to come to America with him. From the stories I've been told, her family was devastated by the decision. They had expected her to remain in Chianti with her family, helping sustain their centuries-old winery and vineyards." Colton caught a glance from Kelsey-Rose. "She hasn't ever returned home. I was born four years later in California, but my father moved us to North Texas when I was just six months old. I've never lived anywhere else."

"I can't imagine your mom giving up her family like that, Colton. I don't think I could go a week without seeing my dad and sisters."

"She's stayed in contact with them over the years, but my father won't allow her to visit. I don't think the rift will ever be mended. Father resented her family's interference and forbade her to see them, which is why

I've never met any of my mother's relatives. It's not allowed."

Colton went to the refrigerator and pulled out two bottles of apple juice. He loosened the caps and then handed one to Kelsey-Rose. "My father ran our lives and our household just like he runs his companies. Heavy-handed and uncompromising."

"I'm sorry. He sounds like a demanding father. I can't imagine my dad ever being that kind of man. We've always been close."

Colton took a sip from the juice bottle, then screwed the lid on again. "I've always been closest to my mother. My father isn't the type of man you get close to. Actually, he has always been obsessed with perfection and wealth. I don't think he knew I existed until I turned sixteen and went on the payroll." Colton stood opposite Kelsey-Rose at the counter, sipping juice instead of making eye contact.

"What made him cut you out of his will?" Did she have a right to ask? "I don't mean to pry. You don't have to tell me if you'd rather not."

Colton leaned against the counter, giving his gaze back to Kelsey-Rose. After hesitating, he answered, "I couldn't be trusted." Then he shifted.

"Why would your father think that?"

"It's a long story. One I haven't told in a while, but suffice it to say that employees of the largest newspaper my father owns were investigated and charged with blackmail, hacking, gifts for favors, police bribery, and exercising improper influence in the pursuit of stories. It turned into quite the scandal, and the emerging accusations resulted in several high-profile resignations and numerous arrests and convictions."

Kelsey-Rose set down her bottled juice. "The dark days?"

Colton nodded. "I was convinced Father was innocent of orchestrating such a thing, so I agreed to work covertly with the authorities, thinking I would become the hero by clearing his name, guarding his reputation, and saving his business. I thought, finally, he would be proud of me, but it didn't work out that way." He downed the last swallow of his drink and then dropped the plastic bottle into the trash. "It's sad to think that I'm nearly thirty-five years old and still trying to find a way to impress my father."

"So, he knew about it all?" she asked.

"Not only did he know about it—he was ultimately responsible for it. He was charged initially, but because of his position, he was given a plea deal for his testimony against some of the state's most powerful leaders and politicians who didn't care about getting their hands dirty, clawing their way to the top for their own success. He knew secrets that none of them wanted known, and he helped set up their adversaries for failure. There's still one big-time trial left, but my father is a free man, working and living as if nothing underhanded ever happened." Colton shrugged. "When I realized he wasn't as blameless as I thought, I confronted him. He said, 'Did you honestly think the big stories just fell in our laps? That we were just in the right place at the right time?' Then he said if I was ever going to be a success, I'd have to make the big stories happen, not sit around waiting for them to be handed to me." He glanced at Kelsey-Rose with a gaze measuring her heart. "He said that I was his only failure and his biggest disappointment."

An audible gasp came from Kelsey-Rose. "That's a

terrible thing for a father to say to his son. Colton, I can't imagine how awful that must have made you feel."

"There weren't many highlights in our father-son relationship, but that was certainly one of the most surprising to me. I'd made every newspaper he'd put me in charge of a success—or at least I thought I had. But it was never good enough. Now I realize the success was him behind the scenes the whole time."

"So, your father wasn't reporting the news. He was creating the news."

Colton cast her a look. "With every tabloid tactic known."

CHAPTER 15

Free barked and scratched on the door, wanting to go out. He spun in circles and barked again.

"Uh-oh, it's an emergency." Kelsey-Rose went for his leash. "He only spins when he can't hold it anymore." She clipped on his leash and opened the front door, looking back at Colton. "Do you want to come? We're just going to the playground at Wiggins Park."

Colton smiled. "You go ahead. I think he needs some alone time with you."

The Jack Russell terrier spun and spun again.

With Free beside her on his leash, Kelsey-Rose jogged across the back parking lot. The minute they neared the first tree, the dog pulled her to it and hiked his leg.

Free was still peeing when the patrol car pulled up alongside them.

Kelsey-Rose glanced at the officer but then looked back at the terrier. Over her shoulder, she called, "Hey,

Eddie." If she ignored her brother-in-law, maybe he would just say hello, and drive on.

But Eddie shifted into park and then leaned with his elbow out the window. "Thought you were going to Galveston for the weekend."

"No," she said, hoping to dissuade further conversation. She was almost thirty years old, and she was tired of being treated like the baby of the family just because she was the only single daughter. "I decided to stay in town."

Eddie turned off the car's engine and got out. His black uniform was crisp and clean, and his plain black leather holster, buffed to a shine, secured his duty weapon. He stood with both hands resting on his hips. "Kelsey-Rose, I saw your car here last night."

Her head jerked up. "Did you say anything to anyone?" *You don't need permission. You don't need permission. You don't need permission!* Colton's voice echoed in her head.

"No, I didn't even mention it to Mae, but your big sister will find out about it sooner or later." Eddie glanced across the parking lot to Colton's building. "Is this thing between you and him serious?"

"No." Kelsey-Rose shook her head. "Of course not." At the sound of her own words, her heart skipped a beat. She couldn't lie about Colton. "Maybe. I don't know."

Eddie looked down at the ground. "Look, kid," he said before aiming his focus at her again. "I'm not ever going to judge you. You should know that after all these years. But you're like my own little sister, and I don't want you to get hurt. I've never had one, but I've heard that a broken heart is worse than taking a bullet."

Kelsey-Rose had to smile. She glanced at him. "You've never been shot before either."

"True," Eddie said. "Ten years as chief. I've been lucky." He adjusted his equipment belt. "The thing is, word is going to get out—more than it already has—and you're gonna pay the price for it from all these people who are waiting for you and Dax to get married." Eddie looked at her. "Is it fair? No. Is it going to happen anyway? Yes, it is. I don't want that for you, Kelsey-Rose. You deserve better."

Kelsey-Rose had never needed her brother-in-law as a confidant, but she'd always known he was worthy. After hesitating, she said, "What if Colton Wilde *is* my *better*?"

Eddie looked down again, then squatted to pet Free who sat staring up at him. Quiet, he scratched behind the dog's ear. He whispered, "Good boy," before patting his head again. Eddie stood. He opened the driver's side door to his patrol car and then leveled a look at Kelsey-Rose. "Then grab hold and don't ever let go, no matter what anyone says."

Kelsey-Rose stepped in, encircling his neck with her arms, and hugged him, then she handed him the leash. "Take Free home with you for the weekend so he can play with Finn?"

"I'm on patrol, Kelsey-Rose. I'm not a dog taxi."

"Please?" she asked, smiling.

Eddie sighed. "Fine." He opened the back passenger door for Free, who jumped inside. "But he's going to have to eat Finn's food. I'm not stopping to buy that expensive crap you feed him."

"Good enough." Kelsey-Rose laughed. "Thank you, Eddie," she said. "For everything."

When Kelsey-Rose returned to the vintage apartment, Colton was standing at the kitchen island, typing on his laptop. With his back turned to her, he asked, "Everything okay?"

"Fine," she said. She stood back, quietly taking him in as he typed.

There had never been a man like Colton Wilde within a hundred miles of Topaz. He had liberated her lonesome soul, and she already knew that one night would never be enough.

"How did you let go?"

Colton stopped typing and swiveled a look to her. "Let go of what?"

"Carly." Kelsey-Rose didn't move, not even an eye shift. "How did you break the bond—the tie that held you two together? I don't know how to do that."

Colton closed his laptop and focused his attention on her. "I didn't have a choice."

"Neither did I." Kelsey-Rose went into the kitchen, filled a glass with water, and drank most of it down as if refilling her gumption. "There's a ten-year-old tether tied to me that has a whole town full of people pulling it so tight that I can't breathe sometimes." When he didn't answer, she asked again. "Just tell me. How did you do it?"

Colton went to her and took her by the hand, leading her back to his barstool. He sat, pulling her closer until she stood between his knees, directly in front of him. He took her nearly empty glass of water and set it down on the countertop. Holding both of her hands, he gazed thoughtfully into her eyes. Softly, he said, "I stopped giving it my attention."

Kelsey-Rose shook her head, trying to understand his answer.

"The more attention you give to something, the

bigger presence it has in your life. I had to redirect my thinking by pulling my focus away from the constant thoughts of Carly and all of the things that had gone wrong. I turned the attention I'd been giving it inward to myself instead. The only way I could move forward on my own was to find whatever was left of the best version of myself in the ashes of our relationship and shake off the loneliness and sorrow, and just let Carly go."

Kelsey-Rose stared through the honesty, hanging on to his every word.

But his circumstances were different. Carly had left on her own. She couldn't be expected to let Shane go—she had to carry his death forever. She owned the burden of it.

Shaken by the advice, she reached for her glass, but when she tried to bring the last of its water to her lips, she realized her hand was noticeably trembling. She set the glass down, trying to calm her nerves by tracing the embossed design with her fingertips.

"You had no reason to hold yourself responsible for Carly leaving. And you didn't have a whole town reminding you of what happened."

Colton lowered his head, a blameworthy smile taking shape. "Yeah, I did." He looked up at her. "All of North Texas, and even people from three other states where we—I mean he—has dailies still hold me accountable for their loss of revenue, which ruined their newspaper jobs, too. And they're mostly right. The big difference between you and me is that it's obvious your family stood by you."

He was right. Her family had been her salvation. Dax had been, too. "That's something I don't understand, Colton," Kelsey-Rose said. "Your mother shut you out, too?"

Colton took a breath. "There's a little more to it. My mother was the one who tipped me off. She came to me in private, scared of how deeply my father was involved with disreputable dealings. Things were getting scary, I guess." He scoffed a laugh. "But I'm a newspaperman. A good one, I thought. How could something that big go unnoticed by me? I couldn't bring myself to believe her. A mistake I'll regret for the rest of my life. She asked me to help her convince my father to retire. I knew I'd inherit it all if he did, but there was no way I could believe my father would be running a big newspaper corporation using blackmail and pure tabloid tactics, printing enormously influential stories without the least bit of merit. But my mother is a good woman — trustworthy and strong. She's the philanthropist of our family. And she'd been right all along. I never should have doubted her." Colton looked at Kelsey-Rose with a regretful smile. "The man I trusted and admired had used me as a pawn and her as a shield."

"Have you talked to her since it all happened?"

"'Lily Wilde no longer accepts calls from her son,'" Colton quoted. "I've tried."

"But you didn't do anything wrong," Kelsey-Rose said. Sensing his pain, she brushed the line of his jaw with her fingertips. To lighten the mood, she said, "And here I thought you were just a rich boy who'd been handed everything without earning it."

Serious, Colton said, "Maybe I was once. Not anymore. I've learned that I can't change my past, only my future. That's all I have control over." He glanced at her with a forced smile. "I'd say this conversation took us off the fun track of our secret weekend together. I'm sorry. I shouldn't have laid all that on you."

Kelsey-Rose leaned in with a kiss for him.

"Knowing helps me understand why you've come to Topaz, Colton. Now it's easier for me to understand the urgency you have to make the newspaper successful. Before, I thought it might just be a toy."

The moment that statement was out of her mouth, she realized what she'd said. Reliance faded from his blue-gray eyes. She saw his expression harden. Saw the color deepen on his face.

Colton pulled back. "I'm not willing to fail at this, Kelsey-Rose. I have to know that I can do this on my own. I won't become the same man as my father. I need you to know that."

"I know. I'm sorry if I sounded insensitive. I didn't mean it that way. Is there anything I can do to help? Something that might jumpstart new interest in the paper?"

He straightened his posture into that of a professional businessman—his glance landing squarely on the redheaded woman whose opinion mattered to him.

"If I print an 'Insider's Report' on the front page of *The Blue Topaz Times* disclosing the facts about my father's downfall, sales will skyrocket, probably in ten or twenty counties since I've never publicly talked about my side of it, which means advertising dollars will start rolling in, but I'll become part of the news. People will pick sides, and I know how you feel about that. And nobody wants to be the front-page headline of a negative story, especially where crimes are involved."

Kelsey-Rose stiffened. Being part of the news hit too close to home. "You don't have to worry about making a decision like that here in Topaz because the town's leaders won't allow any crime reports to be printed in the newspaper, and definitely not on page one."

Colton snapped into an attentive stance. "Since when?"

"Since almost forever. The Revival Coalition says that printing negative news adversely affects the tourist trade and home sales. They don't want the town or its citizens painted in a negative light. Real news stories around here don't get printed unless there's a positive spin to them."

"Well, I've got news for the coalition," Colton said, the indignant ire of a newspaperman blazing. "They might have had a nice tidy little deal with the former owner of the newspaper, but they don't have one with me."

Butting heads with the town leaders wasn't what worried Kelsey-Rose. Colton had come to Topaz to start a new life and splashing his troubles across the front page probably wasn't the best way to do it.

When he pulled a piece of paper out of his pocket with a name and phone number written on it, Kelsey-Rose sensed trouble. She gave a caring, but cautionary stroke to his arm. "Think it through, Colton. Don't make any rash decisions."

"It's way too late for that." Colton picked up his phone and dialed, turning away when his call was answered by a recorded greeting.

"Trent, it's Colton. I assume this is important, or you wouldn't have called." Then, "Call me when you get this message."

He turned back to the woman who had unknowingly powered his will.

"One more call," he said to Kelsey-Rose in askance of her tolerance. Then he dialed his mother's assistant.

"Richard," he said when a man answered. "I was surprised to hear from you."

Colton pressed the phone closer to his ear and walked to the trio of windows, looking out. He was well aware that he had major trust issues, so when he heard, "Your mother needs you to come home," he didn't have to force himself to ask why.

Most people he'd known would simply have said, *I'm on my way,* but he'd learned that things were not always what they seemed. His life was more complicated now, and he'd learned not to trust even the most trusted.

"For what reason?" Colton asked. At the answer, he whirled around, focusing on Kelsey-Rose. "Tell her I'll be there as soon as I can."

When he clicked off, Kelsey-Rose asked, "What's wrong?"

"It's my father," he said, his voice shaken. "He's been shot."

CHAPTER 16

"I'm sorry," Colton said to Kelsey-Rose. "But I've got to go."

"Yes, of course," she said.

She followed him into the bedroom, where he took a travel bag from his closet and set it on the unmade bed, then he went to a tall, antique Italian armoire—walnut swathed in exquisite burl mahogany, bordered with satinwood marquetry in an intricate laurel leaf pattern. He pulled open its drawers and took out T-shirts, socks, and underwear, arranging them inside his bag, and then he opened the right-side door of the massive piece and took three shirts off their hangers.

When Colton turned with the clothing, his focus fell again to Kelsey-Rose.

"I hate to leave you right now." He took a deep breath, releasing it slowly.

"It's okay, Colton. You need to go, but I'm worried you're too upset to drive all the way to Dallas. I can have you at Austin-Bergstrom Airport in an hour."

"Thank you," he said softly. "I appreciate it—I

really do—but even if a flight is available right away, it's still an hour drive to Austin, and preflight check-in is an hour before departure. Then it's more than an hour in the air, renting a car, and fighting the traffic out of DFW…I'd get there about the same time as if I drove it myself. And this way, I'll have my car." He lowered his gaze. "I just don't know what to expect when I arrive, so I need to be completely self-reliant."

Kelsey-Rose nodded. "Tell me how I can help."

Colton tossed the shirts onto the bed beside his bag, and then he went to Kelsey-Rose.

"I hate to ask you this, but I'd rather that no one knows about my father. Not yet, anyway. Not until I have more information. I'll call Mack and tell him that I'm leaving for a few days on a family emergency. I'll leave him in charge, but I don't want to go into the rest of the story." He reached for her, his hand sliding down her arm until he had hold of her hand. "Can you keep this a secret?"

"Yes," Kelsey-Rose told him. "Whatever you need."

"Good." He smiled. "Thank you."

When Colton was finished packing, he zipped the travel bag, grabbed his Armani leather jacket, and took the keys to his Corvette out of the polished wood valet tray atop his bureau, only to stop and whirl around with a look for Kelsey-Rose at the sound of a knock.

"Let's hope this isn't another unexpected surprise." He carried his things into the living room and then set down the travel bag before he opened the front door.

At the sight of a uniformed officer, Kelsey-Rose blurted out, "Eddie, what are you doing here? We just talked about this! I don't need your permission to be here."

"You're right," her brother-in-law said. "You don't need my permission, but that's not why I'm here."

Colton shot her a look of angst. "Kelsey-Rose, I'm sorry, but I have to go."

"Go," she said, compassion filtering her tone. "I'll lock up if that's okay."

"Yes, that's great." He leaned for a kiss, lingering before whispering, "I'll call you as soon as I can."

With no explanation for Eddie, Colton maneuvered past him and took the stairs down.

"Can I come in?" Eddie asked Kelsey-Rose.

"Sure. Yeah, I guess so." She moved aside for him.

The demeanor of her sister's husband had changed from when she'd seen him just over an hour ago.

Eddie removed his hat, holding it waist high as if his call were official. "There's been an accident."

"An accident?" Her question formed a barricade that only a wisp of air could penetrate. "Who…"

Her brother-in-law steadied his focus. "It's your dad." He grabbed for Kelsey-Rose when her balance faltered. "Here, just sit for a minute." Eddie eased her down onto the leather sofa.

"Is he okay?" she asked. "Do you know what happened?"

"I don't have all the details, but he's been CareFlited to Memorial Hospital. Mae and Rainey are on their way with Nina, so they should be there in about thirty minutes. I told them that I'd find you, and we'd be there as soon as we could."

Misty-eyed, she stood. "Tell me what you know."

"The DPS officer that I spoke to said Harley was hauling the Longhorns into town for the parade this morning when he came across a teenage girl pulled off onto the shoulder of the road. She had a flat tire, so your dad stopped to help. He was loosening the lug nuts when a speeding pickup clipped another vehicle. That driver lost control and crashed into the girl's car while your dad was changing the tire."

Shaken, Kelsey-Rose glanced around, finding her purse and sweatshirt. "We should go. Are we taking your patrol car?"

"Yes, absolutely."

A HUNDRED MILES NORTH OF TOPAZ, THE HORIZON flattened into a sweeping panorama, masquerading as a vast limitless sea lacking any significant hue. Colton already missed the rolling hills fluffed with trees that had been traded in for this level earth, barely green. The terrain was weathered by the low light of a late November day, leaving the landscape hard and nondescript, just like his life felt, except when his thoughts found Kelsey-Rose. She was the color in his rainbow. Air to his lungs. A bastion of light in his darkness.

On the way, Colton called his mother twice, but each time, when her voicemail answered, he had chosen to disconnect rather than leave her a message. Perhaps her phone was turned off or silenced, or maybe reception was bad. He didn't want to jump to any conclusions, but the only way he would ever be sure it was truly her that wanted to hear from him now was if he spoke to her directly. Until then, he would have to rely on Richard, Lily Wilde's trusted, longtime assistant.

The University Medical Center in Dallas was the location he had been given, so he took I-30 to Exposition Avenue, then inched through the traffic, heavy with families already drawn to Fair Park for the annual, season-long Christmas event that energized the sprawling downtown district.

Colton parked in the lot of the six-story hospital, closest to the entrance, and then rode the elevator inside to Level 3 where the Surgical Trauma Intensive Care unit was located, exiting directly into a waiting area with a nurse's station.

There, behind a wall and door of glass, seated in square box-like chairs, was Lily Wilde and her assistant, Richard, with another man Colton did not recognize. He approached the nurse's station, pointing to the room visibly draped in a vine-like forest of machines, monitors, cables, and hoses. The only movement came from caregivers.

"Excuse me," he said quietly at the desk. When a nurse looked up at him, he explained, "I'm Colton Wilde. Lily Wilde is my mother. I'm here to see her." He could not bring himself to say that he was there for his father, too.

The ebony-haired nurse in shocking pink scrubs held up a halting hand. "I'll need to check. Wait here."

Colton watched the nurse slide open the glass door to the critical care room, and then he saw his mother look up, finding him with her eyes. She stood and started for the door, motioning the two men inside the room to stay seated.

Haggard-looking, his mother walked across the speckled-gray terrazzo floor toward him. Her herringbone tweed jacket left open at the front revealed a wrinkled blouse tucked sloppily into the waistband of her sage green straight-leg pants. Her shoulder-length chocolate-brown hair was mussed. She was not at all the polished, well-put-together woman that he knew.

"Mother," he said when she reached for his hand. "How are you? You look tired. How is Father?"

Businesslike, Lily Wilde motioned him toward a solid wood door with a brass plate: *Family Room.* The windowless room was empty when they entered. She closed the door.

"Colton," she said. "Your father was shot while getting into his car to come home last night." Her emotions were in check. "The police think it was a targeted attack, but they don't know from whom." She glanced back at the closed door before she looked at him again. "An undercover officer is here…in case. They're going to want to talk to you."

"Of course. I'll help however I can." Then he asked, "How serious is it?"

"Serious. The bullet entered the right side of his brain. It's too risky to remove it."

He stepped back, looking up at the ceiling, his hands on his hips before his focus found her again. "Did they try?" he asked. "Did they do *anything*?"

"They've done a craniectomy for clot evaluation and removal of debris," she explained.

"And?" Colton wanted the facts. The results. He was a newspaperman.

"Colton, you should know…" Her brown eyes had a thin layer of moisture, giving off a glint beneath the overhead light, her soft voice filtering through his consciousness to the place where his boyhood memories were kept. "He's in a coma with minimal brainstem function."

She'd had time to process the facts. He had not. Like a gut punch, a hard breath blew out of his lungs, and then time stopped.

Breathe, he willed himself. *Breathe.* But he couldn't.

His mother reached for Colton's face, softly brushing her hands down his jawline, tears filling the void in her hard-set eyes ringed with dark circles.

It took all of his effort to inhale again, but when he did, he pulled together the grit he'd inherited from both parents.

Colton knew his mother understood—she'd been on the board of this hospital for twenty years—but he had to confirm anyway. He spoke to her gently, his words breaking at one point. "His chance of surviving this kind of brain trauma is unlikely. I assume they've told you that already."

She nodded. "Yes. I've been told to prepare for the worst."

Lily Wilde had never been an emotional person, so the fact that she was holding herself together was not a surprise to him, but there was more to her composure. He knew her too well to believe that sheer hope and fortitude had steadied her.

"What else aren't you telling me?"

There was a hesitation that held more strength than grief in her firmed stature. "You're still in his will."

Colton shook his head. "No, he told me himself that—"

She took hold of her son's arm. "He never signed the change. If your father dies," she stopped and then corrected herself. "*When*..." She nodded her acceptance of the word. "All of Wilde Enterprises Media and at least half of your father's other holdings will belong to you. I have no intention of contesting the will."

There wasn't a single thing that felt real in his world at the moment. He was on foreign ground. A fictional character in a movie whose script he hadn't read. Stuck in a reality that could flip in an instant.

"None of that matters anymore." There was only one thing that Colton cared about now. "Are you safe? What about the person who shot him? Is anyone in custody?"

"No, and the police don't have many leads." His mother took his hand and tightened her grip. "But it's not me—or you—who needed to be silenced."

Colton nodded. He understood. His father's enemies had taken steps to prevent him from testifying against them. He didn't intend to glamorize it or distort the truth by pretending that his father was trying to do the right thing, but in a way, Peter Wilde had done them a favor by never including them in his dealings. Inadvertently or not, he had protected his wife and son.

"What do you need me to do?" he asked his mother.

"As soon as the will is probated, I want you to sell," she said. "Sell the newspapers. It's why I came to you for help in the first place. The business your father spent his life building is the monster that killed him."

"No, Mother," Colton said, shaking his head. "*He* became the monster. I'm sorry, but he created this end for himself. It wasn't the business that did this to him. Newspapers have worth. It's the most important thing I learned from him. They're a bond between a government and its people. They are the voice of injustice. When they're managed right, newspapers have the power to bring a community together. I believe in the need to report the news—to inform people—but the truthful and honest way."

She took him by the shoulders, focusing on him with an urgency in her eyes. "Colton, when the political world realizes that you've inherited Wilde Enterprises, half will never trust you, and half will manipulate you into doing their bidding. They'll see you as your father's son, and then those people and their money will find a way to turn you into a monster, too. Politics is a serious business that most people don't understand, and it doesn't care whom it uses, whom it fools, or whom it kills to win."

"I'm a different man than him."

His mother glanced at the closed door again, ensuring their privacy. "I can't force you to do the right thing anymore than I could force your father, but I can't let greed and privilege ruin you, too. Those in power seek out influential media sources, and you're stepping into the position of being the one who can give them what they need. It's deadly ground."

Colton nodded. His understanding was greater now than ever before. How could he have been so naïve to the influence and control that his father wielded in the political underworld?

"What will you do…after?" Death wasn't an easy subject to discuss.

His mother glanced down, lips tight, then after a moment she walked softly to the door and opened it a crack, looking out before closing it again. She walked back to Colton. "I intend to go home to Italy. My family has waited too long for my return. Everything has been arranged for weeks."

"You were planning to leave Father?"

"Yes," she said.

"Were you going to tell me?"

With a nervous hand, his mother swept a flyaway tendril of brown hair from her face. "I intended to call as soon as I landed in Florence." Then she reached for Colton's hand again. "I'd like you to come, too. Your uncle has work for you. It can be a fresh start for both of us."

He didn't want to disappoint her. This wasn't the time. "I understand."

"Good." His mother squeezed his hand longer than needed, a sigh of relief easing her grip. She motioned to the ICU area on the other side of the door. "Colton, you probably need to say goodbye to your father. I don't know how much longer he might have left."

CHAPTER 17

Faith is the strength by which a shattered world shall emerge into the light. The Helen Keller quote, painted in cursive, encircled an artist's vision of a sunrise over the sea. It was an offering of hope that hung in the hospital waiting room where Kelsey-Rose sat with Nina, Mae and Eddie, and Rainey.

"Where's Emma?" Kelsey-Rose asked her sister, just needing to hear sound in the silence of the room.

Rainey sat leaned forward in her chair, hands tightly clasped, her long blonde hair splayed over her shoulders. She was focused on the floor. "She's with Harry. He drove over from Austin last night for the parade. He rode on the Goat River Films float today."

It was the first time since hearing about the accident that Kelsey-Rose thought about the holiday event. She glanced at her brother-in-law. "What happened to the Longhorns? Were they hurt in the accident?"

"No," Eddie told her. "They weren't involved. Ty and Cullen came and got the truck and trailer and hauled the cattle back to the ranch."

"Thank God," Kelsey-Rose mumbled.

When the waiting room door opened, everyone jutted up from their seats, silently staring at the man in blue scrubs, wearing black-rimmed glasses with a stethoscope draped around his neck. His ID badge had his photo and *Physician* listed with the name: Steve Jenkins.

"Are you the Flowers family?"

Memorial Hospital was an hour northeast of Topaz, so although it was the closest *serious* hospital, the people —its workers, the staff, the nurses, the doctors—were all strangers today, no matter how much influence they had on the care of their loved one who was so well-known in his own hometown.

"Yes," Nina blurted out. "How is my husband? Please tell me good news."

His focus went to her. "Mrs. Flowers?"

"Yes," she said. "Nina."

The doctor reached for a cursory handshake. "I'm Dr. Jenkins." He began—methodical, unemotional, and clearly clinical. "Surgery for your husband's hip and pelvic fracture went well, but he's suffered a mid-to-lower thoracic spinal cord injury." He flipped through a few papers on a clipboard that he held before continuing. "T7 through T9, to be specific."

"What does that mean?" Kelsey-Rose asked.

The surgeon glanced at her before his eyes wandered through the other faces fixated on him. "Thoracic vertebrae." He stopped but then restarted when no one spoke. "Sensation and motor control are typically innervated by the T7, T8, and T9 segments of the spinal cord." At their continued silence, he took a breath, releasing it before turning his attention back to Nina. "Since signals from the brain cannot easily get past this area of a spinal cord injury, individuals often experience paralysis below this point."

Nina reached for Mae, drawing her closer. "Are you saying my husband is paralyzed?"

"It's possible for spinal cord injuries to initially appear worse than they actually are due to inflammation, which is a response triggered by the biochemical processes that cause swelling, so depending on certain circumstances, paralysis isn't always permanent." He gave a quick study of the faces in the room again. "But for now…yes."

Paralyzed. When Nina broke into tears, Mae and Rainey went to her, holding her up in a fellowship of arms.

But Kelsey-Rose stayed focused on the doctor. "Is he awake? Can we see him?"

"He's in recovery, but he will probably be moved to the ICU within the hour. As soon as he's settled, I'll have the nurses notify you, but no more than two people can be in the room with him, and then it's only for a short time."

"Okay," Kelsey-Rose said, information swirling in her head. "Thank you."

In an instant, her world had changed. The man who had never failed to walk life's hardest path with her was no longer able to walk at all.

But he was alive. And there was hope.

IN HIS MOMENT OF ALONENESS IN THE DIMLY LIT room, where the beeps and clicks of life-sustaining machines seemed the only difference between a mortuary and a hospital room, Colton stood at his father's bedside.

He stared down at the fifty-nine-year-old who looked like he was sleeping, though not peacefully. A finger twitched, but the nurse had explained it was just a spontaneous movement and she had advised Colton not to read anything into it.

Life looked different on the brink of death.

His father had been fit, healthy, and energetic. His mind and memory sharp. But now, in this bed that seemed too small, wearing a ventilator that pushed air into his lungs then pulled it back out again, this man didn't look at all like the person who was his father.

Colton's memories skipped through the years—a flat rock skimming the waters of time.

Peter Wilde had given him everything except love. Even in this unconscious state, love felt no different now than it had five years ago. Ten years ago. Thirty-five years ago. If all but love counted, they'd lived an enviable life. The difference was that Peter Wilde had earned his way to the top, through ill-gotten means or not. But it had been different for Colton. Privilege had been gifted to him.

That was the one truth he intended to change.

Colton reached for his father's hand and steadied the twitch, and then he gave the man a decisive nod before silently walking out of the room.

When Colton stepped outside the glass-walled room, an undercover police officer reentered, taking a seat in the chair by the door.

"Mr. Wilde," Richard, the personal assistant, called to Colton. When he glanced up, the dark-haired, well-dressed man who stood alone waved him over.

Colton crossed to him. "Do you know where my

mother is?"

Richard motioned with his eyes to the family waiting room. "She's speaking to detectives who have asked to see you." When Colton started toward the private room, the assistant stepped in front, stopping him. Low and with no obvious emotion, he said, "She's asked that you refrain from discussing the will."

When Colton opened the door, the two detectives looked up. "You wanted to see me?" he asked them.

"Are you Colton Wilde?" one of the men asked.

"Yes."

"Colton," his mother injected, "this is Detective Garcia and Smith. They would like to talk with you about the shooting."

"Of course." Colton reached with a handshake for each man. "How can I help?"

Detective Garcia seemed barely old enough to have earned the title of detective, but he took the lead with a hard-nosed approach.

"Do you mind telling us where you were last night around six forty-five?"

"I was home," Colton told him before realizing his answer was ill-defined. "In Topaz. That's where I live now. I bought a business and moved there last month."

"What kind of business?"

"A newspaper." He smiled. "My first. On my own anyway."

"How did you buy it?"

Colton pulled back with raised brows. "That's none of your business unless you can tell me how that question relates to my father's shooting."

Detective Garcia leveled an icy stare. "We've talked to several people today, Mr. Wilde, and they all seem to think you had the biggest grudge of all against your father." He glanced at his partner, then at Lily Wilde before looking back at Colton. "So, I'm going to ask you again, how far in debt did you have to go to buy that new business and home for yourself?"

Colton looked down with a disingenuous smile. When he looked up again, his demeanor had hardened. "My finances are private, but I can assure you, I have more than enough money to retain an attorney if I need one. Do I need one?"

The older detective glanced at his partner before speaking directly to Colton. "Detective Garcia comes off a little strong, Mr. Wilde. He's young, you know?"

Colton hated the good cop, bad cop routine but he understood it. "What's your real question?" he asked. He knew he sounded gruff and to the point, but he didn't care.

Detective Smith grinned, his eyes never leaving Colton. "Look, we're just trying to clear people off the list. We know your father intended to cut you out of his will, and we also know he hadn't done that yet, so you stand to inherit a lot. That clearly makes you a suspect." He shifted. "You're a smart man. You know where we're going with this."

Colton looked at his mother. She'd told him not to talk about the will, but he wasn't sure how not to answer.

His mother stared back at him for a moment, then she turned to the detective. "I've asked Colton not to discuss his father's will with anyone."

"We're not just anyone," Detective Garcia said.

"I know, but I don't want my son to become a target for anyone who has a grudge against my husband."

"I get it, Mrs. Wilde," Detective Smith told her. "But we can either talk here, or we can talk to your son at the station. One way or another, we're going to get answers to our questions."

"Mother," Colton went to her, "remember when I said that I intended to manage things the truthful and honest way? I meant that for my personal life, too." He wasn't trying to scold his mother for her caution, but he wanted her and everyone else to understand that he was not the same kind of man as his father. He'd sworn to himself that he never would be.

Lily Wilde looked down with a nod. "All right, Colton." When she looked up again, her focus was on the detectives. "The truth is, Colton didn't know his inheritance was intact until I told him tonight after he arrived here. He had no idea that he still stood to inherit his father's holdings."

Detective Smith jerked a look at Colton. "Is that right? You didn't know?"

"That's right," Colton said. "I thought my father cut me out of his will months ago."

Doubtful, Detective Garcia stood with his hands resting on his hips. "You must have had a tidy little sum from somebody to bankroll a new business and a home. Do you have partners?"

"No." Reluctantly, Colton disclosed, "I invested well when I worked for my father, and I sold the condominium I owned on Leonard Street last month."

Detective Smith nodded. "That would do it. What's the name of your newspaper?"

"*The Blue Topaz Times*. I own the business and the building. The newspaper offices are on the lower level, and I live on the upper floor." He looked at his mother. "It's an old historic place. You'd like it."

His mother smiled, a glisten in her eyes. "It took courage to do what you did, Colton. I'm proud of you."

CHAPTER 18

The first few hours at the hospital with Harley Flowers were full of crying. Nina cried, Mae cried, even Eddie shed a tear at not being able to console his wife who was normally the strength of the family. And Rainey—maybe Rainey cried most of all.

But Kelsey-Rose was steady and dry-eyed. She couldn't explain it, really. She was numb. Numb and terrified. When she looked at her father, his hair whiter now than the day before, it was as if his remaining years were unraveling right before her eyes.

The truth though, was that Harley Flowers had always been good at everything he did, and if he hadn't been good at something initially, he had taught himself how to be. Whatever future lay ahead for him, Kelsey-Rose intended to remind him of that.

She had hold of his hand when he awoke from a medically induced sleep. In a voice still hoarse from the intubation tube they'd removed, he asked her, "Where's Nina?"

Kelsey-Rose smiled in recognition of his effort. "Mae took her downstairs to the hospital cafeteria while you were sleeping. She'll be back soon. How are you feeling?"

Low and raspy, he said, "Like I was hit by a train."

"Well," Kelsey-Rose tried to lighten the moment, "almost."

Harley glanced up at his daughter, but his gaze wandered. "I think I remember her saying the girl was okay. She said the steers were, too. Was that real, or was I dreaming?"

It was just like her father to worry about everyone but himself. "Yeah," she said. "Eddie had to leave, but before he did, he got a statement from the hospital. They said the teenager you stopped to help had a few bruises and a broken arm, but she wasn't even admitted to the hospital. And Ty and Cullen took the Longhorns home. They're perfectly fine."

Harley nodded. "But they missed the parade?"

Kelsey-Rose patted his hand. "Yes, but it's okay, Daddy. You don't need to worry about that right now."

"Yes, I do," he said, his vocal cords laboring through the words. "We have more parades. The holiday schedule is on my desk. We committed to providing the Longhorns. If those steers don't show up, we'll have to refund a lot of money, and we'll owe a penalty. It's in the contract."

The pain and strain were evident on his face and in his voice as he spoke.

"Daddy, everybody will understand. The accident even made the Austin news."

"Doesn't matter, honey." He squeezed his eyes shut with a grimace. "People still want what they want."

"I'll ask Ty and Cullen—"

"No. Ty and Cullen are reliable, but they're used to being told where to go and when, and they're no good at picking up payments and communicating. Cullen has been with us for over twenty years, and nothing has changed. He's not suddenly going to become businessman enough to run the ranch." He winced and then took a breath, coughing and wincing again. "This is a bad time to have this happen."

"There's never a good time, Daddy. You just need to focus on getting well and doing your rehab."

Her father squeezed her hand. "They told you I might never walk again, didn't they?"

"Don't say that, Daddy." She squeezed back. "You're going to beat this. I believe in you. You can do anything you set your mind to, and we're all going to help you."

He glanced up at her again. "I hope so, honey." Then he cleared his throat, and as firmly as his hoarse voice could, he said, "I'm going to need you to take over the ranch. For a while, anyway. You're the only one who can do it."

Years' worth of grief and overwhelming guilt haunted her whenever she thought about running the ranch, even though it'd once been her undisputed future. After college and marriage, she and Shane had planned to come home to the Forty Flowers. Their children would grow up on the same ground she'd grown up on herself. Her father had supported Mae through her real estate licensing, built her a real estate office, and gifted her one hundred acres of prime Forty Flowers land. For Rainey, he'd also given one hundred acres of prime land, but he'd built her a country-style three-bedroom home near a creek on the land so that she would never be dependent on the husband who had always found other places to be.

The ranch, though, had always belonged to Kelsey-Rose. But one careless misstep—one stupid dare—and her future had vanished. Not only had it been her fault that Shane died, but she had almost lost the Forty Flowers Ranch in a lawsuit over his death. Yet her father never blamed her or lost faith in her, although she had none in herself.

When Nina reentered the room, a glisten was in Kelsey-Rose's eyes.

"Is everything all right?" Nina asked. "I didn't mean to be gone so long."

"Everything is fine. Daddy and I were just talking."

The beeps and clicks of hospital monitors overshadowed the mood of the tender moment, but Nina went straight to her husband and leaned down, kissing his forehead and smiling. "It's good to see you awake and talking," she said softly to him.

He looked at her, but his eyes were aquiver trying to focus. "I've asked Kelsey-Rose to take over the ranch for a while."

When Nina glanced at her, Kelsey-Rose released the hold she had on her father's hand. "But it's been so long. I can't remember how to do most of what's needed. It's ten years since I've had anything at all to do with ranch operations." She cleared her throat. "You really don't need help from me. You'll do fine with the bills and the livestock commitments, Nina. Ty and Cullen can handle the stock good enough by themselves, and what they have trouble with, I can lend a hand to on the weekends, or in the evenings, if it can't wait." She stepped away from the bed and its high railing. "Besides, I have the flower shop."

Nina hardened her stance. "And who do you think will take care of your father while I'm trying to manage the Forty Flowers and keep my full-time job? Our medical insurance is through my employer. I can't risk losing it." Her tone was unforgiving. "He's paralyzed, Kelsey-Rose. It might be weeks, or maybe months before he can even come home, and this hospital is more than an hour away from the ranch."

It was rare to see her stepmother angry, but she had a right. Nina had never pretended to be a ranching woman, and their lives might be on the verge of changing forever. The stress of it all was overwhelming.

The hardest thing to push aside was her conscience, but Kelsey-Rose managed a nod. Words, though—those were different. They had cemented themselves inside her, so it took a minute to chip away at their freedom, but as soon as she did, she said, "Of course, I'll handle the ranch. Maybe Rainey can help with the flower shop."

Nina gave a relieved sigh, her hand massaging the tense wrinkles that had deepened on her forehead. "Good. You girls need to pull together on this. Lord knows, your father has stood by each of you no matter the circumstances, and he needs all of you now. We both do."

"I'll do my best." Her words were so close to a whisper, she had to force them out. Kelsey-Rose reached for her father's hand again and gently took hold. "I won't let you down, Daddy."

"I know you won't." Fatigue was closing his eyelids as his words became a mumble. "I trust you, girls, to do what needs to be done."

Trust, she realized, was what this broken man

needed most. It was the one healing gift she could give to him.

When Kelsey-Rose returned to her sisters, other people had gathered in the waiting room for their own sick or injured families. The room was no longer theirs alone. In a chair along the wall, Rainey sat holding her two-year-old daughter, Emma. Both had red eyes and faces wet with tears.

"What's going on?" Kelsey-Rose mouthed to her older sister, Mae, for privacy among the strangers with tears of their own.

But Mae had never been a quiet or discreet woman. "Harry drove Emma here all the way from Topaz just to drop her off and tell Rainey he's filing for divorce. He's met a woman he can't live without." Then somewhat quieter, she said, "And at a time like this...that bastard."

"Oh, no." Kelsey-Rose went to Rainey and knelt at her chair, wrapping her arms around the sobbing mother and daughter. "I'm so sorry," she whispered.

Rainey nodded. "I really thought we could work things out."

"Hey," Kelsey-Rose said, wiping her sister's tears. "Sometimes things happen for the best, you know?"

Mae sat down in the chair next to Rainey. "You don't need him. He's nothing but a half-rate actor who barely made enough money to support the two of you anyway. You can get your real estate license and come work with me. You can start a new life."

"Or..." Kelsey-Rose stood. "You can run the flower shop." She reached, affectionately smoothing her niece's blonde hair, ignoring the look of surprise on Rainey's face. "Emma can stay with you every day after preschool, or all the time, if that's what you want."

Stunned, Rainey stared up at her sister. "You wouldn't fire Rita just to give me her job, would you? She's worked at the shop as long as you."

Kelsey-Rose loved that about Rainey. Her younger sister had been the one to inherit their father's compassion for people. "No," she answered. "I'm offering you *my* job, not Rita's job. You would really be helping me out if you could run the flower shop, for a few months anyway."

"Why?" Rainey stood, propping Emma on her hip. "Where are you going?"

"Daddy needs me at the ranch." It sounded better—stronger—to blurt it out, burying the feelings behind it.

"Is he just giving up?" Tears started down Rainey's cheeks again. "We can't let him do that!" she shouted, causing the others in the room to grow quiet and stare. "You go back in there and tell him he won't be paralyzed forever!"

"Rainey, stop," Mae said, reeling in the emotions of her sister. "We're all hoping Daddy will walk again, but there is a very real possibility that he might not." Then she looked at Kelsey-Rose. "And, of course, he asked you to run the ranch. He's been waiting for you to come home for ten years. It's not an option anymore."

Mae had never had a problem taking charge, and in a way, Kelsey-Rose was glad. She and Eddie had never had children, so Mae took her role as older sister as seriously as if it were motherhood.

"Now," Mae focused on Kelsey-Rose, "what else did Daddy say to you?"

At that moment, a memory that had long been forgotten flashed through her mind. In this same hospital, maybe even this same waiting room, Kelsey-Rose had learned about the death of her mother. At four years old, she had huddled with her two sisters and cried. Now, maybe for the first time, she recalled her father's words that day. "I trust you, girls, to take care of each other. To do what needs to be done."

Reflectively, softly, Kelsey-Rose mumbled, "He trusts us." She was being gentle, maybe more for her own sake than theirs, but the words hardened her as she spoke them. She glanced from one sister to the other. More firmly, she said, "He trusts us to do what needs to be done, and that's exactly what we're going to do."

CHAPTER 19

The Italian-style villa would always feel like home, even though Colton hadn't lived in the place for over ten years.

He walked the house alone—the Dainite rubber soles of his oxfords silencing the sound of his steps on the marble floor. Everything in the home was in order, lights were subtly lit, the air temperature a tad too cool, just the way his father had preferred.

Steen, the house manager who resided in his own private quarters on the grounds, had let Colton into the home, but only after calling Lily Wilde for express permission to do so, and then he had left.

In the quiet, deserted-feeling mansion, Colton roamed the rooms and hallways, allowing the furnishings to jog his memories of the life he'd once lived on this Tuscan-inspired estate. Just off the foyer was his father's office, its doors uncharacteristically left open rather than locked. He entered, breathing in the subtle cigar-scented air. The tall cherrywood library shelves, filled with books categorized by subject, gave the room elegance, intellect, and a calming solitude. He went to his father's desk, fingering a white star-tipped pen before returning it to its holder, and then he pulled out the dark cognac-colored leather chair and sat. Tired, he leaned back, resting his eyes, envisioning his father. Reflection on a life now fading couldn't be helped. He drifted off, trying hard to find his good memories.

At midnight the clock chimed, waking Colton. He sat forward in the chair, tapping the banker's lamp on the desk for light. Only then did he realize that Peter Wilde's last will and testament, signed and dated three years earlier, lay before him. Beside it was a crisp new will, unsigned. Colton glanced at the black Montblanc pen he'd returned to its holder earlier. Would his father have signed the replacement had he never been shot?

As any competent newspaper reporter would, Colton rubbed the sleep from his eyes and scooted the chair closer to the desk for a better look. He laid the two multipage wills side-by-side, and then, line-by-line, he compared the two documents. The unsigned will was what he'd expected, but the document that was three years old—the valid will—had a few surprises. Of his father's holdings, two were entirely unknown to Colton, including a weekly newspaper in the northernmost county in Texas, which made sense since its distribution crossed two state lines, and a penthouse condominium in the Dallas Arts District. He knew the building well. It had tight security and housed many of the wealthiest people in the world. But why his father had needed it was a mystery.

Colton set about researching his suspicions when a glance caught sight of a newspaper in the trash. He got up and retrieved the paper. He unfolded it to the front-page banner: *The Blue Topaz Times*. His father had known exactly where Colton was all along and what he was doing. This issue was a week old and had a mailing label. Peter Wilde had been a subscriber, for how long, he didn't know. While the *Wall Street Journal* and the *Dallas News*, along with copies of every newspaper Wilde Enterprises owned, had their own prominent place on the credenza behind his father's desk, it was only *The Blue Topaz Times* that had ended up in the trash. Opinions didn't always have to be voiced. Sometimes actions spoke louder.

At four in the morning, his mother arrived home, unexpectedly since she hadn't phoned. At the brief chirp of an alarm, Colton got up from the desk and went to the foyer.

Lily Wilde entered and pressed the code. She was head down, preoccupied in thought, as she crossed the floor without any notice at all of her son.

"Mother," Colton said, his voice halting her steps. "I thought you planned to stay at the hospital until…"

Lily Wilde turned, looking at her son. Regret, apology, and a whiff of grief stuttered her breath and wet her eyes. "Colton, your father has died," she said.

It was instinctive. He went to his mother and took her in his arms. He held her close. Felt her tears on his shirt, but he said nothing. This was her time, not his. He simply hugged her until she gathered her strength.

The man who had been Colton's ruler for nearly thirty-five years was no longer ruling.

When she finally pulled away from her son, she simply said, "It's over now. We need to make decisions and move on."

But Colton had already moved on. He was molding a new existence in Topaz. His own merits meant something to the people there. He owned a business that would be a true test of his abilities. And then there was Kelsey-Rose. There was something magical about her. He wanted more of her.

He had once enjoyed the rush of city noise and lights at night, and he'd thought that here was where he belonged. But now—after starting a new life in Topaz—he felt different about it all. There, he had strength, value, and an inner soul he'd felt he always had but could never find. He was becoming the man he wanted to be, but maybe most importantly, he had things that he needed to prove to himself.

"It's been a long night, Mother," he said to her. "We can talk more after we've had some sleep. Our heads need time to clear."

She nodded. A brief smile came when her eyes met his. "I'm glad you're back, Colton."

Back. Colton didn't know how to respond, so he said nothing at all. His mother had been right about one thing, though. Decisions needed to be made.

ALTHOUGH IT WAS SUNDAY, DEAN KENNEDY HAD come when Lily Wilde called him. Colton stood with her in his father's office, listening to her steady voice as she informed the attorney of her husband's passing.

"What about the will?" she asked.

Dean picked up the newer document off the desk and glanced at the signature page before he looked at Colton. "Peter had me draw this new will, removing you from the inheritance. He said he told you."

Colton said nothing. He simply stood and stared back at the attorney.

"Peter had a temper." Lily Wilde's professional

stature was unswerving. "You probably know that better than anyone. He was angry when he asked you to do that."

Dean Kennedy had been Peter Wilde's attorney for two decades. He had been one of the few men who had been trusted.

The attorney hesitated, his gaze measuring her intent. "This wasn't the first revision. He requested these new changes two days ago, Lily. And he wasn't mad two days ago. I have a clear understanding of Peter's intentions."

Without so much as an exhale, Lily said, "And how many times over the last few years had Peter's *intentions* been to fire you, Dean?" Her question was a challenge. "But in the end, he reconsidered, didn't he?" She took the signed will off the desk and used it to give a terse wave to the man. "My question is, is this will still valid? Legal advice, Dean, that's what I'm looking for from you—not your personal opinion on the matter."

Again, Dean glanced at Colton, but just for a moment. Then, "Lily, you have grounds to contest the will. You *should* contest the will. We need to talk about this in private."

"No need," she said. "As Peter's wife, I can assure you that once he had a chance to look over the new will, he decided not to sign it. He had no intention of approving the changes. That's why he didn't come to you with it."

Colton glanced at his mother. Her stance hadn't changed, but her eyes were not as steady. *She was lying.* She was lying to protect him.

After she'd arrived home in the early morning hours, there had been a brief time of grief and regret, but then before sunrise, Lily Wilde had gone to bed, sleeping for a few hours while Colton had done the same, but then she'd risen, showered, made herself a presentable widow dressed all in black, and called the attorney. She had not discussed her plans with Colton before doing so. She'd simply awoken him, told him to dress and meet her in his father's office. There, they had waited together for Dean Kennedy's arrival.

"The signed will is valid." He handed the unsigned document back to Lily Wilde. "I can start the probate procedure tomorrow."

"Good," she said. "Do that." She left the office, ushering the attorney to the front door. "Thank you for coming at my request today." After opening the door for his exit, she reached for a handshake. "I'll wait to hear from you."

After closing the door, Lily Wilde leaned back against it with her focus on Colton. "Now that we have that taken care of, we need to contact the funeral home and choose an urn."

CHAPTER 20

Halting Baley, her chestnut mare, on a ridge, Kelsey-Rose watched the morning shadows inch across the lower elevations. Here and there, in the distance, the metal rooftops of exotic game lodges and luxury estates dotted the landscape, drawing a definitive line—invisible as it was—between the old world of ranching and the new world of developments.

Farther to the south, in the haze of a day unfolding, she was able to see the outskirts of Topaz and the road that led into town.

From the saddle, Kelsey-Rose urged Baley forward toward the herd of longhorns that were grazing in the low valley. "Come on, girl." She needed to take stock of the ranch and its workings again. A thing that had been so natural to her once.

At a slow pace, the horse and rider descended the hill, weaving around prickly pear cacti and rocks. Ty and Cullen were moving the herd to the south pasture, slow but steady. They were good cowhands. Honest and hardworking. And in spite of their age difference, the two got along well. When needed, they shared their bunkhouse with day workers and rarely complained.

The Forty Flowers Ranch had been in the family for eighty-plus years, and not a single acre of it had ever been sold, except the one-hundred-acre parcels that were gifted to Mae and to Rainey, but keeping it in the family made those acceptable deeds.

The understanding, handed down from her grandfather, made it clear that the only way a ranch could stay in the same family for generations was if a deep love for the land existed with pride in its heritage. A family had to make sacrifices in order to keep a ranch in operation. It was more than just a job. It was a way to survive and preserve a way of life. As families grew, they had to work together to ensure that at least one family member —the one who loved ranching the most—stayed with the operation, allowing the others to pursue different careers of their choice. But everyone, whether they worked the ranch or not, understood the land had to be protected, so they supported it however they could without question.

As Kelsey-Rose neared the herd, she could tell that the cattle that needed branding had recently seen the hot iron without any help from her. The Bar Double F brand was a special mark that announced, "These cattle belong to us. Leave them alone." She had learned early on in her life that on this land, you ride for the brand, and you protect it with all you've got.

When Cullen spotted Kelsey-Rose, he turned his mount and headed for her, stopping just a few feet away.

"Miss Flowers," the cowboy said, tipping his hat with his misshapen left hand as if she were a guest rather than a wrangler. "Didn't expect to see you. Can I help you with something?"

"Hey, Cullen," she said. The scent of rain on the horizon turned her head. "We expecting rain today?"

"Maybe." He shrugged, giving a glance to the sky. "You can't trust a weatherman, but the purple sage bloomed yesterday, so I'd say we've got a good chance." Then he asked, "Any news on Harley?"

"Yeah," Kelsey-Rose said. "A little, anyway." Baley turned, lowering her head to nibble on a barely green clump of grass, nudging Kelsey-Rose closer to Cullen and his Quarter Horse. "Right now, Dad is paralyzed, but it might not be permanent. We don't know yet."

"Sorry to hear that. Anything we can do?" Cullen asked.

"Keep doing what you're doing. Take care of the herd. Daddy asked me to run things for a while, so I need to take a look at the schedule. I know the Longhorns have a lot of appearances in these next six weeks or so. As soon as I know what's going on, I'll ride out to the bunkhouse so that me, you, and Ty can talk about it."

"Yes, ma'am," Cullen said with a nod. "Did Harley tell you that we got a head count comin' up?"

"No," Kelsey-Rose said. "He didn't mention it. Is the herd scattered?"

"We got a few that we haven't been able to account for in the last few days, including a cow-calf pair and a heifer that's due any day," he glanced back at the herd, "but our focus has been off, what with the accident and all."

"Well, I hope they stayed mothered-up. I saw coyotes running this morning."

"They've been real active all week under the full

moon," Cullen said, taking off his cowboy hat and then refitting it on his head.

"Right," Kelsey-Rose said, nodding. "I'll meet you both at the horse barn at six tomorrow morning, and we'll go look for the mamas and babies. We'll find them."

Kelsey-Rose rode back, taking in the beauty of the day that she felt guilty about noticing. At the barn, she dismounted, giving a pat to Baley. She uncinched the horse, removed the saddle and bridle, and turned the mare out into the paddock, then she forked fresh hay into the feeders and filled the big steel trough with water from the hose. Inside the barn, she opened the stalls and turned out the other four horses to roam and graze, too.

She couldn't remember the ranch ever being so quiet. Without her father, the spirit was gone from it, or maybe it was just gone from her.

In his office, she found the printed schedule for event appearances on his desk, just where he'd said it would be. He was undeniably an organized and detail-oriented man, so the schedule had everything she would need, including dates and times, names and phone numbers, and all of the event locations with unloading and setup instructions.

One entire desk drawer was devoted to three critical elements: financing, genetics, and marketing. Another drawer held at least a dozen ledgers, all complete except for the top book. She pulled it out of the drawer and opened it to the ribbon-marked page. His accounting with handwritten entries was up-to-date, including notes on who had outstanding balances. His old-fashion ways made her smile. If she stayed long, she would download bookkeeping software onto his computer and transfer it all. Recordkeeping by hand was not one of her strong points.

The two Longhorns, Sequoia Sam and Speckled Pete, were scheduled to appear at Topaz High School for a pre-Thanksgiving event, and then on Saturday, they were booked for the Wild Game Dinner and Dance. It was an annual post-Thanksgiving event that he had attended for the last twenty years. After that, the schedule listed events twice a week until after the New Year. A busy schedule indeed.

Kelsey-Rose turned on the desktop copier and made two copies—one to take for her and one for Cullen and Ty when she met with them the next morning.

On the desk by where she had laid the blue ledger was a manila file marked *Meat Orders*. She opened it to find a list of beef orders waiting for delivery.

Kelsey-Rose closed the file, took a deep breath, exhaling slowly, and then leaned back in the chair with her eyes closed. She needed to find and hold on to a rational perspective on this unforeseen situation. Positive thoughts were what she needed.

Her father was alive, and today, at least, there was hope, however slight, that he might recover and walk again. Until then, she couldn't allow herself to be crushed by the extra load of ranch duties. He had never let her down, and she didn't intend to disappoint him. She just needed to figure out how not to.

When the light gradually dimmed through the south-facing windows in the office, sunset made itself known. Kelsey-Rose stood, stretching with a yawn. Sitting at a desk all day wasn't her idea of real ranching, but at least now she had a better grasp on the current state of things. So much had changed in the last ten years, but probably not the things that needed changing. The experience of owning her own business, different as it might be, had made her smarter than she'd once been about money matters and marketing. And although she was good at customer service, she hadn't inherited her father's cowboy personality—the one everyone loved.

She missed Free, her Jack Russell terrier, who was still stranded at a neighbor's house with Finn, Mae and Eddie's dog. And she missed Colton. Most of all, she regretted not being at the hospital to see and hear all that was happening.

Kelsey-Rose picked up her phone and checked for missed calls and text messages. She had lots. Calls from well-wishers and longtime family friends, even a call from Dax with twelve text messages. She had a voice-mail message from Robert, her friend, who was concerned after hearing about the accident. But nothing from Colton. He said he would call her when he could, she needed to trust that he would.

Just as she started to type a text to Dax, her phone rang with a call from Rainey.

She answered without a greeting. "Is everything okay?"

"Daddy's fine," Rainey answered. "But he's worried. Did you get the mail today?"

"Daddy's worried about the mail?"

"Yeah. You need to go get it. He said a five-thousand-dollar check should be there. You need to deposit it, and then go pay Rusty's Meat Processing for the order that needs to be picked up." Rainey paused. "Then you've got to deliver the orders. The file is on his desk."

"Tell him I already found the file," Kelsey-Rose said.

"Have the doctors been back in with any new information?"

Instead of answering, Rainey started to cry. Emotions were running high for everyone, but her sister had been hit by a second jolt, when in the midst of crisis, she'd learned her husband was divorcing her.

"Rainey, it's going to be okay," Kelsey-Rose spoke gently. "You and Emma are going to be fine, and Daddy is going to come out of this. Honestly, I'm glad you'll be rid of Harry."

"He's Emma's father. I won't ever be rid of him." Another sob broke free. "And I love him, Kelsey-Rose."

The burden of heartbreak was a heavy weight. She knew what it was like to love a man so deeply that a place is carved into your heart forever. Death and divorce had a strange commonality when love refused to let go.

"I know, little sister," Kelsey-Rose said softly. "There's still a chance you can work it out with him. Don't give up yet, okay?"

"Okay." The word carried its own intense grief and doubt. "Will you be back tomorrow?"

"I wish I could, Rainey, but we've got a head count coming up, and that list of Daddy's meat orders is already two days overdue. I need to pick it up from Rusty's and get it delivered. And Boyd from The Purple Sage has already left two messages on the ranch phone. He's nice, he said everyone was sorry to hear about Daddy's accident, but they're out of steaks."

"Do you want me to call Boyd and talk to him? His son is in my dance class, and he's been to see me a few times to make sure that I don't tell anyone that his son is a brilliant dancer. He's embarrassed about it, you know?"

Kelsey-Rose laughed. "He should be proud of his son, but his good ol' boy Texas pride is getting in the way, huh?"

"Yeah, I guess so. It's a shame. Dylan is really talented. But Boyd owes me a favor, or he thinks he does. Do you want me to call him and ask for a few more days?"

"Wouldn't hurt," Kelsey-Rose said. "See if Wednesday afternoon will work, okay? I've got to help find a cow-calf pair tomorrow that's been missing for a few days, and I've got a hay delivery, too. And I need to get ready for the head count." An unintended sigh came out. "Rainey, I don't know how Daddy does all of this. There's a lot more than I remember."

A moment of silence from her sister set her thoughts in motion.

"Has he been working this hard all along, just waiting for my help this whole time?" The guilt of it all cut through her. "I thought Cullen had taken on more responsibility."

"Kelsey-Rose, Daddy understood," Rainey said. "But in his mind, he knew that someday you would come home all on your own. He said the ranch was in your soul, and you just needed time."

"I should have realized he needed help. We could have hired another hand." Kelsey-Rose said.

"Daddy wouldn't hire anyone else. He said that job was yours, and he worried that if he took on another cowboy, you might never realize that you needed to come back. You were born to be a ranching woman, he said. He never gave up on you."

Shane's death had shut the door on that dream forever. She had no right to live the life that he had died for. The ranch, the horses, the longhorns, the sheer Western existence—it had taken the man she loved. She had been so caught up in living life as a rancher and a rider that she had never imagined it could snuff out a life so devoted to it. Memories of him and their love had stalemated any rational decision.

Now, a decade later, she was back on the ranch, thinking thoughts about Colton. The man had breathed life back into her again. He was completely different from Dax, or even Shane. He had set her heart on fire so blazingly hot that it was hard to remember how deeply heartbroken she was.

Kelsey-Rose lifted her focus, gazing out the office windows at the headlights appearing on their private ranch road, headed toward the house. "Rainey, I've got to go. Someone's here. I'll call you tomorrow, okay?"

After hanging up, she slipped her phone into the back pocket of her blue jeans and went to the front door, opening it.

Dax, still wearing his light blue mechanic's shirt with a sewn-on name label and jeans that bore oil stains, walked to the house, holding the keys to his Honda Accord in one hand and carrying a white plastic sack in his other.

"Hungry?" he asked, holding up the bag with *Marta's Homemade Tamales* printed in red.

"I was getting ready to text you. How did you know I was here?"

"When you didn't answer my call or texts, I went to see Eddie at the station. He told me you were staying at the ranch."

Dax knew her so well. Better than most. And he was right—she was hungry, and Marta's tamales were exactly what she would have requested had she been asked. Not only that, she was lonesome for someone to talk to tonight.

He leaned in and kissed her, and then walked the food through the house to the kitchen. At the breakfast table, the two of them ate while Kelsey-Rose filled him in on the details of her father's recovery.

"He asked me to run the ranch."

Dax snickered a laugh. "He asks you to do that at least five or six times every year. What did you say this time?"

Kelsey-Rose fidgeted in her seat. "I had to say yes, Dax. He's paralyzed. There's no one else to run it."

He sat back with surprise in his eyes. "What about the flower shop?"

"Rainey will have to run it for a while."

"Are you going to be okay doing that?"

He was one of the few who understood her troubled heart. "I don't have a choice."

"Okay," he said. "Well, I can help out at the ranch between my hours at the auto shop. What do you need me to do?"

Kelsey-Rose smiled, reaching across the table for his hand. "Dax, you're like the worst cowboy ever. I know your heart is in the right place, but you've never been a good rider, and you don't like cattle. But thank you for the offer."

Offended, he leaned back in his chair. "But I can drive the hell out of a truck. Not every job on a ranch involves horses and cows, right? I can drive the rig for you."

"And then do what? Unload the steers? Run the events?" She smiled, wanting him to see that she appreciated his offer, but the hurt in his eyes said he didn't feel appreciated at all. "My knight in shining armor," she said sweetly. "Those are cowboy jobs. And besides, what would Cullen and Ty do if they didn't get to haul the longhorns?"

The sun had been down for several hours, with the mood in the room just as low, when Dax asked, "Did you ever love me?"

Kelsey-Rose scooted to the edge of her chair and looked directly into his dark brown eyes. "I thought I did at one point, maybe a year or two after, but then I realized it was just loneliness that I was feeling. I'm sorry." She reached for him, taking hold of his hand. "I've always tried to be honest."

"Don't apologize. You have been honest. I guess I just thought that someday you might realize that I was the best man for you, and then we'd get married, have a bunch of kids, and live that happily ever after everyone talks about."

For a long while, neither spoke.

Finally, as gently as she could, she said, "Waiting until December won't change my mind. You know that, right?"

Dax glanced at her. "What about your once and forever promise? You're the one who doesn't give up on those, Kelsey-Rose."

She couldn't admit to him that she had already given up, because if she did, she would have to confess that she had fallen madly, if reluctantly, in love with Colton Wilde.

CHAPTER 21

The Tuscan-inspired stone-clad estate with an Italian red tile roof impressed everyone who had ever visited the estate. Its manicured grounds with mature landscaping and arched walkways between buildings were the epitome of his mother's affluent Italian heritage.

Colton was outside waiting when the Realtor arrived in her black Mercedes.

The blonde woman stepped out of her car wearing a beige business suit with a too-tight blazer detailed with black leather lapels and pockets, flaring open at the bosom to reveal a thin, clingy white blouse.

"Mr. Wilde?" She extended her hand. "I'm Bridget Fyve." As they shook, she said, "I know it sounds like there should be four more of me, but I'm the one and only." She handed him her business card with her photo and name covering half. "You'll notice my name is spelled f-y-v-e, not f-i-v-e. It's a pleasure to meet you."

Colton shook hands. "Thank you for coming. Dean

Kennedy highly recommended you. He said the two of you have worked together before?"

"Lots." Bridget glanced at the estate grounds. "Very nice. Shall we go inside?"

After a full tour of the home, additional buildings, and the grounds they returned together to the study. When Bridget set her satchel down at the octagonal meeting table, Colton went to retrieve his mother for the signature needed on the listing agreement.

At Lily Wilde's entrance, Bridget reached for a handshake, saying, "I'm sorry to hear of the loss of your husband."

"That's an odd expression, isn't it?" Lily asked, taking a seat at the table. "My husband isn't lost. I know exactly where he is, but thank you for your condolences."

Taken aback, Bridget hesitated, but then pulled out a preprinted listing agreement with everything filled in except for the asking price and a few other blank spaces. She laid it on the table.

"I assume you've brought a comparative market analysis for our review?" Colton asked.

"Yes, absolutely." The Realtor handed him another document, and then seated herself when Colton did.

Sharing the CMA with his mother, Colton flipped past the cover sheet and a few others, finally coming to a page that listed similar homes in the area currently for sale. He pointed to a photo he recognized of a neighboring property. To his mother, he said, "I didn't know Jim and Adele were selling?"

His mother nodded. "Jim has two new television shows in production. They're relocating to California."

"Well," Colton said, raising his brow in disappointment. "Their home is similar to ours in size and design.

If you want a quick sale, you'll need to price well below them."

With her business stature intact, his mother said, "I suggest we review these others before we start lowering the price, Colton."

After an hour of discussion, his mother signed the real estate listing form and then stood.

"We have one more," Bridget said, pulling out a second document.

"The penthouse?" Colton asked. At her nod, he said, "I've inherited the condominium. It was my father's sole and separate property, so I'll be signing for the sale of it. The probate will show that my signature alone is all that is needed."

"You?" Bridget's tone was doubtful. "When Dean showed me the property, he didn't mention that it was yours."

"Is that a problem?" Colton asked.

"No," she said, barely above a mumble. Then more clearly, "Not at all."

The Realtor was thorough, knowledgeable, precise, persuasive, and beautiful. She was also younger than he expected, but she was exactly what they needed to sell the estate and the penthouse as quickly as possible.

Trent Nolver's second call had taken Colton by surprise. He had already refused to provide the rival newspaper with a statement about his father's death, so why Nolver was calling again was a mystery.

"Look, Colton." Trent had the tactful voice of an experienced journalist. "Jakku Ito is an important guy, and he's got big backers. When he bought us last year, he walked in the door and raised the wage floor that day, and he raised it again last week. I'm telling you the truth. He's not someone you want to blow off. And he asked to meet you. He wants to talk—just you and him. No gimmick. The guy's loaded. Let him buy you a meal. Have a drink on his dime. What could it hurt?"

Colton had to admit, he was curious. "When and where?" he asked.

"The Tables at Turtle Creek. Outside, he said."

"When?"

"Four o'clock today?"

"Okay. Tell him I'll be there."

By four o'clock, all Colton wanted was a shot of good single barrel bourbon. Maybe two. These last few days had changed his life entirely, and it felt like his world was still spinning.

The Tables was a favorite restaurant for the wealthy, and those who pretended to be, but Colton had never needed to pretend. He was comfortable and recognized.

He stood just inside the door to the outside area, trying not to appear lost in the day's early crowd, scanning the outdoor diners as if he would recognize someone he had never met.

"Mr. Wilde," the head waiter asked. "Are you meeting Mr. Ito?"

"Yes," Colton said. "Can you point me in the right direction?"

"Absolutely." Without being an obvious pointer, the elder man said, "The dark-haired gentleman, seated near the railing, wearing the black Dolce and Gabbana suit, is Mr. Ito." He waited, then asked, "Shall I present you?"

"No," Colton said, with a generous, but discreet tip to the seasoned headwaiter. "Thank you."

Colton crossed the patio brick floor of the outdoor dining area. "Mr. Ito?" he inquired at the table.

The man looked up and then stood. His stature diminutive. "Yes. Mr. Wilde, I presume?"

"Yes."

They shook hands and then both sat, with the publisher then raising a hand to catch the waiter's attention. When the waiter arrived tableside, Jakku Ito asked Colton, "Would you like something to drink?"

Colton focused on the waiter. "Your best single barrel bourbon, please?"

"Certainly, sir," the waiter said, then to Jakku Ito, he asked, "Would you like another?" When he received a nod, he turned and headed for the bar, leaving the two men.

"So," Colton said, settling back in his chair near a wrought iron railing where a thin beard of ivy grew. "I admit, I am curious about this meeting."

"Are you?" Jakku tittered, then he sipped from his near-empty glass. "I wanted to offer my condolences to you and your mother."

"That's not why you called me here."

"No." When the waiter returned with their drinks, Jakku straightened in his chair, angling an appraising glance at Colton. Then he took a sip of his drink and set it down. "There was no love lost between Peter and myself. He was a brutal foe to his rivals, as anyone will tell you, but perhaps most of all to me. In less than a year, he had almost been successful in convincing even the most knowledgeable of men that I was not trustworthy—a literary hack and a weasel is what he called me—and yet, there he was, slyly, the most cunning and unscrupulous publisher I've encountered in the media world today."

Although his heartbeat thudded at the insolence, Colton remained stoically resolute. He kept his gaze on Jakku Ito, taking a sip of his bourbon before setting down his glass.

"And that's why you called me here? To tell me that my father almost ruined you?"

Colton knew that wasn't the reason, but he couldn't figure out what the reason was, so he stayed seated, keeping hold of a disciplined demeanor.

Jakku Ito leaned closer. "My sources tell me that you're the grand recipient of Peter Wilde's estate, including his chain of newspapers. Are my sources correct?"

A smile. "You mean your sources weren't clever enough to convince a probate clerk to confirm or deny?"

Ito leaned back. He took another sip from his glass. "I'd heard you were more like your mother than your father. I'm beginning to doubt that."

"I am nothing like my father." Colton wasn't smiling anymore. "What is it that you want from me, Mr. Ito?"

"I want your chain of newspapers."

Taken aback, he stared at the publisher. Neither man blinked until Colton stood. He took a business card for Dean Kennedy out of his wallet and dropped it on the table in front of Jakku Ito. "Make an offer." Colton swallowed the last of his bourbon and then set down the glass, tossing a twenty-dollar bill onto the table. He walked out, never looking back.

~

INSTEAD OF THE HOUSE BEING QUIET AND SOMBER, like a mourning might dictate, Colton arrived home from his meeting to find it busy with at least a dozen men and women, wandering through the rooms with notepads, pens, iPads, and cameras. Every light in the house was lit.

"Mother," Colton caught her halfway up the stairs with three other visitors. "May I speak with you, please?"

Lily Wilde acknowledged him with an understanding nod before sending her focus to the upstairs landing where Steen waited. To him, she said, "Please accompany Ms. Murdoch through the upper floor. I'll be up in a moment."

"Yes, Mrs. Wilde," Steen said, waiting for the three who were on the stairs with her to reach the second-floor landing as Colton's mother descended the steps to where he waited.

"Is everything all right, Colton?" his mother asked him.

Colton glanced at the busy horde in the house, ignoring everyone who wasn't wearing a name badge. He looked back at her. "What's going on? Who are these people?"

"Our estate organizer and her staff." Her look with squinted brow settled on him. "I told you about the estate sale, didn't I?"

"No," Colton told her. He glanced at the throng of people again. "Evidently, you forgot to mention it to me."

Lily Wilde put a comforting hand on Colton's arm. "I'm sorry." Then she glanced around the room, her eyes settling on a woman dressed in a conservative black dress and blazer, calmly directing the others.

"Lana," she called. When the woman turned to her, she said, "This is my son."

Lana, tall, svelte, and fiftyish, approached, hand extended. "Mr. Wilde," she said. "I'm Lana Moore from Moore and Murdoch Estate Sales. It's a pleasure to meet you." She handed him a pack of hot pink sticky notes. "Just tag any item you want reserved from the sale. We'll make sure it is set aside with your name." At Colton's silence, she asked him, "Are there any questions I can answer for you?"

He fiddled with the cellophane pack of pink tags. "No. No questions."

In hearing her name called again, Lana turned with a glance then hurried away in answer to two men moving an ornate Italian gilded mirror through the foyer. "The neighbor has already purchased that mirror! You're supposed to deliver it to the house next door."

Colton looked at his mother. "You're selling everything?"

"Everything that you don't want. What else should I do with it? I'm not planning to move it all to Italy." She gave him a thoughtful look. "But I thought you might want to keep a home here in the States. We can have things shipped wherever you decide."

Colton needed time to think. Not about the personal items that seemed to mean less to his mother than they meant to him, but about the direction of his life and how it was all changing too fast.

"Is everything all right?" his mother asked him. "You look a little flushed."

Colton motioned with a glance to the activity within the home. "The cremation is tomorrow. Our visitation is tomorrow. This is not the somber, reflective occasion I expected tonight."

His mother glanced at the doors left open by the movers using dollies and pulled her slate gray cardigan snug. "Are you having a hard time with the cremation? It'll just be the two of us at the funeral home, and we won't be staying long. I mean, Dean will be there, but he just wants to meet with the funeral director to confirm the accuracy of the death certificate and to be sure that it is handled properly and electronically filed."

Colton had to be honest. "I expected more."

"But I'm doing exactly what your father wanted." She started for her husband's office before he could say more. "Come with me. I'll show you."

Colton wasn't trying to argue or question her decisions, but he followed anyway.

Lily Wilde took a document out of a locked drawer and handed it to Colton. "Read it," she said in a tone of sincerity.

He stood, reading, while his mother stayed beside him, silent. The last page was a prewritten death announcement. Colton looked at her. "He wrote his own obituary?"

"Two years ago. You didn't think he would let someone else do it, did you?" She pointed to the blank spaces. "All Dean and I were required to do was fill in the date and place of death."

Colton handed it back to his mother. She was correct. Everything had been taken care of and was being carried out exactly the way Peter Wilde had requested.

He suddenly felt exhausted. "Do you need me for anything else tonight, Mother?"

"No," she glanced back at the activity, "but you

should take a walk through the rooms and tag any items that you want to keep. I told Lana that her crew needed to be finished itemizing by the end of the day on Wednesday. The house goes on the market Thursday, and everything needs to be in order."

He took another look at his mother and then leaned in to kiss her cheek. "I'll look into it tomorrow after the visitation. I'll be in my room for the rest of the evening." He felt out of place in this house now. Almost sickened by the activity. "Call if you need me."

He didn't wait, he simply took the steps up to the second floor, feeling as though the stairs of life were crumbling beneath his feet. As soon as he got into the bedroom that had once been his, he locked the door and called Kelsey-Rose.

CHAPTER 22

Kelsey-Rose was in bed, staring at her phone, willing it to ring when it did. "Hello?"

"It's good to hear your voice," Colton said.

She sat straight up, then threw off her blanket and stood. "Colton, how's your dad? I've been so worried. You said you'd call."

"I know I did. I'm sorry." His tone was quiet as if the whole world were sleeping at nine o'clock at night. "Things have been…chaotic."

"That's okay. It's been chaotic here, too."

A silent moment stilled the conversation, but then Colton asked, "Chaotic for you, too? How? Are you all right? Did something happen?"

"Yeah." Kelsey-Rose hadn't expected her news to be so hard. "After you left—I mean the reason Eddie came last Saturday—Daddy was in a real bad accident."

"Kelsey-Rose...I'm so sorry. I didn't know," he said. "Is he okay?"

"No," she said. "I mean, he is, but not really. He had surgery. He's paralyzed, Colton." The threat of tears graveled her voice. "It might not be permanent. We don't know yet."

"I feel terrible for not calling sooner."

Kelsey-Rose went to the bedroom window with the phone to her ear. She pulled back a lace sheer and looked out into the moonlit night. "Tell me about your dad. I've been worried."

Colton cleared his throat first before he said, "My father passed away Saturday night." He waited until her gasp quieted. "There's been a lot that has happened since then. Decisions had to be made, and things needed to be taken care of."

"I am so sorry, Colton. I should have called when I didn't hear from you. Are you okay? Is your mom all right?"

"Yes, amazingly. And Mother is holding up quite well."

"When are the services?" she asked.

"Visitation is tomorrow morning, and then afterwards is the cremation. We aren't having a public service, but there are still things that need my attention."

"How long will you need to stay?"

"Well, I don't know for sure, but I was hoping you could come and be with me for a few days while I wrap things up. But with your father and all, I suppose that's out of the question, isn't it?"

"Yes, definitely out of the question. I'm sorry." Knowing that he missed her made her miss him all the more. "I wish you were here with me."

"So do I," Colton said. "Is there anything I can do to make things easier for you?"

She stood at the window, listening to a pack of coyotes howl in the distance, faint but there, sending her vision out across the land that lay bathed in moonlight. "Do you have any extra cowboys you can send me?" She laughed, hoping to lighten the tone of things.

"Sweetness," he said affectionately with a tease in his voice. "Handsome cowboys are the last thing I would send to you."

"They don't need to be handsome, just good."

"Good at what?" Colton asked.

"Cowboying. The ranch is in my hands, for now. Daddy needs me until he's back on his feet again." She felt a lump in her throat at the thought he might never be.

"I don't mean to sound insensitive, but what happens to you and the flower shop if his paralysis is permanent?"

For a moment, Kelsey-Rose was quiet, then she said, "I don't know."

THE URN GALLERY HAD A SURREAL FEEL FOR COLTON, but his mother had an eye for exquisite pieces, so she took her time examining each of the displays before summoning him to the wood crafted cremation urns.

"Colton," she said. "This hand turned walnut wood urn is lovely, don't you agree? The craftsmanship is excellent, and the graining of the wood is beautiful."

He went to her, watching as she examined it. "Yes, it's very nice. It should be easy to transport to Italy."

"Yes." She turned to look at her son. "It would, wouldn't it?" Nodding at what she considered his approval.

The details of the cremation had been finalized by phone, so the visitation and urn choice were all that was needed. Choosing the urn had taken longer than the visitation.

Dean Kennedy, their trusted counsel, was waiting for them inside the funeral director's office when Colton and his mother brought in their completed order sheet with her choice of urn. She handed the request to the solemn-faced director.

"Mr. Kennedy will take care of the cost." Lily Wilde reached out to shake the hand of the glum-faced man. "Thank you for your courtesies today. Please deliver the urn with my husband's remains as soon as possible."

Without any acknowledgment to Dean Kennedy, Lily Wilde turned to her son. "Are you ready to go?"

Colton had no notion of how to handle his mother's detached behavior. If she was grieving, it wasn't the kind of grief he expected.

"Yes," he answered simply, not able to avoid the curious glance from Dean Kennedy. "Mother and I are having lunch together—her request. Would you like to join us?" he asked.

"No," Lily Wilde said, interrupting any opportunity to accept the invitation. "I'm sorry, Dean," she politely apologized. "But this is a private time between a mother and her son. You understand, don't you?"

"Of course," Dean answered, appearing unfazed.

Amphora Ristorante was an elegant Italian restaurant in the upper-class district of Dallas. Lily Wilde had made lunch reservations, so although the dining room was crowded upon their arrival, the two of them were immediately escorted along a Saltillo tile walkway adorned with two-handled terracotta jugs. They were seated at a linen-covered table near a window that looked out onto a terraced herb garden where a wine tasting event was underway.

"A glass of Merlot Bianco, please?" she asked the host upon being seated.

Colton ordered an iced tea for himself, waiting until the man departed with their drink order before scooting his chair closer to his mother for privacy. "Are you all right today?"

"Yes." She looked at him with stoic eyes, although the hint of a smile couldn't be hidden. "I am returning to Italy soon. My home, where my family is waiting for me." Then a comforting quiet settled itself between them. "And my son will finally meet his true heritage."

Their waiter, wearing black slacks and a deep V-cut vest over a long-sleeved white shirt, delivered their drinks. He handed each a menu. "May I suggest the radicchio and Bartlett pear salad with our whole grain mustard vinaigrette and fresh local goat cheese to start your lunch today?"

"Yes," Colton said, grateful for the moment to gather his thoughts. "Thank you."

Quiet while the waiter attended to them, his mother sipped her Merlot Bianco. When they were alone again, his mother set down her glass. "I have a wonderful surprise for you," she told Colton. "Your Uncle Enzo has purchased *World Wineyards* magazine as your welcome home gift." She reached, gently touching his forearm. "You'll no longer be an overlooked American journalist. You'll be the esteemed publisher of one of the wine industry's finest, most respected magazines with a reader circulation of three million."

His chest tightened until it was hard to inhale a breath. Colton leaned back in his chair. He didn't fully understand how or why this was happening, but he couldn't delay any longer. "Mother, I can't go to Italy with you."

"Of course, you can." The ease of her smile somehow softened the darkness in her brown eyes. "You're quite wealthy now, my son. It's just as it should be. There's nothing to hold you back, and once you're out of the States, no one will associate you with your father. It will truly be a fresh start. You'll hold a respectable status in literary circles."

"Mother," Colton said. "I want you to know that I look forward to finally meeting Uncle Enzo and your other brothers. My grandparents, too. And I appreciate what they're doing for us, but—"

She sat back. "No buts, Colton." Her tone turned hard. Uneasy. "You can't stay here."

His curiosity about her recent attitude change had the better of him now. "Why can't I stay here?" he asked her. "What is it that you're not telling me?"

"You just can't..." she stopped when the server delivered their salads. When he started to speak, she held up her hand. "Not now," she snapped. At the waiter's nod and departure, her tone intensified. "You can't stay here. The invitation to come to Italy was not a question. Everything is already set for you."

Colton didn't like to be pushed, but with his mother in mourning, he felt a gentleness was due. "Wilde Publishing is my own company. I started it without any help from anyone, and I'm building it from the ground up." He spoke discreetly. "I've laid out a finely detailed plan that I believe in. I am not going to just walk away from it." The demeanor of grief between them was lost for the moment. "*The Blue Topaz Times* is my first publication, but if I'm successful, I have more lined up. And now that I've acquired a sizable inheritance, building Wilde Publishing into a respectable company won't be as difficult or take as long as I expected."

His mother shook her head as if he didn't understand. "Newspapers are failing all over the world. Their time is over." She started to eat her salad as if the conversation was over, but after one bite, she put her fork down and looked at Colton again. "To compete against digital and all of the social media platforms in today's media world is ridiculous. Newspapers are outdated and useless. Surely, you know that's true."

"I disagree." Colton was willing to argue this point. "It's true that newspapers are closing their doors, but it's the economy that is their biggest enemy, and economies are always changing. When they shut down, it leaves struggling communities, most of them small, as the hardest hit by the decline of local journalism." His tone became more impassioned. "Most towns that lose their newspaper don't get a replacement, digital or otherwise, and that leaves 70 million residents—over one-fifth of this country's population—to live in areas with no local news organizations."

Again, his mother shook her head. "Which is exactly why I don't understand your taking such an ardent stand in defense of an industry that weaponizes information and prides itself on secrecy. This needs to be a business decision, not some heroic stride to prove that you are better than your father."

"Confidentiality is different than secrecy." Colton pushed his salad away. "This decision is based on my principles in an industry that I've loved and believed in for a long time. Not every media outlet weaponizes information. And I'm not trying to prove anything to anyone but me." He stopped. After gathering his thoughts, he softly started again. "I have a chance to syndicate and also to create a digital platform that will allow me to reach a lot of other communities that need local news. Maybe not tomorrow, or next month, or maybe not even next year, but the opportunity is there for me."

"I won't let you do this."

"Mother, I love you, but it's not your choice. I've spent my life trying to prove to myself that I am capable of making a difference, and I have to try." He reached for her hand and pulled it to his lips, leaving a kiss just above her wedding ring. Then he leaned back in his chair again. When her glare started to fade, he said, "And I've met someone. Her name is Kelsey-Rose, and she lives in Topaz. I want to be with her more than anyone I've ever known."

His mother pulled her napkin to her lips and dabbed. "This is all because of a woman?"

"No," Colton said, attempting to correct what appeared to be a misunderstanding. "She has nothing to do with my decisions, but she is a businesswoman herself, so she understands the things I want and why I want them. I like having her in my life, and I would like to see where the relationship might go." When his mother's eyes became glassy, she looked away, watching the people come and go from the outdoor wine tasting event. Colton called softly for her attention. "Mother, she makes me very happy, and she gives me reasons to believe in myself."

Lily Wilde looked up, refocusing on her son. She smiled at him, a tremble on her lips. "If she can do that, I won't stand in your way."

CHAPTER 23

Finding the pairs had been harder than Kelsey-Rose remembered, but after a few hours, they'd located the missing cow and her calf near a creek bed, staying in close to another young cow and her day-old newborn. Herding them back was a slow process, but before long, they were where they needed to be.

Kelsey-Rose and the two ranch hands sat their horses, overlooking one part of the herd, verbally mapping out their plan for the day's head count. "How many fields are we counting?"

"Three," Cullen told her. "We got the north field in pregnant cows and young steers, the west field in young calves, and the east field in bulls and heifers."

Ty, without any warning that the quiet cowboy planned to speak, shouted out, "Anybody know the best way to count cattle?"

Cullen glanced at Kelsey-Rose with a questioning brow, but then he looked back at Ty. "I think so," he said to the younger cowboy. "I mean, I done it for years now." In a respectful Texas drawl, he asked, "But what do you think is the best way to count cattle?"

Ty laughed, giving his knee a slap. "I use a *cowculator.*" Then he roared with laughter.

Not expecting the range humor, Kelsey-Rose sputtered a laugh, only to have Cullen say, "Don't humor him, ma'am. It only gets worse if you do."

The end of the day brought a successful head count to a close under cloudy gray skies with sundown leaving a bluish-purple hue in the western sky. A sprinkling of rain was falling, but the moment the droplets hit the dirt, they evaporated into sheer nothingness, which did no good at all for the drought.

After leaving Cullen and Ty, Kelsey-Rose, riding Baley, trotted toward home. When the barn came into view, the horse and rider settled into a slow rhythmic walk.

Her straw cowboy hat and suede jacket shielded her upper body from the elements, but raindrops on her blue jeans and bare hands somehow gave her a quiet peace about all the bad happening around her. Perhaps the slower they walked, the less time she would spend in the worry and sadness of it all. Out on the range, life was different for her. It always had been.

In the morning, Kelsey-Rose brewed coffee and toasted a bagel, and then made calls to the customers on her father's list. She fingered the check that had arrived in the mail for the sale of two steers. There wasn't a thing she could do with it unless she drove into town and deposited it herself. She hadn't been on the ranch bank account for ten years, and she didn't have any of her father's passwords. Why hadn't she realized that she was too far removed to help in the event of a crisis? She'd caused these hardships herself, and she knew it.

She should have listened more closely when her father had tried to reason with her. His words felt like a haunting today: *I still have a lot to teach you. You've got to learn more about our ranch operations and the managerial process of it all. The production, recordkeeping, finances, and marketing will all fall to you one day, and it takes time to learn it all.*

She understood now. But *now* was quickly becoming too late.

In town, Kelsey-Rose waited at the bank door with the five-thousand-dollar check. When the door was unlocked and pushed open for her, she entered, greeting the bank manager.

"Good morning, Bryce. How's Susie doing at her new job?" she asked. The man had been four years ahead of her in school, but he and Mae had been classmates.

"She likes it." Bryce smiled. "I think teaching geography to third graders is her true calling. She loves those kids already, and it has only been three months. How's your dad doing after the accident?"

"He's going to have a tough recovery." Kelsey-Rose handed him the check. "That's sort of why I'm here. I need your help."

"Sure," he said, glancing at the check. "Do you just need this deposited into the ranch account?"

"Yeah, but I also need to be able to draw on the account, like to pay Rusty's Meat Processing for a big order that I need to pick up and deliver today."

"That shouldn't be a problem. What do you need?"

"Really?" she asked. "I thought it would be harder since I can't write checks on the account."

"Why can't you write any checks? Are you out?"

"No..." she said, confused. "Don't I need Daddy's authorization to do that?"

"You're on the account," Bryce said. Then with a raised brow, he said, "I mean, unless something has changed. Let's go into my office and take a look."

Kelsey-Rose followed, the heels of her Justin boots tapping against the wood floor all the way to his office.

"Have a seat," the manager said. He went around the desk to his chair and then sat. "I need to log on, but it'll just take a minute." He smiled at her again. "You're the first customer this morning."

Kelsey-Rose stayed quiet while his computer keys clicked, fidgeting in her chair and scraping bits of mud off her twice-worn jeans.

Bryce stopped typing and pushed back in his chair. "Looks like we just need an updated signature card. Sit tight. I'll get one for you." He stood.

"Wait," she said, standing. "Don't you need Daddy's approval for something like this?"

"Kelsey-Rose, you've been a signer on this account for over fifteen years."

She took a step back—a jolt of skepticism shot through her. "Are you sure?"

"Positive. You've never been off this account. Do you need some temporary checks while you're in town today?"

With an unintended nod, she said, "Yes. That would be great."

Kelsey-Rose walked out of the bank with a book of temporary checks and an account balance that would solve the day's problems.

On her way to Rusty's, she drove by Say It With Flowers, noticing that Rainey's car was not in the parking lot behind the building like she expected. She pulled in and stopped, and then entered through the back door.

"Hi Rita," she said to her employee. "Where's Rainey?"

Rita had been employed part-time at the shop since before Kelsey-Rose bought it, and although the older woman only worked half days Monday through Friday, she was responsible, knowledgeable, and dependable.

"I haven't seen her," Rita said, putting the bunch of gladiolas she was trimming into a container of water. "But I'm glad to see you. How's your father?"

Kelsey-Rose shook her head. "I haven't had an update since yesterday." She pulled her phone out of her back pocket. "No cell service where the cattle roam. I need to call and check this morning." Then she slipped the phone back into her jeans pocket. "But last I heard, there's been no change in his paralysis. Everything else seems to be improving. I still can't believe it happened."

Rita pulled Kelsey-Rose into a hug. "It will all turn out okay."

She knew Rita meant well, but words just weren't enough. Things don't turn out okay all on their own. "Thank you," she said.

Kelsey-Rose stepped away to call her sister. When Rainey answered, she said, "Hey, sis, where are you? Rita leaves at noon, and I don't have anyone to cover the afternoon shift."

"Today?" Rainey asked. "Oh, not today, Kelsey-Rose. You know I can't leave Daddy. Mae had to drive back to Topaz for some real estate appointments that couldn't be moved, so it's just me and Emma here with Nina. Without us, Daddy would be all alone."

"Rainey, we're all doing what we need to do, and

you agreed to run the flower shop until I could come back. The ranch is a handful, and that's where Daddy needs me."

"I just can't." Emotions shook her voice. "Maybe next week, okay?"

Kelsey-Rose didn't normally let her temper make decisions for her, but this time it couldn't be helped. She ended the call without a goodbye and put the phone back into her pocket.

"Problem?" Rita asked politely, restocking the floral cooler with trimmed gladiolas.

Rita was in her late sixties and one year away from full retirement. She hadn't enjoyed a day of perfect health in years. Her energy was waning, and so was her interest and commitment.

"That's putting it mildly," Kelsey-Rose said. "Is there any chance you can work full-time for a while?"

Rita closed the cooler door. "Working a whole day is too hard on me, Kelsey-Rose." She reached down and rubbed her knees. "Arthritis is the bigger boss. But maybe I could work until one or two in the afternoon for the next week or so instead of leaving at noon? That would get you through the lunch hour, at least."

"That would be a big help, Rita. Thank you."

With a promise to be back at the flower shop by two o'clock, Kelsey-Rose left with the ranch checkbook and drove to Rusty's Meat Processing. She paid the bill and then loaded the frozen meat orders into heavy ice chests in the back of her sea blue Santa Fe and delivered the orders as promised.

It was ten minutes past two when she pulled into the flower shop parking lot again. The closed sign was hung, the lights were off, and the doors were locked.

She'd never had a nervous breakdown, but she was feeling one coming on.

By the time Kelsey-Rose got inside, turned on the lights, and had the front door unlocked, the phone had started to ring. She answered while pressing the mode button on the cash register to open for business.

"Well, hello," Danielle London said. "I've called three times in the last ten minutes, but no one answered."

"Hi, Dani," Kelsey-Rose said. "I'm sorry." Her once, long-ago best friend was the only person she had ever been close to while growing up who had also lost a parent. "Did you hear about Daddy's accident?"

"Yeah, it's been the talk of the town. You know how it is," she said. "Are you doing okay?"

"To tell you the truth, Dani, I think I'm about to lose my mind."

"Talk to me. Tell me what's going on."

It all came pouring out of Kelsey-Rose, some in angry words, some morose, but mostly sad and scared. "I just don't know how to do it all without shutting down the shop. I can't let Daddy down, Dani."

"Okay, I have a thought," Dani said. "What if after the holiday, I come down to the shop every day at two o'clock so that Rita can go home."

"And run the shop? You'd be willing to do that for me?"

The two had worked afternoons together in the flower shop all the way through high school.

"Of course I would, Kelsey-Rose. You were there for me every day for months after my mom and dad died. You even helped me study for my accounting degree, remember?"

They'd been just eighteen years old then. Their lives

were changed forever, and then one year later, Shane had died. The devastation of another death had been too much for either to bear, and they'd drifted apart as friends. Kelsey-Rose had recoiled from life itself while Dani was just rising from the depths. They'd been headed in different directions ever since.

"The cash register is different now than when we were in high school," Kelsey-Rose said.

Dani laughed. "Honey, everything is different from when we were teenagers."

"I'll have to close 'til Monday. I just don't have enough time or people to open on Black Friday or the weekend."

"Just tell Rita that I'll be in at one o'clock on Monday instead of two for her to teach me the register. Numbers are the one thing I understand."

The emotion of it all surprised her, but Kelsey-Rose managed to say, "Dani, this means a lot—"

"Hey," Dani stopped her. "I'm not ever gonna *not* be there for you. It's not a big deal. You've got more important things to do. Besides," she chuckled, "it'll be fun."

CHAPTER 24

Life in the small town of Topaz seemed half a world away and completely foreign compared to the one Colton had been living in Dallas, and returning to Central Texas with millions more than he'd left with was harder than he imagined.

He hadn't told Kelsey-Rose, or his staff at *The Blue Topaz Times*, that he was on his way back. He needed time to think without the added psychological pressures associated with how they might react after learning about his inheritance. His staff had grown accustomed to him doing trade-outs instead of paying cash, and Kelsey-Rose—the woman he simply could not get off his mind or out of his urges—had no need or desire for money. *It's overrated,* she'd told him. She was glad he didn't have money. *It changes people into someone they're not,* she had said. He didn't want to change if it meant losing her.

Colton had a different eye on the ranches scattered about the countryside on his way back to Topaz. Rarely did he see a rancher, but cattle were plentiful. Longhorns, however, were not. He realized that he had no idea what a real rancher did all day, but it was what Kelsey-Rose was tasked to do now, and from the stories he'd heard, she was good at it.

When he had first found himself without his father's money, after the shock of being cut out of the will had worn off, he had made a conscious decision to create a new life and career for himself using the knowledge and experience he had in an industry he had loved his entire life. He hadn't ever wanted to ride his father's coattails, and now that he knew the truth about Peter Wilde, he was glad of it. He *was* a different man than his father. Those weren't just words to soothe a mother's broken heart or calm a foe's fatal joust.

Colton needed to prove to himself that he could be successful without any help. But that's not to say he wouldn't use a little of his inheritance to buy flowers for the woman who had set his heart on fire. Money wasn't all bad, in spite of what Kelsey-Rose thought about it. But there probably wasn't a need to show her his bank balance.

When Kelsey-Rose spotted Colton's arctic white Corvette with silver and black stinger stripes stopped at the intersection for a red light, she bolted for the front door, pushing it open, but instead of turning left at the green light for the newspaper office, Colton put the car in reverse and backed up on the empty street, pulling into the back parking lot of Say It With Flowers.

Out-of-control schoolgirl feelings overwhelmed her, but at the moment, all Kelsey-Rose cared about was that Colton was home, and he wanted to see her enough to stop at the flower shop first before going to *The Blue Topaz Times*.

Colton was just getting out of his car when Kelsey-Rose pushed open the back door and ran for him. He caught her as she jumped into his arms, kissing him with her whole heart.

He held on to her, turning round and round with her, finally resting her against his closed Corvette door. Her legs wrapped tightly around him, but her kiss stayed, only wetted by tears.

When their lips parted, Colton said, "I've missed you so much."

"I've missed you, too." She unwound her legs from around his waist and lowered her feet to the ground, but her arms stayed around his neck. "Why didn't you call to tell me you were coming home today?"

Colton swept her red hair back away from her face, his blue-gray eyes studying her, and then he kissed her again. "You are the most beautiful woman..."

Kelsey-Rose laughed. "You only say that when I'm dressed like a bum."

"Really?" he asked, taking a step back to look more carefully. After a head-to-toe scan of her, he said, "Shame on me. I should be telling you how beautiful you are every single time that I see you because you are." He kissed her again.

From the open back door, Kelsey-Rose heard the bell over the front entrance.

"A customer." She took his hand and pulled. "Come with me."

Inside the shop were two browsers, brunette twins, college-aged girls, perusing the floral coolers with *oohs* and *ahhs*.

"Hi, can I help you find something today?" Kelsey-Rose asked them, leaving Colton in the doorway between the back room and the interior shop.

The two closed the glass doors they'd opened and turned. One said, "We're looking for something nice to give to our grandma for putting up with us all this week, but she already has a pretty wreath and a nice Thanksgiving arrangement for the dining table. We're trying to think of something different for her."

The other said, "But she really loves flowers."

Kelsey-Rose thought for a moment, and then she asked them, "Are you Mrs. Cummins's granddaughters from Tulsa?"

"Yeah. Do you know our grandma?"

"For a long time," Kelsey-Rose said with a smile. "I might have the perfect gift for her." She motioned for them.

In the glass cooler behind the cash register, Kelsey-Rose took out an arrangement with a clear hurricane glass candleholder ringed by pastel pink Sarah Bernhardt peonies and white, fuchsia-edged carnations with green sprigs of myrtle. She set the arrangement on the counter for the two customers to see more closely.

One twin leaned in to sniff the fragrant pale cream candle with pink swirls. "Oh, my gosh." She looked at her sister. "Come and smell this!"

Kelsey-Rose smiled as the other inhaled a whiff of the sweet-smelling candle. "That scent is called sun-ripened raspberry," she told them.

"It's amazing." Then the girl touched a blossom. "How did you get peonies this time of the year? I thought they were spring and summer flowers."

"My supplier gets them from lots of different countries, so they carry them almost year-round."

The granddaughters shared a look, and then together, they said, "We'll take it." They paid for the arrangement and, grinning happily at each other, they left the shop with their purchase.

"You're really good," Colton said, strolling to the cash register where Kelsey-Rose stood. "I admire that about you." From behind, he slipped his arms around her waist while she put the cash in the drawer, and then he leaned, kissing her neck just below an ear adorned with a tiny gold hoop.

The feel of him turned Kelsey-Rose around, facing Colton's soft embrace. She glanced at her antique gold wristwatch—the one that once belonged to her grandmother—and she said, "It's almost closing time, and I'll bet your newspaper staff has already locked up and gone home for the holiday. Unless you've given them new hours, they won't be back until Monday."

"I haven't talked to them in a week," he said.

Unable to resist the man whose blue-gray eyes saw right through to her truth, Kelsey-Rose drew him into another kiss, wanting to melt right into him. "Everything feels like it's falling apart, except when I'm with you. Am I crazy?"

"No," he whispered into her ear. "You're no more crazy than I am."

The heat between them was soft and soothing. A silky sheet of intimacy. A warmth to her soul. "Tomorrow is Thanksgiving, you know?"

Colton pulled back, his gaze withdrawing its heightened passion. He relaxed his embrace, toying with an artful red curl draping her shoulder. In a thoughtful and understanding tone, he said, "You'll want to spend the day with your family, especially now."

"Yes," Kelsey-Rose said. "We're planning Thanksgiving dinner at the hospital cafeteria so that we can be near Daddy." She couldn't help but smile at the look of disappointment on his face. "We've never spent holidays apart. Not ever. Would you like to join us?"

With a grin, he pulled her to him again. "I would love to."

"Come home with me then. It gets lonely out there on the ranch all by myself. We'll be all alone, and you can stay the night. We can drive to the hospital together tomorrow."

"Well, I am still packed."

"Good," she said. "I have to meet up with Mae's neighbor at my house in about twenty minutes. She's been taking care of Free all week, and she's dropping him off for me tonight. I'll grab some things for tomorrow, and then we can head out to the ranch. I'll find something for dinner, and if you're not too tired from driving all day, maybe we can sit together on the couch, talk, watch a movie..."

"And then, if I'm not tired yet..." Colton laughed at her blush.

The sun was setting, and a chill pervaded the air when Kelsey-Rose turned onto Mustang Drive in her sea blue Santa Fe, followed by Colton in his Corvette.

She noticed the slowing of his car in her rearview mirror as it drove the rural subdivision of 1960s houses on a blacktopped country road without street lights or curbing. Most of the front lawns were scraggly and badly in need of an arborist.

At the end of the street was her small shamrock-green house with ruby red and white window trim and an attached carport but no garage.

Kelsey-Rose pulled in and parked beneath its slate

gray metal roof. She got out, holding her Resistol hat and purse.

Colton turned in and parked behind her in the driveway.

The home was on a corner double lot, totaling half an acre. It was treeless, unfenced, and bare except for the star jasmine in the backyard, but her front porch had a welcoming feel to it, brightened by pots of pansies in full bloom, straddling a red wooden bench beneath a window at the front door.

Colton stepped out of the Corvette. "This whole time, I thought you lived in town."

"I do," she said. "We're still in the city limits, but barely. Come on inside."

After unlocking and opening the front door, Kelsey-Rose entered and walked across the polished wood floor to a standing coatrack and hung her purse and her straw cowboy hat, then she turned back to Colton, who was inside but still at the door.

"What do you think?" She motioned around the room. "This is my home sweet home."

Soft, airy white curtains with white sheers ran the length of one wall, even framing the entrance door, and also hung at the other windows. In the middle of the comfortable living room, beneath a rustic wood coffee table, was a soft gray rug squared by a couch and a double wide armchair, each swathed with flowy white coverings. Lots of throw pillows in various shades of gray decorated each. The walls—painted such an incredibly pale blue—were hard to distinguish from the color white.

Colton's gaze landed on an old wood door with peeling white paint, leaning against the far wall.

Hanging next to it was a sign made of barn wood that read: *Antiques were built to last.*

All around were farmhouse-style treasures from a bygone era, artistically placed, but in the center of the square coffee table was a modern trio of steel pipe and glass candleholders with teal-colored candles, giving the room a slight sea breeze scent.

On the wall opposite the couch was a waist-high credenza, painted white with glass doors and metal handles. Above it was an eighty-five-inch mounted television, taking up one-third of the wall space. Fresh flowers in turquoise cowboy boot vases were positioned on each end, with a clear, thick glass bowl set in the middle filled with raw topaz stones.

Beside the credenza, on the floor, was an old flat-topped wooden steamer trunk with original leather straps that elevated a reclaimed wood cubbyhole DVD shelf. It was stocked with old movies.

At the sight of the television, Colton laughed. "You have a bigger TV than I do."

Kelsey-Rose laughed, too. "I told you. You're not the only one who loves old movies."

She went to the front door, closing and locking it behind Colton, and then turned to him. "I don't know what it is about you, but I can't keep my hands to myself when you're near me."

The woman she had always wanted to be was emerging. Kelsey-Rose wrapped her arms around his neck, kissing Colton. A month ago, she would have never had it in her to do such a thing, but it felt so natural to her now. This man had changed her.

Colton, succumbing to the woman that he found so hard to resist, slid his hands down the backside of her jeans, pulling her snugly to him.

"So," he whispered to her, "the big question is, should we make love first, or drive to the ranch for a quiet dinner?"

In an unexpected move, he slipped a hand where she didn't expect it to go, drawing a moan from her. "I'm not really that hungry," she said to him.

She found herself moving into his embrace as naturally as if they had known each other for centuries. Electricity sparked as they kissed—long lingering tongue-entwined kisses, igniting a passion in her that, until him, she had never known existed.

When the doorbell rang, Colton said, "Don't go. Don't answer it."

But Kelsey-Rose stepped back. "It's probably Free." She smiled at the urgency in his eyes.

She went to the door and opened it, laughing when Free barked and jumped up on the screen door, clawing to get inside.

"Hi, Sylvia," Kelsey-Rose greeted the dark-haired woman as she opened the door for Free. "Thank you for bringing him home. I hope he wasn't too much trouble."

"Oh, no, he was a good boy," she said. Then, "Mae said you're running the ranch for a while now."

Free circled Colton, sniffing every square inch that his nose could reach.

With a shrug, Kelsey-Rose said, "That's where Daddy needs me, so that's where I'll be until..." She stopped. "Hey, do I owe you anything for taking care of Free?"

"No." Sylvia shook her head. "Eddie brought over their food, so Free and Finn just kept me company while he was at work or at the hospital." She turned to walk back to her car parked on the street, saying, "You're all in my prayers."

"Thank you, Sylvia," Kelsey-Rose called out before closing the door.

She dropped to her knees and patted her thighs, calling Free to her. He came bounding, jumping and licking her face. Kelsey-Rose picked up the terrier and kissed him square on the lips before holding him close to her in a hug. "I've missed you so much!"

Colton watched, silent until then. "No wonder that dog came and never left."

Kelsey-Rose stood, laughing. "He's my constant. He never lets me down." She carried Free into the kitchen before lowering him to the floor. She spooned food into his dish and refilled his water bowl. As Free ate, she glanced at Colton, rolling her eyes in a tease. "So, I suppose you want me to wash off the dog kisses."

He laughed. "If you wouldn't mind."

"Tell you what," she said. "I need a shower." She started out of the room, saying, "Help yourself to whatever is in the fridge to drink. It seems like it's been so long since I've been home that I can't even remember what's in there." She gave him a smile. "I'll be quick. Make yourself at home."

COLTON WAS ON A KNEE, PERUSING THE TITLES OF her old movies when he heard a knock on the door. He glanced at the bedroom where Kelsey-Rose had disappeared on her way to the shower, and not seeing her reemerge, he stood and went to the door, opening it.

On the other side of the screen door stood Dax. His head was down, raising only when Colton greeted him.

"Dax, isn't it?" Colton asked, already knowing his name.

"Yeah," Dax said. "Mind if I come in?"

Colton opened the door to the man wearing a blue mechanic's work shirt and shop pants. "I didn't even hear you drive up. Kelsey-Rose is in the shower. Maybe you should come back later."

"No," Dax said. "I live across the street. I saw your car. It's you that I want to talk to."

"Okay," Colton said to the man with ebony-black hair, buzzed short. "Then come on in."

Dax walked to the couch and sat, letting Free jump up and climb onto his lap. The dog cocked an ear and stared at Colton, seeming to have already chosen sides. With a gentle hand on the dog, Dax looked at Colton as if to say *sit,* and then he waited.

Obliging, Colton went to the double wide armchair and took a seat.

"Until you, I always thought Kelsey-Rose would end up with me." Dax picked the dog up off his lap and set him down beside him on the couch, and then he leaned forward, hands clasped with his eyes on Colton. "Kelsey-Rose should be mine. I don't mean that I deserve her, or own her—I mean, I always thought she would choose me. Shane was my best friend, and I promised him I would take care of her. It was probably the last thing he ever heard me say. I don't even know how to let go of that promise. Can you understand that?"

The reality of the deathbed promise settled inside of Colton. His compassion for the vow felt real for the first time. It *was* real. It wasn't just a ruse this man was using to trap an amazing and beautiful woman.

Colton nodded. "I can't even imagine the trauma that the two of you have shared."

"Look," Dax said, unfazed by the gentleness of the remark. He straightened on the couch, focused on Colton. "I love Kelsey-Rose. I will always love her. But she's never been in love with me. I'm not fooled about that. Shane was always the one and only man she has ever loved." He lowered his head. "Until maybe you." A moment passed before he looked up again. "It's been hard for me to admit, but I think she might be falling in love with you." Dax stood, shooting a cold direct stare at Colton. "I don't know you, but I know that I don't trust you. The thing is, I know that Kelsey-Rose is too good for me. That's not lost on me. But she's also too good for you." He walked to the door and opened it, glancing back at Colton. "I'm not giving up on her, so if you want her, you're going to have to fight harder."

Colton stood as Dax left the house, shutting the door behind him. Hearing barefoot steps in the short hallway, he turned to see Kelsey-Rose, wearing a tan knee-length bathrobe, emerging with her hair wrapped in a twisty towel.

"Hey," she said. "Were you talking to someone?"

"No," Colton answered, not intending to mislead her. He needed time to process what he had just heard. "Maybe you heard me talking to the dog."

"Aww, my two guys are bonding," she said.

CHAPTER 25

Kelsey-Rose wore a bathrobe better than any other woman Colton had ever known. He had been without her for too long, and although she had said they would be all alone at the Forty Flowers Ranch, the thought of waiting much longer took more patience than he might have.

"Did you find something to drink in the fridge?" she asked.

"No," he said softly. "I didn't even look. I guess I got caught up in looking through your collection of movies." He went to the cubbyhole DVD shelf and pulled out a case, holding it up for her to see. "You have *The Magnificent Ambersons*."

"Joseph Cotten and Dolores Costello. What incredible performances."

Colton waved the DVD back and forth. "Do you know how hard it is to find this old movie?"

"We can take it to the ranch with us and watch it if you want," Kelsey-Rose offered.

"Yes," he said. His gaze skimmed the length of her, hair towel to bare feet. He set the movie down.

Colton knew that Dax had a right to fight for this woman—he would be crazy not to—but Dax would never be able to give her the kind of life Colton could. He knew, though, that playing the wealth card wouldn't impress Kelsey-Rose Flowers. He needed to win her the old-fashioned way. An honest-to-goodness genuine love affair.

That wouldn't be hard for him, because he was fairly certain that he had already fallen in love with her, and he was not willing to give her up.

"Are we going to be here much longer?" Colton asked. The urge to untie the belt on her robe was intense, but it would be regrettable timing if Dax came knocking again. The situation might upset Kelsey-Rose beyond resolving. He wanted this to be about the two of them without guilt or regret.

"I just need to grab some clothes to take to the ranch. It will just take me a few minutes."

When her phone rang, she looked at the caller ID and then turned to Colton. "It's Robert. My friend who used to own the newspaper. Do you mind if I take it?"

"Of course not. Take however long you need," he said.

Kelsey-Rose answered, "Hi Robert," she said, then, "Can you hang on for just a minute?" She looked at Colton. "Do you mind letting Free out for a pee break? You'll just need to keep an eye on him. He likes to chase the neighbor's cat." Then she returned to her call.

Colton looked at the terrier, who sat, head cocked, staring at him. "So," he said to the dog. "You want to try this bonding thing?"

When Free ran to the back door, Colton followed,

stopping only to pick up a neon green ball in a basket stacked with other dog toys before they stepped out into the backyard together.

~

FOR NO PARTICULAR REASON, KELSEY-ROSE WENT TO her bedroom and closed the door to talk to Robert. It wasn't that she was trying to hide her conversation from Colton, she had just always had the luxury of a private best friend talk when she spoke to Robert. It was one of the things she loved about their friendship.

"I want to know how your dad is doing, Kelsey-Rose," Robert said. "And I want you to tell me how you're handling it all. And don't tell me that you're fine because I know how it feels to have a medical crisis with someone you love."

He was the most honest and compassionate person she had ever known.

"I'm scared, Robert. I think the doctors are just stringing us along, spoon-feeding us bits and pieces of information in their updates, like we'll handle it better if they just give one puzzle piece at a time to us."

"So, what's the last thing they told you?" Robert didn't deny her interpretation of the information.

"The surgeon said that the T7 through the T9 vertebras were damaged in the wreck. He called it a thoracic spinal cord injury, but he said that due to inflammation, the paralysis might not be permanent." She took a breath. "He's out of ICU now, but it's been five days, and there hasn't been much change in Daddy's condition."

"Kelsey-Rose," Robert said. "You're a strong and resilient young woman. You're smart, too. I can tell you what I think, but you're not going to want to hear it."

Tears welled in her eyes. "I already know the answer."

"Okay, then," Robert said softly. "So, pull yourself up by your bootstraps, and let's talk about what you need to do."

For the next several minutes, they talked about the ranch and her feelings about it, and then out of the blue, Kelsey-Rose blurted out, "You know the man who bought the newspaper from you?"

"Colton someone, right?"

"Colton Wilde," she confirmed.

"Yes, is everything all right at the newspaper?"

"The newspaper is fine," she told him. "But I might not be."

Robert was quiet for a moment, but then he asked, "What does that mean, Kelsey-Rose?"

"Robert, I think I've fallen in love with him."

"Well, what do you know about that..." Robert chuckled before putting away his pleased tone. "You've been keeping secrets from me, Kelsey-Rose."

She smiled but hoped he couldn't hear it in her voice. "I've never met a man like him, Robert. I'm not sure how to handle my feelings."

"Does he feel the same about you?"

"I think so," she said. "I hope so."

"Then follow your instincts, Kelsey-Rose. Don't overthink it. And don't judge him on every misstep, okay?"

"You mean 'don't judge his every step,' don't you?"

Robert laughed. "No, we're talking about men, Kelsey-Rose. We have more missteps than steps.

Forgive him the ones that need forgiving. The perfect man doesn't exist."

KELSEY-ROSE AWOKE WITH COLTON ASLEEP BESIDE her. A night alone at the ranch with him was life in a different world. She had changed, and so had her heart. She was in love. Madly and deeply.

Her skin bare, she slipped out from beneath the cotton comforter and quietly went to the shower. When she returned, he was still sleeping. She stood at his bedside, staring down at the man who had just shown her a new world.

A chocolate-brown curl eluded his passion-mussed hair, falling softly onto his forehead. She reached, wanting to gently sweep it back, but she didn't want to wake him, so she withdrew her hand, gazing instead at his closed eyes, imagining the blue beneath his resting lids. If time could stand still, now would be one of the magical moments she would cherish forever.

Kelsey-Rose went to the closet where some of her clothes still hung from previous stays. She quietly slid the hangers down the wooden rod, wishing she had allowed herself to own and wear a more feminine wardrobe, but until now, all that had done was draw unwanted male attention. She glanced back at Colton. Now she wanted that attention. She wanted him to look at her as if she were a beautiful, desirable woman, but the truth was, she had nothing to enhance her appearance for this amazing man. She hadn't been prepared for *him*. Had she known he was the one she was waiting for all these years, she would have bought a dress.

She looked back at her closet. Pushing one hanger

after another down the rod until she came to the last one where a wine-colored cotton dress with a horseshoe print hung. It was old but barely worn. She pulled off the dry cleaner's clear garment bag and held up the dress. It was knee-length, short-sleeved, and had a V-neck with a smocked waistline. She looked back at the closet. Everything else was jeans, work shirts, or sweatshirts.

Kelsey-Rose took off her robe and slipped the dress on over her bra and panties.

Then her gaze fell to the boot box on the closet floor. A ten-year-old Christmas gift from Shane that had been given to her two weeks before his death. It had taken a year for her to open the gift, a year to cry over it, and a year before she put the boots back into the box unworn.

Kelsey-Rose sat down in the white wicker rocker and opened the box once again. The light-brown full-grain leather boots were embroidered with burgundy roses. She slipped them onto her feet and stood.

She was crying when Colton awoke.

Without a word, Colton threw back the covers and went to Kelsey-Rose, holding her close until she had no tears left.

"I'm sorry," she said to him. "I didn't mean to cry."

Colton gently lifted her chin, his gaze meeting hers. "Your broken heart is learning how to heal. You don't ever have to apologize, and you don't ever have to explain. Not to me. Not to anyone."

When Colton went to shower, Kelsey-Rose washed and dried her face and put on a little makeup, and then she hung a small topaz gemstone necklace around her neck.

She went to the kitchen, where she fed Free and

then took him outside. In her boots and dress, she threw the ball for the terrier while phoning her neighbor, Leah, on Mustang Drive. She made arrangements to drop off Free, promising to pick him up on the way back to the ranch at the end of the day.

When she went back to the house with the dog, Colton was waiting at the door, watching them through the oval glass pane. He was dressed in charcoal gray slacks and a fine twill long-sleeved gray dress shirt with a button-down collar and button cuffs.

"Wow," Kelsey-Rose said. She briefly looked away to catch her breath. "You look great. Really great."

Colton took her by the hand and pulled her to him. In a dance with no music, he swayed with her between his arms. "My girl, beautiful and sweet. It takes my breath away just to look into your eyes."

For a few moments, the world stilled—perfect in every way.

The morning was cool, but Kelsey-Rose hadn't thought to bring a sweater. She had chill bumps when Colton opened the Corvette door for her, but Free jumped inside first.

Kelsey-Rose lifted the terrier and then got inside, setting him on her lap as Colton closed the door.

After dropping Free off with Leah, Kelsey-Rose jogged across the yard to her own house and went inside for her cable-knit cardigan sweater. She had it draped over her arm when she came out, trotting back to Colton's car, her long red hair in a gentle bounce the whole way. Once inside, she leaned for a kiss. "Okay, let's go see Daddy," she said.

Although the highway entrance was less than a mile away, the holiday traffic became evident before they reached the on-ramp. It was heavy but steady. Maybe leaving at ten in the morning on Thanksgiving Day hadn't been the best idea, but the time she had spent with Colton was irreplaceable.

As they moved into the slow traffic, Colton asked, "Do you like music?"

"Doesn't everyone?" she asked him.

"No, not really. Lots of people prefer silence." He glanced at her, smiling the moment his eyes met hers. "I have no issue with silence. Sometimes, though, it's a dark hollow space where thoughts I don't want choose to gather, so music helps me close the door on that part of my mind, and it opens another that I much prefer." He reached for her hand, giving it a squeeze, holding it even after he finished speaking.

Kelsey-Rose held his hand in both of hers. "I'd love to hear your favorite music."

Colton pressed the button for his player, and the voice of an Italian tenor, gifted beyond this lifetime, filled the car with song. She didn't speak Italian, but she didn't need to know the language to be overwhelmed by the beauty of the music. She closed her eyes and leaned her head back, absorbed in the sound.

After two songs, Colton lowered the volume on the player and asked, "What do you think?"

Kelsey-Rose looked at him with tears in her eyes. "It was so incredibly beautiful."

Colton smiled. "I'm glad you think so. I listen to his music a lot."

"Do you speak Italian?"

With his eyes steady on the road ahead, Colton held her hand a little tighter. Quietly, he said, *"Mi sto innamorando di te."*

Kelsey-Rose took a breath, surprised by the beauty of his Italian tone.

"What does that mean?" she asked him.

Colton glanced at her. "I'm falling in love with you."

THE HOSPITAL SEEMED DESERTED EXCEPT FOR THE woman at the reception desk. As Colton and Kelsey-Rose walked across the empty lobby, past the receptionist, he asked the woman in an offhanded way, "Don't people visit on the holidays?"

"Just a few," she answered with a regretful smile.

Colton was quiet in the elevator. The death of his father was still raw and real, but today wasn't about his father—it was about Kelsey-Rose's father. It was about Kelsey-Rose.

When they stepped off the elevator, they were in a gray, white, and deep purple waiting room on the third floor, where her father's newly assigned room was located. Surrealist paintings hung on the walls, depicting oddly-colored Texas landscapes swirling with lavender dust devils.

Two-year-old Emma, wearing a yellow dress and matching shoes, slid off her mother's lap and ran, arms out, for Kelsey-Rose, who swooped her up, hugging the girl. "I've missed you so much," Kelsey-Rose told her with a kiss.

"I have new crayons," Emma said to her.

"You do? Maybe we can color together later."

The girl was smiling when Kelsey-Rose put her down.

Nina hugged Kelsey-Rose as Rainey, and Mae and Eddie, gathered for a hug, too.

Eddie shook hands with Colton. "Good to see you

again. Sorry you're having to spend Thanksgiving in a hospital."

"I'm sorry anyone is," Colton told him.

Mae reached for Kelsey-Rose's bare arm and lifted it high. "Since when did you start showing off your arms and legs? I don't think I've seen this skinny thing for a decade." Then she dropped her sister's arm and stepped back, staring at her dress and pointing to the smocked waist and V-neck. "And look at you! You've got curves, after all."

A blush heated her cheeks. "You're embarrassing me," Kelsey-Rose told Mae.

"Well, I'm sorry, honey, but I haven't seen you dress like a girl in a long time."

"Mae," Nina said in a motherly tone. "Stop picking on your sister." Then to Kelsey-Rose, she said, "Your daddy has been waiting for you. Would you like to go see him for a few minutes before we all barge in? Everyone else has already had some private time with him this morning."

"Yes." She looked at Colton. "Will you come?"

"If you want, yes."

When Colton pushed open the door to room 340, he held it for Kelsey-Rose and then followed her inside. The room was quieter than his own father's hospital room had been. This private room had a window with far fewer cords, cables, machines, and beeps.

Harley Flowers turned his head at the opening of the door. When his eyes came to rest on his daughter, he said, "Where have you been, honey?" He gave her a weakened smile. "I thought maybe you weren't coming."

Kelsey-Rose went to him and kissed his forehead,

and then took hold of his hand. "Of course, I would come, Daddy. It's Thanksgiving."

"How's the ranch?" he asked. "Is everything okay?"

"It's just fine. Nothing to worry about."

He nodded, took a breath, and then closed his eyes for a moment before reopening them, his gaze landing on Colton. His eyes shifted to Kelsey-Rose before swinging back to Colton again, his disorientation either pain or medication driven.

Without explanation, Colton reintroduced himself. "Colton Wilde," he said. "I bought *The Blue Topaz Times*. You were my Realtor."

"Right," Harley Flowers said, not convincing anyone that he remembered. He looked at Kelsey-Rose. "Is Dax here, too?"

"No, Daddy," she said. She glanced apologetically at Colton. "Colton came with me today."

When the door opened again, a nurse with a hypodermic needle entered and went straight to the bed. She nodded at Kelsey-Rose and Colton before she spoke to Harley. "Okay, I can give you that pain shot now." When she finished, she said, "You'll be feeling better in no time. Ring the buzzer if you need me." She left the room, closing the door.

Kelsey-Rose touched his hand again. "Do those shots help?" she asked her father.

"Yes," he said, pushing a button on his bed rail, slightly elevating the angle of his bed. "And they work fast." Her father's gaze widened with clarity. "Are you wearing a dress?"

"Just an old one," Kelsey-Rose answered.

Then his focus found Colton again. "Sure, yes, I remember you. I'm sorry. I've been a little foggy lately."

"Understandable," Colton said. He reached for a

polite handshake. "I was sorry to hear about your accident."

Harley Flowers glanced at his daughter, and then back to Colton, whose hand rested midway down Kelsey-Rose's back. "I take it you two are dating now?"

"Yes, sir," Colton answered.

"Daddy, we should talk about that later."

"How 'bout we talk about it now?" he said to Kelsey-Rose. "While that pain shot is working." Again, he looked at Colton. "That doesn't mean I disapprove." He took hold of his daughter's hand, firming his grip a little. "But she's more fragile than she looks, and I don't want her hurt. Kelsey-Rose is also promised to another man, and her world has already been turned upside down once in this lifetime, and I won't have it again."

"Daddy, don't...please? And I never agreed to marry Dax. We can all sit down and talk about it when you're home from the hospital, okay?"

After an uncertain, but acknowledging half smile, he said, "That's going to be a while, honey. By the time I get home again, you two could be head over heels in love, or you will have already broken each other's hearts."

Kelsey-Rose glanced at Colton, her eyes seeking answers. When Colton smiled and gently nodded to her, her father readjusted his handhold, interlacing her fingers with his.

"Well," her father said. "Looking at the two of you, I can see that I'm too late. If you have any honest words, I'll be glad to listen."

"I have them, Daddy. I just wasn't ready to say them yet." Kelsey-Rose looked at Colton. "But I've wanted to." She pulled her father's hand to her lips, kissing the back of it before returning it to him, then she gently released their hold, and reached for Colton's hand. "For the first time in so many years, I finally want to look at tomorrow, not yesterday, and I don't have to try to be happy anymore, or even pretend that I am. When I'm with Colton, it just happens."

With his hand around her waist, Colton urged her a little closer.

But her father kept his focus on the man who was courting his daughter. He was silent, but it was clear he was waiting for more words.

When Colton spoke, his gaze found Kelsey-Rose. "We haven't seen a lot of each other this past week, but we're enjoying the time we've had together. The moment I met her, my world changed, and every day that I am with her, it changes a little more. I assure you, I understand how special she is."

He'd asked for honest words, yet neither had chosen to be completely honest. Kelsey-Rose had wanted to tell him that she was in love with Colton, but not here. Not with him lying in a hospital bed, unable to move his legs or retain a clear thought without medication.

"Well, let me state the obvious," her father said. "You two are completely different." He pointed to Colton first. "You're a newspaperman with a lot of money who has probably never had to go a day without having whatever you wanted, and I've never seen a speck of dust on your oxfords." He switched to his daughter. "And you, Kelsey-Rose, are a rancher's daughter who rides and ropes and gets dirty, and only loves the simple things in life like flowers. How do you two plan to navigate that?"

"Daddy, this is just the pain medicine talking."

"No," her father said. "It's the pain itself *not* talking."

Colton never wavered. "I don't have a blueprint in my back pocket, and I don't have all the answers, but I don't think anyone does." He glanced out the window and back. "We'd like to spend more time together."

"Well, Kelsey-Rose," her father said. "In that case, I want you to do something for me."

"Yes, of course. What is it, Daddy?"

"I want you to tell Dax before he finds out from someone else."

CHAPTER 26

The cafeteria had twenty tables with two to four ladder-back chairs with padded seats stationed at each. Only one table was occupied by a man and woman sipping coffee from paper cups when Kelsey-Rose, Colton, and her family entered the quiet dining room. Food and drink vending machines lined the wall at the entrance.

"There's no one here," Rainey said. "And it's almost noon. Are you sure they're open today?" She carried her toddler high on her hip while the girl cried to be released, her hands grabbing for the machines filled with snacks and candy. "I can't feed Emma from a vending machine."

"I talked to them earlier in the week about Thanksgiving," Nina assured her. "They're open and serving a turkey dinner today."

Eddie tapped Colton on the shoulder. "Let's rearrange this place."

The two men moved four tables close together in the dining area and then spaced chairs so that the family would be seated as if they were at one long dinner table.

In the food service line, each person slid their tray along, serving themselves buffet-style from steamer pans beneath a plexiglass shield. Sliced turkey, meatloaf, mashed potatoes, brown gravy, green beans, squash casserole, sandwich bread and bread rolls, garden salad, macaroni and cheese, vegetable lasagna, and lemongrass tofu. At the end was a display case with pumpkin pie, apple crisp, chocolate cake, and squares of lime gelatin with whipped topping.

On a different wall was the drink station, where they each filled a red plastic tumbler with their choice and then carried their glasses back to the table, along with stacks of paper napkins and packets of salt and pepper.

After laying a napkin across her lap, Nina looked at Kelsey-Rose, who sat between her and Colton, and asked, "Did your daddy talk your leg off about the ranch this morning? You were in there for a while. It seems like you and those longhorns are all he wants to talk about."

"Not really," Kelsey-Rose said, taking a bite from her plate. "He just had one question, I think."

"One?" Mae asked. "He calls me every day and asks about you and the ranch and wants to know why he hasn't heard from you."

"Well, you need to remember," Kelsey-Rose said. "There's no cell service out in the pastures with the cattle, but I haven't had any messages from Daddy either."

"He doesn't want to call you," Rainey said without looking up from feeding Emma. "If it sounds like things aren't going well, he'll worry himself sick. He just wants all of us to tell him how you're doing, but you don't call us either."

Kelsey-Rose slammed down her fork. "Well, if you were in town running the flower shop like you promised, it would be a lot easier to talk to you."

From beneath the table, Colton took hold of Kelsey-Rose's hand. "Hospitals make people edgy," he said to the family.

"He's right," Eddie agreed. "Maybe we should talk about something else." He glanced at Colton. "So, how did you get stuck spending Thanksgiving with us in a hospital dining room and not with your own family?" he asked. "I'm sure it would have been a lot better than this cafeteria food."

Kelsey-Rose shot him a look. "He's not *stuck*. I asked Colton to come and so he did. I don't always have to invite Dax, do I?"

"All right," Mae said, putting her drink down a little too hard. "Let's not take offense to everything anyone says, okay? Eddie didn't mean anything by that, Kelsey-Rose. We're not an arguing family, especially not on a holiday, right?" she reminded everyone. "At least we're all here together. Daddy might not be sitting at the table with us, but he's not far away. That's what matters."

Eddie sat back, chewing a bite of tough turkey. "Never said anything about Dax, Kelsey-Rose. All I'm saying is that Colton would have had a better dinner with his own family." He motioned to the table. "I mean, come on, if we were at the ranch today, Harley would be frying a turkey again this year, and I can guarantee you, it would have tasted a lot better than this crap we're eating now. Tell me I'm wrong."

Mae snickered. "You're not wrong."

Eddie looked back at Colton, which sent everyone's eyes to him, except for Kelsey-Rose. "So, I'm curious, doesn't your family celebrate Thanksgiving?"

Colton glanced at each face at the table. No one understood the immensity of the subject Eddie had broached.

From the corner of her eye, Kelsey-Rose saw Colton put down his fork.

When his father was shot, Colton had asked her not to talk about it with anyone, so she hadn't, but she was hoping that he would explain it now. It wasn't the kind of secret she wanted to keep from her family, and she was feeling a bit deceitful about not telling them what had happened to this man that she had been sleeping with and loving.

Colton glanced at Kelsey-Rose. "So, you didn't tell them?"

"No," she said. "You asked me not to tell anyone." She squeezed the hand she held under the table where no one could see. "I never want to be the person you can't trust. This is your story, not mine."

Colton turned to the people seated at the long makeshift dining table, crowded together for a family holiday meal in a cold and unhappy environment. They were important people to Kelsey-Rose.

"To tell you the truth, Eddie," Colton said to her brother-in-law and the local police chief, "my father was shot and killed last week. I've been up north in the Dallas area attending to my mother and the personal affairs of my father."

Everyone, except two-year-old Emma and Kelsey-Rose, put down their utensils and stared wide-eyed at Colton.

"Are you serious?" Mae asked him.

Kelsey-Rose glared at Mae, who ignored her stare except for a glance. "Why would he say it if he wasn't serious?"

Mae kept her attention on Colton. "I am so sorry," she said to him. "We didn't know."

Colton nodded. "I asked Kelsey-Rose not to tell anyone about the shooting."

Mae glanced back at her sister again, and then she got up from her seat and went around the table. She hugged Kelsey-Rose, who stayed seated and silent. "I am so sorry, little sister. I can be such an ass sometimes."

But Eddie had a different expression. The eyes of a police officer settled on Colton.

"Was it a robbery?" Eddie asked.

"No," Colton said, taking another bite of his food.

"Road rage? Drug related? Home invasion?"

Colton looked across the table at Eddie. Plainly, he said, "Homicide."

"Random or targeted?"

"Targeted."

"Okay," Mae said. "Enough of that talk at the dinner table." She nudged Eddie with her elbow. "Maybe you could pull yourself away from your work long enough to help me make this an enjoyable family gathering today, huh?"

Rainey got up from the table, pulling Emma out of her highchair. "I think that ship has sailed, Mae. We're going back in with Daddy. He's more pleasant."

CHAPTER 27

Darkness had fallen by the time Colton and Kelsey-Rose picked up Free from Leah's house. With the Jack Russell terrier perched on her lap, they drove back to the ranch.

At the house, Kelsey-Rose fed Free, and with Colton seated at the kitchen table, she called the bunkhouse for an update from Cullen. "Sorry to be gone so long today. I hope you guys had a good holiday meal."

Neither man was married, and neither had a serious girlfriend, which made them perfect ranch hands, but Cullen had good cooking skills, especially for a man stranded on a cattle ranch for days at a time. He had deep fried enough turkeys and chickens in his life that she was certain he and Ty hadn't gone hungry.

"So, the horses have been fed, and you've checked the herd?" After a moment, Kelsey-Rose gave a relieved sigh. "Okay," she said. "That's great, Cullen. Thank you. How about I go check the cattle at dawn so that you and Ty can sleep in tomorrow morning?" A moment of silence followed, then she said, "No, I insist. You two go into town for a nice breakfast on me. I'll see you about noon, okay?"

After ending the call, Kelsey-Rose turned to Colton, who had Free at his feet, petting the dog.

"Looks like you're checking cattle with me tomorrow morning," she said to Colton. It was more a statement than a question. "You're comfortable in a western saddle for a couple of hours, right?" The polo saddle had a flat seat with long, reasonably straight saddle flaps, whereas the Western saddle was heavier and built for a long day of riding.

Colton grinned at her. "I think I can handle it. Will I be able to add cowpuncher to my resume by day's end?"

Kelsey-Rose laughed right out loud. "I'll let you know tomorrow whether or not you've earned that title, but having you along with me while I check the herd would be nice."

She opened the fridge and rummaged through the shelves and drawers, finding nothing suitable for dinner, and it had been hours since they'd eaten Thanksgiving turkey at the hospital. With the refrigerator still open, she turned to Colton.

"I wanted tonight to be perfect, but with all the stores and restaurants in town closed for the holiday, and Nina gone all week, dinner looks pretty skimpy." She looked again through the refrigerator. "We've got eggs, milk, lettuce, carrots, jam..." She turned to him. "We could have a peanut butter and jam sandwich. It's a homemade peach jam."

Colton gave Free a last pat, and then he got up and went to Kelsey-Rose, taking her in his arms. "I don't care what we eat, but let's find something because you're going to need all your strength tonight. I've been waiting all day to get you alone." He smiled at her. "I have a definite ravishing in mind."

"We're not alone." She laughed, pushing herself back in a tease, and then she pointed to the Jack Russell, who had his round brown eyes focused on the two of them. "Free is here. And besides, I don't need strength to give in to you. I would only need strength *not* to."

Colton laughed. "Okay." He got serious. "Do you think Harley and Nina will mind if we rummage through their freezer?"

"Of course not, but they have three freezers, and then another eight in the insulated shed out back for their customer orders, but anything stocked in those freezers is frozen so rock hard it would take an hour, at least, to thaw it. And I actually hate thawing meat in the microwave."

Colton didn't seem fazed.

"So, let's look through one of the freezers in the house and see what we can find."

In the big pantry room freezer, they came across half a dozen frozen pizzas. Sifting through the various flat boxes, Colton chose one and pulled it out. Together, they both said, "Pepperoni."

While sharing the oven-cooked pizza at the kitchen breakfast table, Colton asked Kelsey-Rose, "If you're willing, I'd like to hear the story of how your fiancé died."

She knew the question would come up eventually. He was, after all, a newspaperman, and details in a story mattered. If he truly was falling in love with her—his Italian words ringing in her ears—then learning about the one event that had changed her life and her future would be important. He deserved to know before it was too late. But still, she hesitated.

"Kelsey-Rose," he said, gentle and sincere. "I feel like this story is the secret to your soul that no one but you can share with me. It's important."

She got up and pulled a bottle of Merlot from the kitchen wine rack. She opened it with an electric opener and poured him a glass, but for herself, she filled a tumbler with sweet tea and then sat again. "Colton, it's not something I usually talk about. To anyone."

"I'm not anyone," he said. "But this...this I need to know. I *want* to know. There are too many things that I thought I understood, especially lately, only to find out that I was so far off base with my perceptions that it was astonishing. I don't want to find out that I've done the same with you." He reached across the table and took her hand. "Do you understand?"

Kelsey-Rose focused on him and his blue-gray eyes, assessing the risk. It was hard to open a door that might lose him to her forever.

"No, I really don't understand, but I'll tell you whatever you need to know because you're different from everyone else and because I—" She couldn't bring herself to say the words she wanted to say, so more quietly, she said, "And because I care about you."

Colton smiled. Softly. Gently. "I want to know all there is to know about you." His tone was one of encouragement. "Everything that has happened to you. And then, if you don't want to, we'll never have to talk about it again." When her emotions showed, he said, "Tears give a sparkle to your beautiful blue eyes."

Kelsey-Rose took a deep breath. She started to reach for him, wanting to hold him, but just one touch might drop her to her knees in shame. He would never look at her the same again. Her gaze through misty eyes hardened on him. "What happens if you decide I'm not the person you thought I was after I tell you? What if you find out that you can't trust me? That you can't depend on me? What if you decide that I am one of God's greatest failures?"

Colton sat back, his eyes studying her. "What if I don't?"

Kelsey-Rose dropped what was left of her second slice of pepperoni pizza onto her plate. She stood, inhaling a stuttered breath without looking at him. "You've got to let me say this without any interruption, okay?"

"Okay," he said. Putting down his pizza.

"The Sunday that you came out here for dinner, I told you that Shane was a rodeo champ, but he was also a ranch hand here at the Forty Flowers. He had worked here since he was sixteen and he could ride just about any horse, no matter how wild they were. So, while he was here, he turned himself into a saddle bronc rider. He broke just about every horse on this ranch. It was his dream to be number one in the world. His mind and his body rode those broncs with a rhythm so perfect that no other rider could hold a candle to him in the arena."

For a moment, she could almost see him again.

"He was just nineteen, but he could win the saddle bronc event at almost any rodeo. He would always say that he was just lucky and drew good bucking horses, but it was more than that, Colton. Watching him was pure magic.

"Daddy and Cullen, and a ranch hand named Sissy, had tried to break a horse named Four-Bidden for a month or more, but they never got past getting a saddle on him. He just wouldn't take the weight of a man. Daddy would never let Shane ride him because he didn't want Shane hurt before it was time for him to leave for the Las Vegas National Finals Rodeo, which was just a week away at the time. The whole town pitched in and bought Shane a plane ticket to Vegas so that he wouldn't have to drive all that way. What they were really doing, though, was giving him more time at home before he left for the rodeo, and then on to college. He had already given up so much for me. It was sort of a reward, I guess, for me letting him go."

She took a gulping swallow of her sweet tea, then set her glass back down on the table.

"That day, Sissy was out with the herd while Daddy and Cullen were working with Four-Bidden, trying to turn that crazy horse into a ranch horse, but that roan would bite you and kick you and try to stomp the life out of you. He'd bitten a hunk out of Cullen's hand, right between his thumb and forefinger, and Daddy thought for sure Cullen was going to lose a thumb.

He wrapped Cullen's hand and got him to the truck, and then they started out for the hospital, but Shane and me were still astraddle the fence where we'd been when it happened. Daddy pulled up close to us in his truck and yelled out the window for us to stay away from that horse. He said he would get the saddle off him and turn him out when they got back."

She looked at Colton, and for a moment, she was so buried in the past, she saw a stranger. Maybe that made it easier.

"I swear," she said. "That horse watched them drive off, nodding at them like he'd just won a fight. He was the meanest horse I'd ever seen, and he'd never been ridden. Not once. That was a challenge to Shane, and I knew it because for over a year, he'd never been thrown here on this ranch, and we had some great broncs that went on to buck at some of the biggest rodeos in the country. Shane had ridden them all."

Memories filled her eyes with tears again.

"As soon as Daddy was out of sight, I went into the house, grabbed his half-full bottle of whiskey, and took it back out to the corral with two shot glasses, but Shane never took a drink." She looked down for a moment to gather her thoughts, then started again. "Whiskey is a mean drink. Four shots later, I was mouthing off to Shane, threatening to dump him and find another guy if he didn't marry me before college and take me with him. I just couldn't stand the thought of ever being without him."

Kelsey-Rose glanced at Colton, but when she found his expression unchanged, she went to the kitchen door, looking out through its window. "Ironic, isn't it?"

She was facing the defining moment of her true self once again. Unintended, her hand went to the door handle. If she opened it and walked out—as far into the darkness as she could—maybe she would never have to come back to this moment again. But then she felt Colton's hand on hers, and she released the handle.

"Kelsey-Rose," he whispered to her. "It's okay. Finish your story for me."

A sob broke free from her. She couldn't look at Colton.

"Shane said to me, 'What do I have to do to prove to you that I love you and I'm coming back? I'm coming back and we're going to get married and we're going to have a dozen kids and raise them right here.

Every one of them will be a rodeo champion, and we'll all be famous for it.'

"I was still yelling such mean things at him when Dax drove up and pulled his car right to the fence. He got out, saying, 'Kelsey-Rose, are you still mad about him leaving? I'll bet people half a mile away can hear you!'" She wiped her tears with the back of her hand. "God, I was such an awful person back then. But the worst part was, I knew Dax had always had a major crush on me, so I walked over to him and threw my arms around his neck, glad for him to put his arms around me in return. I didn't even flinch when he slipped his hand up under my flimsy blouse, thinking Shane couldn't see him, but then I turned so that Shane *could* see, and I said, 'Prove that you love me, or else.'

"Shane got mad and asked me how he was supposed to do that, and so I dared him to ride Four-Bidden. If he could stay on him for eight seconds, I'd shut up and wait for him, but if he couldn't, he'd have to give up college and stay with me forever. I thought we'd travel the circuit together, living in a rodeo motel, and in the off-season, we'd learn to run the ranch."

Kelsey-Rose looked up at Colton, trying hard not to cry again. "This is so hard. And you haven't said hardly anything."

"I know it is, but I promised I wouldn't interrupt, remember?"

"Yes. Okay." She nodded, turning her face away from Colton. "I'd never seen Shane so mad. He looked like he wanted to strangle both me and Dax, but instead, he jumped the fence into the round pen, and he rose into the saddle that day like he was a ghost with Four-Bidden still as a hill for him, but the minute his weight was on that bronc, it went wild. In that first burst, Four-Bidden jumped high and came straight down on the ground with his four feet together like he was hog-tied—and then there were no feet on the ground. Next thing you knew, his back hooves were touching his nose. I'd never seen a ride like it.

"Shane stayed on when that bronc turned, running head down, right at the fence Dax and me had climbed to watch from, but when we scrambled down off it, that horse suddenly stopped, then reared straight up on his hind legs, falling back and taking Shane with him. Four-Bidden broke his neck in that fall. He was dead in an instant with Shane trapped beneath him, the saddle horn crushing his chest. He was barely alive. We both went over the fence to help him. We tried to move that dead horse off of Shane, but with just the two of us, we couldn't budge it."

She stood, bawling, reaching for the door handle again, needing air, but Colton stopped her and took her in his arms.

"My God, Kelsey-Rose." He held her.

She cried until the overflow of guilt and shame washed some of the old pain away, leaving just enough room inside of her for a moment of strength to rise.

"It took twenty minutes for the EMTs to get to the ranch," she said. "But Shane was gone by then. Before he died, I told him I was sorry, and I promised I would never love another man but him."

THAT NIGHT, WITH KELSEY-ROSE FITFULLY ASLEEP IN his arms and the dog nuzzled beneath the blankets with them, Colton couldn't stop thinking about her story. He understood so much more about this woman now. He understood her heart. He understood her feelings of shame and regret. And he understood the fracture that might never heal.

But maybe, most importantly, he knew why Kelsey-Rose would never love him like she had loved Shane.

CHAPTER 28

Boundaries to the Forty Flowers crossed three county lines. In parts of the ranch, the Llano River flowed intermittently, crossing the land for a time before seeming to disappear into the karst, only to reemerge a few miles later, sprouting tributaries along the way. As the waters of time had always done, the mere trickle of a stream had the ability to carve canyons and caverns into the limestone cap of the Edwards Plateau.

The two rode the ridgeline until an area of the escarpment descended, allowing them to navigate their way down the moderate slope.

Kelsey-Rose glanced at Colton, who rode the grade uneasy, the reins taut. "Hey, loosen up on those reins," she advised. "When in doubt, let your horse do the thinking."

At the bottom was a stream where water flowed freely, but only in the middle channel of an otherwise dry creek bed.

"We call this Topaz Trench," Kelsey-Rose

explained. She dismounted and went straight to a tiny glint and picked up a fingertip-size pebble. She held it up, catching a sunray, then she walked to the water's edge and squatted, dunking the small stone.

She had been quiet all morning.

Colton dismounted and followed her, holding the split lead to the Forty Flowers sorrel named Cinnabar. "Did you just find topaz lying right on top of the ground?"

She swished the nugget in the waters of the stream, rubbing off the dirt with her fingers. "Almost positive," she told him. "I need to clean it up a bit and look again to be sure." Kelsey-Rose held the stone up a second time to the sunlight and then stood with it. She handed the little nugget to Colton, who took it from her. "Blue topaz," she said. "You should keep it. I've always thought of them as wishing stones."

Colton rotated the piece between his fingers, then he held it up to the sun like Kelsey-Rose had done. "How do you know this isn't quartz?"

"After so many years of finding it, you just know, but we can give it a quick test if you're doubtful. Topaz will scratch steel, whereas steel will scratch quartz. It's a hardness factor."

He held up the crystalline piece, championing the find. "I believe you. Thank you." Colton gave her an appreciative smile. "It will remind me that there is more than one rare gem on this ranch." Then he thumbed the blue-tinted rock into his jeans pocket and glanced around at their surroundings again. "I feel absolutely alive out here on this land. This is real life. I can feel it way down deep." He looked at her. "I never felt this way in the city. This is a different world. It's balanced and freeing. I guess I didn't know what I was missing."

But Kelsey-Rose had her thoughts miles away today. She hadn't been able to focus on the cattle, or the ranch and its commitments, or even Colton for that matter. Unlike him, her world was spinning off-kilter, and she knew why.

She walked Baley closer to Colton and his sorrel. "Hey, I've got to take Sequoia Sam and Speckled Pete to an appearance in San Saba tomorrow."

"What's the occasion? A holiday parade?" Colton asked.

"No." She shook her head. "Complimentary Christmas card photos for the locals. A few businesses went in together on the idea, and it seems to be a big hit. Families get to pose with the longhorns, and a professional photographer will be on-site to take photographs. We're supposed to be there for two hours, but it's a one-hour drive each way."

"Can I come along and help?" Colton asked. "My office is closed until Monday."

For a moment, Kelsey-Rose was quiet. "I don't think so, Colton," she said. "Dax called early this morning while you were in the shower. He really wants to help, and I think it's a good idea." She mounted Baley. "Maybe we can get together again on Sunday? We'll see, okay?"

Colton stood, holding the reins to Cinnabar, staring at Kelsey-Rose. "Is everything okay? Have I done something wrong?"

"No," Kelsey-Rose told him. "Not at all." She looked toward the horizon, where her gaze stayed. "But about last night," she said. "I've only told two other people what I told you—Daddy and Robert. I don't even think my sisters know the whole truth, so I'd appreciate it if you could just keep it to yourself." Then her gaze traveled straight up, gauging the sun directly overhead before she looked back at him. "We should get back so that I can update Cullen and Ty on the stats for the herd today."

Colton mounted Cinnabar, and then he said, "Kelsey-Rose, are you trying to tell me that you might need some time? I don't want to misunderstand."

"Maybe," she said, her emotion had a frozen-in-time feeling. "I think so."

Just as he caught the glisten of a tear, she tightened her fingers on the reins and leaned forward, raising slightly out of the saddle, sending Baley into a gallop toward home.

WHEN THEY RETURNED TO THE HORSE BARN, COLTON wanted to help, but Kelsey-Rose had found a tough ranchwoman's attitude, and she told him to go home. She would call him, she'd said. Colton felt dismissed. It wasn't a feeling he'd had very often, and he wasn't completely comfortable with it.

He drove back to *The Blue Topaz Times* building, confused and confounded by the day.

Instead of going upstairs to his apartment in a sulking mood, Colton went downstairs to the history room in the newspaper office. He remembered John Pixley and his grandson, Kyle, saying Shane had died just a couple weeks after Joe Pixley was killed, so he went to the wall of cabinets and opened the one that held the December issues from ten years ago. He pulled out the weeklies for that month and laid them on the study table. His eyes found the big bold headline even before his brain registered the words:

HOMETOWN HERO TRAGICALLY DIES.

Colton pulled out the issue and unfolded the crease to see the entire front page. A photo of Audley Shane Delany, a handsome young cowboy with a black felt Stetson, holding a gold championship belt buckle, was above the fold.

He read the newspaper story, which basically gave the same rendition that Kelsey-Rose had recited, but some of the details had been left out. Her drinking, her flirtatious dare with Dax, and her ultimate challenge to ride, all had been left out. Were they important details to the story, or were they just important to him? He read the article again. And again.

The story was complete except for Kelsey-Rose's influence on the accident. Perhaps the omission is how the previous publisher, her friend Robert Wood, had protected Kelsey-Rose from public scorn.

Colton spent most of the night searching every issue after the first that made any mention of Shane Delany. He also searched the office files for paper copies of submitted articles and the notes associated with each. He read through everything. Something felt off, but he couldn't put his finger on what it was.

He hated to start thinking like his father, but it seemed the only logical way to get to the answers he needed. And the date of the tragedy had not escaped him.

~

CULLEN DROVE, MUCH TO DAX'S DISMAY, TO THE SAN Saba event on Saturday with Kelsey-Rose. It was sunny and almost warm, but still, elves in winter suits,

Santa Claus in his jolly red jacket, and Mrs. Claus in a fur and felt dress sat on hay bales in the shopping center's parking lot, right in front of the corralled Texas Longhorns for photo ops with the local families. A silk screen of snow-tipped bluebonnets hung between lamp posts as the backdrop.

During a midday break from the photography event, Kelsey-Rose and Dax walked across the street to a park. Under a dozen or more pecan trees, most over one hundred years old, they found a secluded concrete bench.

"We need to talk," Kelsey-Rose told him as she sat.

"No, we don't," Dax said, prepared for the topic. "This thing between you and him needs to stop." He turned his head so that his assertive glance landed hard. "You and me, Kelsey-Rose, that's the only love story in this town. And I don't want to be mean about it, but before you crawl into bed with somebody else, we need to make this commitment final. Ten years, I've waited. I kept my promise to you. Now I need to keep my promise to Shane."

"I don't love you, Dax. I never have."

Dax gave her an embittered smile. "I don't even know if I care anymore." He stood. "People are tired of waiting for us to get married, and so am I. You'll need help running the ranch now that Harley is paralyzed, and you know that newspaper guy can't help you with that. I doubt he can even ride a horse." Dax reached down and softly took hold of her hand. "Marry me, Kelsey-Rose. I can give you all the babies you want. I might not be able to make them rodeo champions, but who really even cares about that anymore? I've got a ring at home for you."

Kelsey-Rose stood. She pulled her hand back. "I'm

in love with Colton." She looked at Dax, truly believing that if he understood, he would care. "He's the man that I want to spend my life with, have babies with, and whose arms *I* want to die in someday. I just don't ever want to be without him." Tears welled. "I haven't even told him yet."

Dax laughed. "Be serious, Kelsey-Rose. The man is like a millionaire or something. And you hate those fake people."

"No," she said. "He doesn't have any money, Dax. Everyone thinks he does, but he doesn't."

"Kelsey-Rose..." His tone was patronizing. "Everybody knows he's loaded. You just wait and see, he won't stay around here for long. Why would he?"

Softly, she said, "Maybe because of me."

Dax stepped back, giving her a head-to-toe evaluation, and then he motioned to the length of her. His eyes had hardened with temper. "Look at you. Do you look like the girlfriend of some rich guy? You're just convenient to him right now. He doesn't care about you, Kelsey-Rose."

She looked down at herself in blue jeans, scuffed up boots, and an old blue-and-pink plaid work shirt that had seen better days. Her long red hair was tied into a messy bun, and she hadn't even bothered to put on any makeup this morning.

"See," Dax said after giving her a chance to consider what he'd said. "I don't mind the way you look or dress...you know I never have. But him? He's just using you, Kelsey-Rose. I'm surprised you haven't figured it out yet." He pulled her into a hug. "We're going to set a date. I think December thirty-first is good. Grandma says that we'll get a tax break for the whole year if we're married before the first of January, and then if you get pregnant right away, she says that we'll get another deduction next year." He tipped her chin up, ignoring the tears in her eyes. "That's smart financial planning."

Quietly, she said, "Dax, I don't want to marry you."

"It doesn't matter what you want, baby. The whole town doesn't need to know what you did, right?" He kissed her. "They only need to know that I kept my promise, even if it took ten years."

CHAPTER 29

Sunday had come and gone without a word from Kelsey-Rose. Colton had picked up his phone to call her several times, but he had always put it back down again. She had made it clear that she needed time.

He regretted asking her about Shane. It had dredged up too many memories, and instead of bringing the two of them closer like he'd intended, it had pushed her right back into the arms of Dax, whom she had chosen instead of him to help her with the San Saba event.

The relationship was odd, even though he understood why it existed.

He was almost dressed and ready for a full workday when his phone rang. His caller ID didn't register.

"Colton Wilde," he answered.

"Bridget Fyve here. I have good news. Your counteroffer was accepted!"

Colton sat. "That is good news." He had never even

seen his father's penthouse in the Dallas Arts District, yet it sold sight unseen in less than thirty days to a cash buyer. It seemed odd that neither had set foot in the place, but 4.2 million was being exchanged for it. "Have the title company email the closing papers to me so I can review them," he said. Then, "Oh, I'll need them to arrange for a mobile notary that isn't local or find a suitable closing location in the Austin area for me. I don't want anyone from around here knowing about it. I'm learning that there is no privacy in a small town."

"The title company has an office in Georgetown. I'll set it up for Tuesday, okay?"

"Afternoon, if possible."

Colton ended the call. His bottom line was feeling a lot more comfortable.

Halfway down the Scarlett O'Hara stairs, his phone rang again. He stopped when he saw the caller ID. "Mother," he answered. "Good morning. Is everything all right?"

He ignored the inquisitive glances from his staff, half a room away.

"You're leaving before the sale?" he asked her. He turned away from the prying eyes of his managing editor and the advertising manager and walked to the back door. Opening it, he stepped out into the parking lot for privacy.

"Yes," she told him. "There is no reason for me to stay. I've had Dean draw up a power of attorney, which will allow you to sign any real estate documents on my behalf. The funds can be wired to me after the sale."

"Yes, of course, I'll be glad to do that for you. Did you hear the penthouse sold? I just spoke with Bridget. I am expecting to sign papers in Georgetown on Tuesday. Why don't you ask Dean to send the power of attorney to that office, and then, when the house sells, I can just sign at the same place."

"Yes, I'll do that," she agreed. Then, she said, "Colton, you never tagged anything to withhold from the estate sale. Was that a mistake?"

His focus fell to the blacktopped parking lot beneath his feet. "No," he replied. "A fresh start and all."

"Well," his mother said. "I couldn't bring myself to sell Peter's watches and his jewelry." She hesitated. A mourning pause. "You know how he loved them. Many pieces have significant value. They're yours, whether or not you want them. You can sell them, put them in a safe deposit box, give them as gifts…or you could keep them, maybe for the children you'll have one day. Sometimes it's nice to hand things down through the generations. I've set some things of my own aside for you, too."

"Thank you, Mother." Colton looked up. The sky was gray, but not from clouds. It was a haze that fit his mood quite well. "Will you send me your travel itinerary?"

"Of course."

They ended their call with *I love you*.

When he'd first moved to Topaz, he hadn't a friend left in the world, or so it seemed. He had never felt more alone in his life, until today. He was losing his mother again, but this time it was to Italy. And the new woman in his life had gone silent, just like Carly had done.

He had decisions to make, both business and personal.

Colton went back into the newsroom where his employees were at work again, either on phone calls or from fingers clicking away on their keyboards, even a camera flashed.

Scott stood when he saw Colton. "Hey, boss," he said. He wore his corduroy jacket and had his camera strap angled across his chest and over a shoulder. "The Historic Homes Tour is this weekend, and they're all decorated for Christmas. I thought I'd go take pictures and maybe write a little history on each home."

Colton gave him a wide-eyed nod. "Scott, that's a great idea. Did you think of that on your own?"

"Yeah." Scott grinned. "Well, I mean, my aunt owns one of the houses, so I guess it was really her idea."

"Well, I'm impressed. I can't wait to see it. Grab lunch for yourself and your aunt while you're out today, and then just bring me the receipt so I can reimburse you the cost."

The heads of both Beth and Mack jerked up, staring at him. Beth said, "What, no trade-out? Are you feeling okay?"

Had it been Mack who'd said it, Colton probably would have laughed, but now, knowing Beth was Dax's grandmother, the jab didn't amuse him.

"Go out and find us some advertisers, Beth. Earn some of that year-end bonus you're expecting."

She grabbed her coat off the rack and headed for the door. "I need a cigarette anyway," she said as she walked past him.

When the back door shut louder than usual, Mack turned his attention to Colton. "Good to have you back."

~

Kelsey-Rose had two reasons to skip out on her afternoon chores at the ranch, and both made her nervous. When she pulled into her regular parking space in the back lot of Say It With Flowers, Dani pulled in beside her, parking alongside. Both women got out of their cars, closing the doors.

"Don't tell me that you didn't trust me to show up today," Dani said to Kelsey-Rose.

"I just wanted to make sure things went well for you and Rita on your first day."

"And…" Dani waited.

Kelsey-Rose smiled. "Okay, and I wanted to be sure that you hadn't changed your mind."

Both laughed on their way inside.

Kelsey-Rose spent an hour training Dani on the cash register, reacquainting her with the list of special requests, the incoming orders, the outgoing deliveries, and giving her a key to the store. Then she printed a list of employee phone numbers and handed it to Dani with everyone's hours. She pointed to the names, saying, "You'll have to call Lexi when you have deliveries, but Aiden is only going to respond to a text." She glanced at Dani with a grin. "I don't think he even knows he can talk on that thing."

After yet another glance from Kelsey-Rose at the building across the street, Dani said, "He's a doll, isn't he?"

Kelsey-Rose snapped her a look. "Who?"

"Colton. The new owner," she said.

Dani was a buxom blonde who had a flair for country fashion. She wore blue jeans, boots that had never seen a cow or a pasture, and a ruby-red Henley shirt. Her long, relaxed blonde hair hung in waves to her thin waist, which was cinched tight by a black leather belt that Kelsey-Rose feared might cut off her oxygen if she had worn it. With long, manicured nails painted deep red, and rhinestones that dangled from her ears and her neck, Danielle London was a knockout in anyone's book.

"You've been looking at his building ever since you got here. Does he ever come in to buy flowers or anything?"

Kelsey-Rose looked again at *The Blue Topaz Times* building. "Yes. Well, sometimes."

"I met him once. I encouraged him to call me." Dani fanned herself. "I'd sure love to have some quality time with that gorgeous man." She walked to the front window; her gaze glued to the newspaper building.

"Did he?" Kelsey-Rose asked, dreading the answer she might hear.

Dani turned to her. "Call me?"

"Yes."

"No." She turned back to the building. "I'm going to have to be a little more aggressive, I think. I'll bet he likes that kind of thing."

"So, well then, okay..." Kelsey-Rose said, so flustered, she knocked over a countertop card rack.

Dani hurried to help her pick up the cards. "I can get this," she said. "You have other things to do. That's why I'm here, remember?"

Kelsey-Rose backed away from the counter. "Do you need anything else?"

"Well, there is one thing that I didn't mention last week. I forgot all about an important meeting with a client who's driving over from Llano on Wednesday. They want anonymity, you know? I like those kinds of clients because they'll stay with you forever once they trust you. Anyway, I can't come in that day."

"Wednesday? This...this Wednesday?" she asked her. *The tenth anniversary of Shane's death.* When Dani nodded, Kelsey-Rose tried to recover from her verbal stumble. "That's...that will be fine."

But it wasn't fine. It was the most important day of the year for her. And she had never missed spending it with Shane. At exactly 12:11 in the afternoon, Kelsey-Rose would be there to lay calla lilies atop his grave, and then sit with him, alone, for seventeen minutes—the length of time it took him to die in her arms.

"Good luck with your new client," she managed to say to Dani before leaving through the back door.

Kelsey-Rose needed to find Colton but her vulnerability right now was too immense. She sat in her Santa Fe in the parking lot, doors locked, engine running, and tried to strengthen her emotions. Without giving it much thought, she picked up her phone and called Robert.

"Hey," she said when he answered.

"Kelsey-Rose, is everything all right?"

"Yeah," she said. "I really miss you, you know?"

"I miss you, too. Do you want to tell me what's wrong?"

"Can't I just call to see how you're doing without something being wrong?"

"Yes," Robert said. "Of course, you can. But I know that tone."

She started to cry and realized she couldn't stop. The two of them stayed connected without words for the next few minutes, both waiting until Kelsey-Rose caught her breath.

"Do you need me to come back for a few days?" Robert asked softly. "You're breaking my heart, girl."

"No," Kelsey-Rose answered. "It's ten years, you know?"

"December fifth, I know," he said. "And you've got some decisions to make, don't you?"

"Yes." It was the only word that came without pain.

"Are you still in love with the new owner of the newspaper?"

"I am," she answered. Then she said, "I told Dax."

"How did that go?"

"Not well."

"He's still holding that teenage antic over your head, isn't he?"

"Yes."

"Kelsey-Rose," Robert said in his stern tone. "The only person you owe an explanation to is Colton Wilde. And the only reason you owe one to him is that—if you love him—he deserves to hear the whole story from you before Dax does whatever he's going to do that will keep you committed to him."

"I've already told him."

"You told Colton?" Robert asked. "You've told him the *whole* story?"

"Every bit."

"Well, Kelsey-Rose, I am proud of you. What did he say?"

"He's been great about it all."

"He sounds like a good man," Robert told her. "So, what are you going to do now?"

"Well, I'm *not* going to marry Dax."

"All right."

"But now's a bad time for the whole town to hear

that I seduced Dax in front of Shane, and that's what made him so mad he got on that horse." She used a tissue to wipe her eyes. "It will start everything all over again, Robert, and Daddy doesn't need any more trouble right now. I think I just need to fade into nothingness again and hope that Dax stays quiet. Just until Daddy is stronger."

"We should have told the whole truth from the beginning."

"Daddy would have lost the ranch in the lawsuit for sure if we had."

"Well, you might lose the man you're in love with now if you don't. I doubt he'll put up with another man having a key to your house, honey."

KELSEY-ROSE WALKED INTO THE NEWSPAPER LOBBY with a resolve of steel that she'd never had before.

"Hi, Lillie," she said. "Is Colton here?"

"Yes, let me buzz him for you."

Less than a minute later, Colton was in the lobby.

"Hi." He smiled. "Come on back." He held the door for Kelsey-Rose. "Let's go upstairs." He glanced at Mack, who was the only one left in the newsroom. "Let me know if you need me."

Mack glanced from Colton to Kelsey-Rose and back again. "All right," he said. "Are you going to be long?"

"Maybe," Colton said. He looked at Kelsey-Rose. "Actually, I'm not sure."

They took the Scarlett O'Hara stairs up to Colton's apartment. As soon as they had privacy, Colton took her in his arms and kissed her, but when they parted lips, he noticed her eyes were red.

"You've been crying," he said. "What happened?"

"Oh." She lowered her head, turning her face away from his view of her. "I was talking to Robert on the phone. I miss him, that's all. It seems like all I do is cry lately."

"It's not supposed to be that way," Colton said.

"What isn't?" She turned back, eyeing him.

"Love." When she didn't respond, he said, "I hope that wasn't a one-sided statement."

Doubts swirled through her mind in a whirlwind. She looked hard at Colton, trying to find the fraud in his eyes. *She was looking for it.* If she found it, she could walk away and go back to a safer life where her heart wasn't in danger of breaking again.

"How can you be falling in love with me, Colton?" She stepped back, scrutinizing his perfectly pressed slacks, the long-sleeved cashmere polo, his polished oxfords—he hadn't suffered at all from losing his life of privilege. Had Dax been right? Was she just a convenience for this gorgeous, virile man who had stolen her heart? Had she lost her balance in the romance of it all?

She hadn't meant for her tone to flare, but it did. "Colton, look at you, and then look at me. Not only am I the worst-dressed woman in this town, especially standing next to you, but I barely know how to be in an intimate relationship, and I know that my inexperience is obvious to you."

There, she'd said it. She had thrown down the gauntlet, called his bluff, challenged the lie.

Colton stepped back, taking a deep breath with him. "What are you doing?"

"You can't possibly love me."

"Why can't I?"

"Because I am not the kind of girl that someone like you falls in love with."

Colton smiled, which she hadn't unexpected.

"What kind of girl should I fall in love with?"

"You know," Kelsey-Rose said, her hand swishing the air in a gesture of the obvious. "A girl who wears jewelry and has salon-styled hair. One who has her nails done." She jutted out a hand, her fingers extended, to prove she hadn't been to a manicurist or painted her nails in what seemed like forever. "Someone with class. Beauty. Manners. Nice clothes. Someone who doesn't ride around on a horse all day or shovel manure." She stood, her hands landing on her hips in defiance. "Someone who knows how to make love to you."

Even though Kelsey-Rose was serious, Colton laughed.

"You're better than you think." He reached for her hand and led her to the leather couch and sat her down, and then he sat on the coffee table, facing her. "You want to tell me what's really going on?"

Kelsey-Rose took a deep breath and said, "I'm in love with you, Colton. I've fallen, madly and deeply in love with you, and that means that I've broken my promise to Shane." She reached out, gently touching his face, needing to feel some part of him. "It was the one honorable thing I've done in my life."

Colton took hold of her hand, caressing it. When she took another deep breath, he said, "And what else?"

"Dax wants to get married on December thirty-first."

Colton brushed a long strand of red hair away from her eyes, curling it behind her ear. "Did you tell him you're in love with another man?"

"I did."

"You did?" Colton straightened, surprised by her answer.

"Yes." Kelsey-Rose nodded. "I thought he would understand, but he didn't."

"So, is that where you got the idea that I couldn't possibly be in love with you? Dax told you that?"

"Yes," she said. "He's right, Colton. In my heart, I know he is. You and I are so different. You deserve someone so much better than me."

"We're the same in all the ways that count, Kelsey-Rose." Colton stood. "I've been doing some research, and there's something that I'm curious about." He looked at her as she sat on the couch. "Why didn't Dax get any of the blame for Shane's decision to ride that horse?"

She glanced up at him. "What do you mean?"

"Well," he said. "I'll be brutally honest. If another man put his hands on any part of you right now, especially right in front of me, I'm pretty sure that one of us would end up needing a doctor. When I think about a teenage boy in love being put in that situation, I can't even imagine what was going through Shane's mind at the time, other than rage."

Kelsey-Rose stood. "I caused it, though. You don't understand—it was all my fault." She gripped his arm. "Please, you can't tell anyone about that, Colton. Daddy almost lost the ranch in a lawsuit based on negligence. If they'd known that my conduct caused Shane to ride that day, I think we would have lost the ranch, for sure."

Colton nodded. "I see. It makes more sense now." He took Kelsey-Rose by the shoulders and looked into her eyes. "I need you to trust me. This is one of those situations that I know how to handle. Genetics, I guess." He lifted her chin, sweetly kissing her. Softly, he said, "The only thing that you need to decide right now, is whether or not you have time to make love to me. I think there are a few things you can teach me."

CHAPTER 30

Late for her Tuesday morning appointment with the Our Best Wishes! greeting card distributor, Kelsey-Rose pulled into the Say It With Flowers parking lot and got out, hurrying inside through the back door, wearing her cowboy hat and the dust that came with it. The minute she made it through the back room and into the shop, she stopped dead in her tracks.

At the cash register was her sister, Rainey, talking to the salesman.

"Rainey?" Kelsey-Rose said. "You're here. Why are you here?"

Her sister raised *I-don't-know* hands into the air. "Daddy said to stop whining and crying about him. He said I needed to pick up the slack and help you run this shop. He said the family needed more from me."

Kelsey-Rose went to her younger sister with a hug. "I'm sorry, Rainey, but I'm so glad you are here."

"Well," Rainey said with a glance around the shop. "I have to admit, I do love this place. I'm only teaching two dance classes a week at the high school this year anyway, and just walking in the door here makes me happy."

"What did you do with Emma today?"

"I took her to preschool. She's been with me ever since Harry filed for divorce. I guess I needed her, but I can't use my two-year-old daughter as my therapist, can I?"

"No," Kelsey-Rose said. "But I'm here to talk if you need me. And you can bring Emma to the shop with you anytime."

Kelsey-Rose turned to the greeting card representative, a middle-aged man in a short-sleeved button-down shirt who stood leaning on the front counter, looking annoyed. "I'm so sorry to keep you waiting," she said to him. Then she motioned toward her sister. "I've turned over management of the shop to Rainey. Let's go into the back and get our next order placed, shall we?"

After the salesman left, Kelsey-Rose showed Rainey where the incoming order receipts were kept, and then instructed her where to file them once the order had been completed. She was taking a shop key off her ring for Rainey when Rita came into the back room.

"There's someone here to see you," she said.

Kelsey-Rose put her hand on her sister's shoulder. "Rainey's in charge now. I've already called Dani to let her know. She'll cover the two afternoons that Rainey has dance classes." Then she looked at her sister. "These customers are all yours."

"No," Rita said. "They want to see you, Kelsey-Rose. They brought a box."

Kelsey-Rose walked to the front of the shop. "Hey!" She smiled at seeing Jack and Paige with a TXUS Seeds display box and then realized that Carter and

Addy were with them. "Oh, my gosh, you're all here!" She hugged her riding friend—a pure down-to-earth country brunette.

Paige gave a wide smile when Jack held up the new display box. "Kelsey-Rose, your idea for these boxes was wonderful. We've already sold all twenty we had made on a trial basis, but we haven't distributed any of them yet. We wanted you to have the first one since it was your idea."

The barnwood cubby box was decorated with red stenciled horseshoes and bluebonnet blossoms, book-ending the TXUS Seeds name. It was already stocked for her with every variety of flower seed they produced.

Jack handed it to Kelsey-Rose. "Our gift to you."

"Free?" she asked. "I can't let you do that. Let me pay you for it." She glanced at the box. "This is like a double delivery of seeds, too."

"No charge," Paige told her, but speaking of *free,* where is that little rascal?"

"He's how I met Kelsey-Rose," Addy said to Jack. "Did we ever tell you that story?"

"Paige told me." He reached for Addy's hand and held it in his. "Ironic how all of my favorite people somehow came together, piecing my life back into order."

Kelsey-Rose smiled at the memory. "I never did find the shoe that dog stole." They all laughed. "He's home with the run of the place right now." Then she looked at Carter, reaching for a handshake. "It's good to see you again. How's the horse therapy program coming along?"

"Really well," Carter said. He glanced at Paige, who nudged him with encouragement. "We'd really like to talk to your father about training a few wild horses.

We're getting several from the Adoption Incentive Program through the Bureau of Land Management. My application was approved last year. I've had some people up there working with them, so the horses are tame enough to move off BLM land now, but they're not tame enough to use as therapy horses yet. Your dad is the man everyone recommends to us. Paige and I would really like to come out to the Forty Flowers sometime soon and talk to him. Do you think you could arrange it for us?"

Kelsey-Rose glanced from Carter to Paige. "I'm sorry," she said. "But Dad had a real bad accident the weekend before Thanksgiving. He's not going to be able to help you."

"Oh, Kelsey-Rose," Paige said, reaching out with a compassionate touch. "We hadn't heard."

"Will he be okay?" Jack asked her.

"He may be paralyzed. We don't know yet whether it's permanent."

"Who's running his ranch?" Carter asked.

"Me." Kelsey-Rose stepped back, showing off her ranch attire. Then she glanced back at Rainey, who was helping Rita clean the floral coolers. "My sister is taking over the flower shop until we can get things worked out."

"I'm sure sorry to hear about that," Carter said. "We'll keep you and your dad in our prayers." He glanced back at Paige. "It's a shame. This would have been good money for your ranch. We have a long-term plan in place."

"Kelsey-Rose," Jack said. "Are your pens empty?"

"Yeah, but you know we don't do much in the way of breaking broncs anymore."

"What if you had one or two designated cowboys to break them and train them for you?"

She laughed. "Sure, that would be great, but we don't. I've just got Cullen and Ty, and they've got their hands full managing the longhorns."

"Do you remember me telling you about my cousin, Jace, who has the Farr Reaches Ranch?"

"Yeah, his grandmother, Hannah Farr, is a legend."

"Well, I talked to Jace a few nights ago. He has a young cowboy working for him by the name of Kid Crisp. He's nice enough, I met him at Jace and Mia's wedding, but Jace says Kid is anxious to get back to training cutting horses and breaking broncs. I hear he's a natural at it. He grew up on The Lost Lonesome Ranch that his father owns, but I guess he and his dad had some father-son trouble. Jace took him on as a favor to his father, but he says that Kid needs a bigger challenge. What if he moved over to your ranch for a while?"

Carter said, "That's a great idea, Kelsey-Rose. Your ranch is already set up for something like this, and we just found out that we've got less than a month to move those horses. We need to find a place pretty fast. We might be able to make this work. What do you think? I could pay Kid's salary if you've got room for him in the bunkhouse. I can email you some numbers tonight."

"I'll need to talk to Daddy about it."

"Okay. Will you call us after you do?"

"Yep." Kelsey-Rose had mixed feelings. She had already taken on too much, and breaking broncs again tied a knot in her stomach.

After her friends had gone, Rainey went to Kelsey-Rose. "I wasn't trying to eavesdrop, but I couldn't help but overhear them asking you to talk to Daddy about bringing in broncs again. You're not going to do that, are you?"

Kelsey-Rose shook her head but didn't say no. "It wouldn't be like before. There's more to it this time. It's a long-term plan. Almost a partnership," she told Rainey. Then she looked at her sister. "But I don't know if I can ever look at a wild horse in that corral again."

Rita held up an order slip. "Rainey, do you want to make this arrangement? The customer came in this morning and asked for it to be delivered by noon."

Rainey looked at the clock on the wall. "That's in twenty minutes."

"I can do it if you want," Rita said. "But you'll need to deliver it. I don't do deliveries anymore."

Kelsey-Rose looked at Rainey. "It's your first arrangement as manager. You can do it. I'll stay and help."

"Please!" Rainey said. "I should have practiced more with you on the holidays."

The two started for the back room together. "Which arrangement was ordered, Rita?" Kelsey-Rose asked.

"It's the *'Big Apology'* bouquet for a man."

Kelsey-Rose looked at her sister with raised brows. "Uh-oh. Someone's in trouble." She grabbed a floral bowl off the shelves and carried it into the back room. "This silver pedestal bowl is for a man, and the cut crystal is for a woman. For this arrangement, you'll need a half dozen apricot-colored roses, a half dozen pure white roses, and white baby's breath."

"Any green foliage?" Rainey asked from the floral cooler.

"In the very back, you'll find sprigs of myrtle. You'll need about ten."

When the arrangement was finished, Rainey asked, "Do we need a ribbon?"

Kelsey-Rose glanced at the laminated page in the manual that lay open with a description of the array. "No." Then she held up the silver container. "This is such a beautiful that a ribbon would actually detract from its loveliness."

"Let's go see who's getting this beautiful arrangement. I can always drop it off for you on my way back to the ranch."

In the shop front, Rainey asked Rita, "Who is this going to?"

"It's going across the street." She pointed to *The Blue Topaz Times* building.

Kelsey-Rose set the arrangement down and reached for the card envelope. "Can I see?"

Rita handed it to her instead of inserting it into the clear cardholder pick.

The laser-printed name and address were on the front. Kelsey-Rose looked at Rainey. "It's for Colton." She turned to Rita. "Did we print the card for the customer?"

"No, the lady handwrote a message herself."

The lady.

"Did you see what she wrote?" Rainey asked Rita.

With a semblance of a glare, Rita said, "Of course not."

Rainey took the card envelope from Kelsey-Rose. "Let's open it."

"No." Kelsey-Rose took it back. "We have a code of ethics." She slid the envelope with the card inside onto the cardholder pick. "I can take it over."

Even though she was dressed for ranch work, not floral work, Kelsey-Rose walked the arrangement across the street. She opened the front door and entered, holding the floral delivery.

"Oh, those are beautiful!" Lillie said when she saw Kelsey-Rose. "And I can smell the roses all the way over here."

Kelsey-Rose gave her a well-practiced smile. "Can I leave them here?"

"Are they for me?" Lillie stood.

"Oh, no, I'm sorry, Lillie. They're for Colton."

Lillie sat down. "Of course, they're not for me." She buzzed the door to the newsroom. "Would you just leave them on his desk? He's gone for the day."

"The whole day?" Kelsey-Rose asked. When Lillie nodded, she said, "Sure. Okay."

She was on her way to Robert's old office when Beth stopped her.

"Well, Kelsey-Rose," Beth said, doing a visual scan of her. "Don't you look…nice."

"I'm working on the ranch today," she told Beth and kept walking.

"Oh, yes, I heard about that. How is Harley anyway?"

Kelsey-Rose stopped and took a deep breath. *Be polite. Be nice. Be professional.* She turned back. Beth was alone in the newsroom. "Daddy is improving every day. Thank you for asking. Now if you'll excuse me, I need to deliver these flowers."

"Are those for Colton?"

"Yes."

"He asked for personal deliveries to be sent upstairs." Beth pointed to the Scarlett O'Hara steps. "I'm sure anywhere will be fine."

Confused, Kelsey-Rose asked, "Is his door unlocked?"

Beth opened the drawer on Mack's desk, took out a key, and held it up. "He's already had one delivery this morning. Something special must be happening. His birthday, maybe? Or is that tomorrow? Anyway, I left the door unlocked in case anything else came for him."

"His birthday?"

"Yes, didn't you know?"

Kelsey-Rose turned and headed for the stairs. She took them up, fast as she could, to the upper floor hallway with its interior brick wall. At the old foyer, she turned the knob, opening his apartment door, and stepped inside.

"Oh!" An unexpected woman met Kelsey-Rose at the door. "Doesn't anyone knock in these primitive little towns?"

"I'm sorry," Kelsey-Rose stopped, completely taken off guard. "I didn't know anyone was here." Then she said, "How did you get inside?"

"My fiancé's employee brought me up." Then distracted, the woman exclaimed, "Oh! My flowers!" She took the arrangement out of Kelsey-Rose's hands and carried it to the coffee table where two wrapped gifts already waited. Romantic music was lightly playing through his sound system. "Colton will be gone all day, but I wanted things ready for him when he arrives home."

The woman was beyond gorgeous with long, nearly elbow-length, sandy-blonde hair in a windblown style, and she wore heavy, but artistic and sexy eye makeup with nude and barely there-colored lip gloss that left her lips very kissable. She wore silver hoop earrings, bigger than Kelsey-Rose had ever dared to wear, and she had diamond platinum tennis bracelets adorning each of her perfectly tanned forearms. The slightly gray, off-the-shoulder, rolled-neck sweatshirt had three-quarter length sleeves, and paired with her ripped distressed jeans, she was in the "sexy elite" class. It hadn't escaped Kelsey-Rose that a diamond ring, at least five carats, was on her ring finger.

"Are you Carly?" Kelsey-Rose asked.

"Colton told you about me? He is the sweetest man." Her stance relaxed. "I want him to wake up with me in his arms on his birthday tomorrow."

"His birthday?"

The woman squeezed her shoulders together in a huggable stance. "This will be one birthday he will never forget."

"I thought you disappeared when his father cut him out of the will."

Carly gave her a surprised look. "Well, that's a lot of information for his little florist to know, but I've heard small towns are like that. And Colton wasn't cut out of anything. Now that his father is dead, he owns the whole Wilde empire. He didn't tell you?"

"No." Kelsey-Rose hated having a conversation with this woman at all, but worse, she hated knowing that Colton had lied to her.

"He's in Georgetown signing papers for the sale of his father's penthouse as we speak. He'll be coming home a few million richer, but I wish he would have asked me first. The place was pure luxury! I think we should have kept it." Carly glanced around the apartment. "This place is a real dump."

Nausea rolled through Kelsey-Rose as she stood staring at the woman.

"Are you waiting for a tip or something?"

"A tip?" she asked.

The woman started toward Colton's bedroom as

"What a Wonderful World" began playing. "I never carry cash, but let me see if he has some on his bureau."

Feeling dazed, Kelsey-Rose turned and left the apartment. She went down the stairs and out through the newsroom without a word to anyone. She crossed the street, got into her Santa Fe parked behind the flower shop, and drove away.

CHAPTER 31

Colton had his leather satchel that held a yellow legal pad and pen, and the current issue of *The Blue Topaz Times* with him as he drove to the auto shop across the street from The Purple Sage restaurant.

When he opened the door, the only person inside was a shop technician standing at the service desk in a light blue mechanic's shirt with a sewn-on name label.

"Hi," Colton looked closer for the name, "Mason." He set his satchel on the counter. "Is Kevin Lawson around today?" He hadn't met the shop owner yet, but Mack was invaluable at providing names.

"Yeah, you got a car that needs looked at?" Mason asked. "I can probably help you with that."

"No, another matter." Colton took out his business card and handed it to the service tech. "Would you give this to Mr. Lawson and ask if I can have a few minutes of his time, please?"

The man read the card and left the service desk,

walking across the clean, motor-oil-scented lobby to a hall of offices.

The music system played traditional country at a level so low that it was hard to hear it.

Soon, the technician came back down the hallway, walking with an older man who had a clean-shaven head, wore tan industrial pants, and a white button-down long-sleeve shirt. A silver nametag was pinned above his right-side pocket.

Colton walked toward him with an outstretched hand. "Mr. Lawson?"

"Yeah," the man said, accepting Colton's hand. "Good to meet you, Mr. Wilde. What can I do for you?" Then he smiled. "I heard you had one of those new Corvette Stingrays. Haven't seen one of them yet, but we'd sure be happy to service it for you. We have a master mechanic here, and not many shops in the state can boast about that."

"Well, thank you," Colton said with courtesy. "But I'd actually like to talk to you about something else. Do you have a minute for me in your office?"

"Sure, sure," he said. "Come on back."

The auto shop owner led Colton to his office and closed the door. "What can I help you with?" He took his seat behind a desk. "You're not trying to sell me advertising, are you?"

Colton laughed without intending to, but what was it about this town that had no faith in newspaper advertising?

"No." He pulled out the most recent issue of *The Blue Topaz Times* and laid it on the desk in front of Kevin Lawson. "I've started a new column called 'This Week in Local History.' Are you familiar with the story of

Shane Delany? This week is the tenth anniversary of his death."

The man sat back in his chair. "Has it been ten years? Yeah," he said. "I remember it. That kid was talented. Good kid, too."

Colton sat forward in his chair. "I understand you have a mechanic working for you, Dax Porter, who was there when it happened."

"Yeah, but he wasn't working for me at the time. He was working out at Pixley's on Highway 29."

"So, I guess he never had a reason to talk to you about it. Is that what you're saying?"

"Well, no," Lawson said. "Actually, that's why I hired the boy in the first place. He's been kind of a hero around here, you know? As a mechanic, he wasn't worth a darn at the time, but people were ready to throw a parade for him after he promised the Delany boy—right there as he lay dying in that horse corral—that he'd take care of Kelsey-Rose for him." He looked at Colton, giving an emotional headshake. "I'll be honest, everybody in town wanted to bring their cars to Dax as a show of support. My business tripled after that. I've had him employed here ever since, and he's become a good mechanic. He was worth the risk."

Colton knew his eyes had settled too hard on the shop owner. He took the current issue of the newspaper and flipped open to the first "This Week in Local History" column about Joe Pixley and then pointed to it. "Would it be okay if I interviewed Dax today for this column? I'll be sure to mention your shop in the article."

"Yeah, sure! Want me to get him for you? You two can use my office."

Colton stood with a smile. "That would be great."

When the office door opened again, Dax stepped inside, wearing blue shop coveralls. He closed the door behind him.

"When they told me someone from the newspaper was here to talk to me, I figured it was you."

"Smart man," Colton said. "Congratulations on cracking the case."

Colton stood several inches taller than Dax. In the nature of a masculine world, it gave him psychological dominance over the opposing man. He knew that, so Colton eyed Dax with a downward sweep of his eyes, wanting to smile when Dax slid his hands uncomfortably into the pockets of his coveralls, slumping his shoulders.

"So, did you come here to tell me to stay away from Kelsey-Rose? Because that's not going to happen. I tried to tell you that already."

"No." Colton shook his head, he picked up the folded newspaper, and he handed it to Dax, then he sat on the edge of the desk, leaving him holding it. "That's the first issue with the new column 'This Week in Local History.'"

Dax looked down at the page. "Oh, yeah. This is Kyle's story."

"That's right," Colton said. "Now I'm doing another story. The one about Shane Delany."

Dax looked up at him. "That's what you wanted to talk to me about?"

"Yes. You were there, right?"

"Yeah." Dax went to the desk and pulled out a chair and sat. He pointed to the column. "Will mine be on the front page?"

"Depends on how it turns out, but, no, probably not."

"Well, that's all right," Dax said, putting down the newspaper. "What do you want to know?"

There was an absolute sparkle in the man's eyes that sent Colton to his satchel for the yellow pad and pen. He laid them on the desk beside him. "Why don't we just start with you telling me what you remember about that day." He had no friendliness in his voice, but that had gone unnoticed.

"Okay." Dax readjusted himself in the chair and started talking.

Colton listened, never taking his eyes off the man with ebony-black hair, buzzed short, wearing a well-trimmed mustache and box beard. He wasn't particularly good-looking and had no charm whatsoever. Kelsey-Rose deserved much better than him. To think that this man had controlled her narrative for a decade and had worked his way into her bed at will made his skin crawl.

After rambling on with the story of Shane Delany for more than several minutes, Dax looked at the pen and notepad beside Colton.

He pointed to them. "Don't you need to write some of this down?"

Colton remained focused on Dax. He patted his shirt pocket. "I record everything, then transcribe it later to use as notes. That way, I don't miss anything."

"Oh, well, okay," he said.

When Dax came to the moment that Shane climbed the fence, Colton stopped him.

"That's where I feel like part of the story is missing," Colton said to him.

"What part?" Dax asked, his question sincere.

"If you and Kelsey-Rose were just talking, carrying on a normal conversation, what made Shane decide—right at that moment—to ride that wild horse?"

"Well," Dax said with a shift of his jaw. "You can ask Kelsey-Rose about that."

"But I'm asking you."

Confidently, Dax said, "Shane was a rodeo man through and through. He wanted to ride every bronc he could find."

"So, for no reason at all, he just climbed the fence and got on that horse?"

Dax squinted his brown eyes, glancing from Colton to the blank pad. "Why do I get the feeling that you're getting at something else?"

"Something else?" Colton stood. "I'm just a newspaperman. People like to talk to me. They tell me things, and then I write an article about it. But I can't write the article unless I know the facts. That doesn't mean every fact will go into the story. It just makes for better reading if I know everything so that I can build my article around it." Colton picked up the pen and legal pad. "For instance, I know that Kelsey-Rose was using you to make Shane jealous, but that doesn't mean it will go into the story. I don't want to hurt Kelsey-Rose. And I know that she drank too much whiskey, and that's probably why she won't take a drink to this day. But the fact that she doesn't indulge in adult beverages doesn't make for much of a story either, does it?" He wrote the word *whiskey* on the legal pad and then put an *X* through the word, setting the pad down so that Dax could see it.

Dax looked at it but then sat back, eyeing Colton.

"And to be honest," Colton said. "I know that you took some liberties in that situation. You wanted Kelsey-Rose, and you were hoping Shane would just get out of town, right? Then you'd have her to yourself." Colton sat on the edge of the desk again. "I'll tell you the truth," he gave a quiet snicker, "just man-to-man. I see the attraction. Who could blame you for putting your hands on that beautiful woman when she already had her arms around you? Her boyfriend was running off and leaving her there all alone. She would need comfort, and it would be easier if she knew who would be there for her."

Dax sat straighter. "And Kelsey-Rose never knew, but Shane always had girls hanging on him at the rodeos. When we'd go to one of his events and Kelsey-Rose wasn't there, girls would follow him everywhere!"

"No kidding?" Colton said. "He must have been a good-looking cowboy."

"He really was," Dax said.

"Did Shane give in to any of those women when it was just you and him?"

"Nah," Dax said. "He used to carry a picture of Kelsey-Rose with him, and anytime he was tempted, he'd just pull out that picture and look at her."

Colton nodded. "So, were you surprised that day when Kelsey-Rose turned around while you had your hand on her breast so that Shane could see the two of you?"

"Yeah," Dax said. "But I didn't want it to look like I was afraid of Shane or anything, so I just gave it a bigger grab, thinking he would either laugh or just get mad and maybe go home. He was leaving in a few days anyway."

"Was that when Shane climbed the fence?"

Dax nodded. "He was really mad. I'd never seen him like that."

"And afterward, you and Kelsey-Rose decided to

keep that part a secret."

"Yeah, it wasn't our fault, and we didn't want it to look like it was."

"And no one ever questioned you about it, huh?"

"No, Shane was always ridin' somebody's horse. Nobody thought anything about it."

"Lucky you, you got the girl after all." Colton stood, putting the legal pad and pen back into his satchel and closing it.

"Are we done?" Dax stood. "You're not using any of that in the story, though. I mean, this is like one of those lawyer things, right, where whatever I said is privileged information?"

"Just the opposite," Colton told him. "I'm going to use everything *you* said. I'll make it clear that you took advantage of a young, heartsick, inebriated teenage girl, which infuriated her boyfriend so much, he climbed onto a bronc that he knew he wasn't permitted to ride, just to prove to her that he loved her."

Dax grabbed Colton by the arm. "You can't do that! If you put that in the paper, I'll tell everybody what Kelsey-Rose did. She was the one who tempted me!"

Colton jerked his arm free. "You want to go public with this, Dax? Because I can do that. Things like that don't scare me—but you should be plenty worried. See, I already have the girl on my side, and I have the police chief on my side, and I have the local newspaper on my side. So, there are two ways we can do this. You can let Kelsey-Rose go, and you can keep on being the hero who lost the girl to a man everybody will love to hate, or I can tell everyone the truth and turn your life into a living hell." Colton leaned in closer. "I don't mind being the bad guy in this situation. It doesn't even make me nervous."

CHAPTER 32

After leaving the auto shop, Colton drove to Georgetown where he signed closing documents for the sale of the penthouse, deciding not to tell Kelsey-Rose about his meeting with Dax until he had her in his arms again.

It took less than twenty minutes to sign for the sale before he was back in his car, pulling out of the parking lot when a call came in from his mother. He pulled back into a parking space and answered. "Hello, Mother."

"Colton, is everything signed?"

"Yes, did I forget something? I'm still here if I need to go back inside."

"No, I just wanted to be sure the sale went as planned. Did you ask them to wire your proceeds?"

Colton laughed. "Yes, Mother. This isn't my first time selling real estate."

"I know it isn't," she said, her tone relaxing. "I'm treating you like a little boy again. Maybe I'm just feeling nostalgic."

Colton smiled at the nurturing sound of her voice. It

had been a long time since he'd heard that tone. "I looked over your itinerary. You have a long flight tomorrow."

"Yes, but in a way, I'm looking forward to it. I need a little time with my feet off the ground. I do hate to leave without seeing you on your birthday, though."

"I'll be thirty-five tomorrow, Mother. Not five. One birthday without you won't kill me."

"Colton, I wish you were coming with me. I don't like leaving you here."

"Mother, we've talked about this. I need to see this through."

"Will you do me a favor?"

"Of course? What is it?"

"I want you to meet with some people your Uncle Enzo has hired. They're in Austin. He found someone close."

Surprised, Colton asked, "Who are these people?"

"Attorneys. Security," she said. "We want to be sure that you are safe and represented by someone we trust."

"That's ridiculous," Colton said.

"Yes, maybe, but since you're so close, I told them that you would meet with them at five today. Will you do this for me? They're taking care of the loose ends where you're concerned, and they also have papers to give you for *World Wineyards* magazine. Enzo doesn't know what to do with it. He bought it for you, not for himself. And they've also picked up the jewelry case for you. I've given them two copies of the insurance with the itemized list and photographs of each piece. One copy is for your records. They've offered a safe deposit box, too."

"Yes. All right." Colton nodded, disappointed that he wasn't going home to Kelsey-Rose. He had so much to tell her. He took the pad and pen from his satchel on the passenger seat, and then he asked, "What's their name and address?"

~

Attorneys Rodney Cadmon and Salima Marvala, along with Daren from Nicholas Security, met Colton in the Four Seasons lobby at five, as agreed. The presidential suite on the ninth floor was reserved for their meeting, with Colton expected to stay the night, giving him time to review the documents and the heirloom jewelry.

After the formalities and explanations of the documents, the two attorneys excused themselves, leaving their two business cards and Daren behind. The man was Colton's height, clean-cut, and a professional suit wearer. "Former secret service," he told Colton.

"Daren, I'm ordering dinner from room service, can I get you something?"

"No, thank you, sir. Please don't let me distract you."

"Okay then," Colton said. Unaccustomed to having personal security, Colton went about his business reviewing the documents provided, making notes, and sipping bourbon after dinner. He picked up his phone several times, wanting to call Kelsey-Rose, but he didn't want to lie to her if she asked where he was for the evening. All of this was part of the conversation he wanted to have with her—but in person, not over the phone. She had been so busy with the ranch lately, that she probably wouldn't even notice him missing for one night.

Daren helped Colton move the jewelry case to the

table in the lounge area of the suite, where he had a view of Lady Bird Lake, with city lights from the night reflecting off the water.

He opened the big case and felt a leftover phase of mourning, almost missing the man who once wore this jewelry. Colton set a few pieces aside for himself, but then the tray of his mother's jewelry caught his eye.

A bridal set, not one belonging to his mother, was in the case. He took it out and held it to the light. The center princess cut diamond was only about two carats, but the floral design, inlaid with small diamonds and wrapping the bans in an infinity setting, was probably another carat.

Curious, Colton opened the file and took out the itemized list of the pieces and found the description for the set. It had belonged to his great-grandmother, Rose. He sat back, inspecting the ring. It was perfect.

IT WAS ALMOST ELEVEN IN THE MORNING BEFORE Colton arrived home. He went up the back steps to his apartment to shower and change into clean clothes before calling Kelsey-Rose.

When he unlocked and opened his door, Carly threw her arms around him, kissing him before whispering, "Happy birthday, my darling."

Colton took her by the shoulders and moved her a step back. "Carly. What are you doing here?"

"I thought you would be back last night. I had a big surprise planned for you."

"Okay, wait..." Colton stepped inside and closed the door. "First, how do you know where I live?"

"Bridget Fyve and I are friends. We've been friends

for a while now. She gave me your address, and she told me the good news."

"My inheritance."

"Yes, aren't you excited?" Carly stepped in and kissed him again. "Why didn't you call to tell me yourself?"

Colton moved away from her, his hands landing on his hips. "I'd already spent probably two months calling you, and all my calls had gone unanswered."

"Oh, sweetheart, you know how I get sometimes."

"I do. Yes."

"Look!" She took his hand and pulled him around the leather couch to the coffee table. "I brought gifts for your birthday." She put her arms around him again. "And then I'm your last gift to do with as you please."

Carly leaned for another kiss, but Colton removed her arms from around him and stepped back again.

"Question number two, Carly. How did you get in here?"

"That older woman who works for you. The stiff one."

"She has a key?"

"Yes, didn't you know?"

"No, I didn't. I'll be sure to take care of that." Colton took Carly by the hand and walked her toward the bedroom. At the door, he said, "Gather your things and get out."

"Get out?"

"Or I can gather them for you." He went inside the bedroom with her following. The bed was unmade, and the blinds were still closed. He went to the bathroom and turned on the light, gathering her makeup, toothbrush, and hair styling things, tossing them all into her travel case. He closed it and handed it to her.

"Colton—"

"Get your clothes, too." When she didn't budge, he said, "Move!"

After her things were gathered, Colton took her by the arm and walked her to the door. He opened it and looked down into the parking lot. "Where's your car?"

"Parked on the street in front," she said. "But just listen—"

He set her travel bag outside. "Then you'll have a short walk." He stepped her out onto the landing and turned to go back inside, but then he stopped and turned back. "I want the ring. You conned me out of it in a good old-fashioned gold digger swindle, and I doubt there's a court in Texas that wouldn't support my right to have it back." He held out his hand.

Carly's face reddened while she pulled off the engagement ring and threw it at him.

Colton bent to pick it up, and then he closed the door.

DRESSED IN DENIM JEANS, A BUTTERSCOTCH PLAID western shirt, and wearing her boots embroidered with burgundy roses, Kelsey-Rose went into the flower shop through the back door.

"Hey, Rainey." She quietly greeted her sister. "It sure is nice to walk in the door and find you here."

Rainey took her by the hand and led her closer to the floral cooler in the back room. She pointed through the glass. "Look. You got a new delivery of the Picasso calla lilies. They came first thing this morning."

Kelsey-Rose smiled when she looked at them. "I was hoping they would be here."

"Are you taking them to Shane this year?"

Kelsey-Rose nodded.

Rainey hugged her, holding on a little longer than usual. "I'll leave you alone to gather the flowers, okay?"

Again, she nodded, her words stalled somewhere between her heart and her lips.

With the bouquet wrapped in white tissue paper, Kelsey-Rose carried ten of the creamy white flowers with dark purple centers across the cemetery to the standing headstone that read Audley Shane Delany. She glanced at the vintage gold Timex watch on her wrist, once worn by her grandmother. She sat down on the grass with the bouquet across her lap.

"I'm a little early this year, Shane." She glanced at her watch again, and then took a deep breath, her eyes welling with tears.

~

FURIOUS, COLTON WALKED THE APARTMENT. BETH had deliberately played into Carly's ruse, using an unknown key to let her inside. He wasn't a fool. Beth was protecting her grandson's interest in Kelsey-Rose.

His gaze fell to the glitzy wrapped gifts on the coffee table. He should have thrown those out with Carly. Then he noticed the floral arrangement. He went to it and pulled off the card, his name and address printed on a Say It With Flowers envelope.

Colton picked up his phone and called Kelsey-Rose. When her voicemail picked up his call, he left a message telling her that he needed to see her.

He grabbed his jacket and his car keys and headed down the stairs. *The flower shop.*

Colton parked on the street and went inside, spotting Rainey restocking cards.

"Rainey, where's Kelsey-Rose?"

She glanced up at him.

"What time is it?"

"Almost noon…why?"

"She should be at the cemetery with Shane by now."

"Rainey, did she see—"

"The flowers?" When Colton nodded, she said, "Afraid so."

Colton turned and pushed open the shop door, running to his car.

From the interior cemetery road, Colton saw Kelsey-Rose at a faraway grave. He stopped the car and turned off the engine, and then he got out. As much as he wanted her—needed her—this was her time, and he wasn't going to take it from her. He leaned against the Corvette, and he waited.

AFTER LAYING THE CALLA LILY BOUQUET ATOP Shane's grave, Kelsey-Rose sat silent, watching the minute hand tick on her grandmother's watch. Every minute that passed held a memory still strong enough to break her heart, but this time, not all of the tears were for Shane. Some were for her. Most were for Colton, the man she intended to apologize for loving today.

When the seventeen minutes ended, Kelsey-Rose stood, looking down at the grave. She dabbed her eyes and then her nose with a tissue.

"I still miss you so much," she said aloud. "I've waited ten years for an answer on how to go on living without you, and when I finally thought I knew, it turns out I was wrong. My whole world is shattered again." A sob broke free. "I'm so sorry I made you leave me."

When a breeze rustled the dry leaves holding tight to the limbs of a red oak, Colton softly whispered, "Hey."

Startled, Kelsey-Rose turned. Her eyes were red. She needed another tissue. "What are you doing here?" She stepped back, putting her hand on Shane's headstone in a defensive move to protect him. "You shouldn't be here."

"I needed to see you." Then looking at the headstone, Colton said, "And I needed to meet Shane. I'm envious of the way he holds your heart."

Kelsey-Rose glanced at the headstone, but to Colton, she said, "You lied to me."

"About what, Kelsey-Rose?" His tone was soft and gentle. "What did I lie about?"

She looked at him again. "Carly, for one. And being broke for another."

"Both were true. I didn't lie. Give me a chance to explain, please?"

When she didn't answer, Colton began, quietly and respectfully.

"When I came to Topaz, I barely had enough money to sustain myself for a year, hoping I could turn *The Blue Topaz Times* into a money-making venture. It was a big risk, but I had no choice. I had nowhere to turn. I don't blame anyone for my failures. I made conscious decisions about everything I did or did not do in my life. Whether they were decisions made from regret, guilt, loyalty, or love—every decision was mine. But I also understood that for every success, I owed my gratitude to someone.

"But *The Blue Topaz Times*—that one was different. For the first time in my life, I did it alone. My first newspaper. It was my own decision to buy the newspaper along with the State Bank Building, and it was my own money that I used, it wasn't my father's money. And not my inheritance either. It was *my* money. Earnings that I'd worked hard for, saved and invested, but I couldn't let that be the end of the story. I gave myself one year to succeed, or not, here in Topaz. On my own, Kelsey-Rose."

She listened, watching him intently.

"The only mistake I made, I think, was in not telling you that I was, after all, heir to my father's fortune. I promise you, though, I didn't know until his dying day. But that doesn't change the goals that I have in place. I have to know that I can make it on my own, without my father's money." He focused on her eyes. "I *need* to know." He glanced up at the wintry-looking sky, taking a minute before beginning again. "Kelsey-Rose, if I give it all up and walk away, just because I inherited a multimillion-dollar portfolio, that will be the ultimate failure, and then I'm afraid you might be right. Money will change me. And I don't want to be that person."

"I don't want you to be that person either, Colton. Whether or not you stay here. What about Carly?"

"Everything I told you about Carly was true. And I had no idea that she was here, or that she even knew where I lived. Turns out my real estate agent and Carly are friends. She didn't get any of that information from me."

"So, you're not together with her?"

"No. Not in the least."

"Is Carly still at your apartment?"

"No. I escorted her out, not very politely."

"So, does that mean—"

"It's always meant that, Kelsey-Rose. Since the day I first laid eyes on you."

She glanced at Shane's headstone, then back at Colton. "I'm always going to love him, you know?"

"I know, and that's okay with me." Colton went to the headstone where Kelsey-Rose stood and put his hand on the cold granite monument. He was silent for a moment, but then he stepped away and took his great-grandmother's ring out of his pocket.

Colton reached for the hand of the woman he loved and presented the ring. "Kelsey-Rose, will you do me the great honor of becoming my wife?"

"Your wife? You're asking me to marry you?"

"Yes, I'm asking you to marry me." He glanced back at the headstone. "I asked Shane for permission a moment ago, and I think he said yes."

From a place she feared would never know true love again, came tears. "Are you sure?"

Colton took Kelsey-Rose in his arms and kissed her, whispering, "I've never been so sure about anything in my life."

She placed her hands on his cheeks. "You'll have to ask Daddy, too."

Colton laughed. "Okay, I'll ask everyone, but I still need to know your answer."

"Yes," she said. "Yes, I'll marry you."

Kelsey-Rose held out her hand while Colton slipped the ring onto her finger.

She looked at him, surprised. "It's a perfect fit."

"Everything about us is."

AUTHOR'S NOTE:

Official State Gem of Texas: Blue Topaz

House Concurrent Resolution No. 12, 61st Legislature, Regular Session (1969) the TEXAS BLUE TOPAZ was declared to be the official State gem of Texas, adopted by the House on March 19, 1969; adopted by the Senate on March 24, 1969. Approved March 26, 1969.

The Texas Blue Topaz was first recognized in Texas in 1904. In the earliest part of the century, arrowhead hunters came across the quartz-like gemstone while searching the creek beds for the projectile points.

The granite plutons in the Llano Uplift, located in Central Texas, are the only masses known to bear topaz in Texas. The largest gem-quality blue topaz crystal ever found in North America came from Mason County, Texas.

A LOOK AT: CHANGE OF FORTUNE

The historical 1849 Gold Rush is no place for a refined young woman on her own, but Quinn MacCann plans to become a businesswoman, independent, and capable of earning her own way in this western romance novel. To escape her wealthy but abusive father with her inherited dowry intact, Quinn marries a stranger—a man so new to the area her powerful father doesn't control him yet—but freedom and independence are more costly than she imagined. With her hopes and dreams buried deep by secrets, she flees to California's gold country, a rugged man's land where only the strong survive. Battling blackmail, fraud, and deception, Quinn must face the most divisive lie of all—her own—in this thrilling tale of love and adventure.

"...come hell or high water, Quinn is going to start her own business... Powerful men will try to destroy her, but she is stronger than they think." —Kathleen O'Neal Gear and W. Michael Gear, *New York Times* bestselling authors

AVAILABLE NOW

ABOUT THE AUTHOR

Karen (K.S.) Jones comes to us from the beautiful Texas Hill Country where she writes Historical Fiction and Contemporary Western Romance. In 2014, *Southern Writers* magazine awarded Karen their grand prize for "Best Short Fiction" of the year, and soon after, her first two novels, *Shadow of the Hawk*, Historical Fiction, and *Black Lightning*, a middle-grade sci-fi/fantasy, saw publication. Her work has garnered numerous literary awards, including the coveted WILLA Award from Women Writing the West in 2016, as well as the 2015 and 2017 Literary Classics International Book Award, the 2015 Chaucer Award, and the 2016 RONE Award. Her newest novel, CHANGE OF FORTUNE, was released this past February and within hours it rose to #30 on Amazon's list of top 100 in American Historical Romances. The novel is already in its third printing.

www.ingramcontent.com/pod-product-compliance
Lightning Source LLC
LaVergne TN
LVHW030917080826
845145LV00013B/2933

* 9 7 8 1 6 3 9 7 7 9 8 6 4 *